Trusting Love

A MIDDLETOWN NOVEL

CHERIE ROBERSON

For information contact cherieroberson.com

ISBN 979-8-9864506-3-6
e-book ISBN 979-8-9864506-2-9
LCCN 2025900560

Cover and book design by Lena Roberson

Edited by Megan Montgomery

Always

For my parents,
Tom and Rose McClarren,
whose fierce love lives
in my every
step, word, smile,
laugh, song, and tear.

&

Forever

For my aunt,
Evie Demsko,
who introduced me to the
Greatest Romance
of all time.

*"There is no remedy for love,
but to love more."*

Henry David Thoreau

ONE

Cara sighed with a tinge of trepidation as she exited Interstate 72. Not the same trepidation as two years ago when she left the hometown she planned to live in forever. Middletown wasn't enemy territory, but every return spun her nerves into high alert. With each visit home, a little more of that dread evaporated. Her efforts to avoid a certain someone had helped.

Cara focused her concerns on Gramps and Nestlé. She was eight miles away from seeing with her own two eyes that Gramps had recovered fully from his ministroke and ten minutes until she could wrap her aging canine buddy in her arms. She would pack porch sits and pond visits and Filippo's Pizza into her short five-day visit and then hustle back to the new normal she'd fought to create.

She saved the good news she received yesterday to share in person with her parents—earning the position as school social worker for Edwardsville Middle School, the same place where she'd interned. Her dad would be elated she'd landed a living wage. Her mom would beam with excitement that she'd taken a job just a few hours from home. This trip would also be a true goodbye to her old life, her old home, her past dreams.

Most people shied away from working with junior high students, but their angst was Cara's favorite challenge. She related to their turmoil. She once thought she would never be happy again, but being a sympathetic ear to help kids navigate life's sadness and rejection gave her renewed passion. Frankly, she was good at her job.

Turning north onto the overpass toward Middletown, she smiled at the quilt of green of the Moore's fields, a far cry from the blinding blizzard she'd inched through the last time she was home in late December. Rolling down her window, she filled her lungs with the richness of fresh country air. By the end of June, this stretch of Route 47 would tunnel through knee-high corn and soybeans.

In the last two years, Middletown had made obvious changes, but so had Cara. While working like crazy to complete her undergraduate and master's degrees in social work, she'd found balance with the past, new friends, and a job as a barista that paid the rent.

She didn't fit into Middletown so neatly anymore. Each return trip felt more and more like a visit. Coming home for good was now as futile as wedging a square peg into a round hole. Christmas break was the last time Cara dared spend more than three days back home. She hid behind the excuse that her classes, an internship, and her side hustle at the coffee shop kept her too busy. Avoidance? Most definitely, but she didn't admit that to her family even though every text, voicemail, and visit from her sister accused her of it. Tori sensed her mood and emotions even from three hours away. Tori could read what she didn't say.

Cara propped her elbow next to the window and leaned on her hand, the breeze caressing her cheek. Before she moved away, Nestlé loved to ride with her, jumping in the backseat at her nod and nuzzling his velvet muzzle against the crook of her neck. Eventually, she'd roll down the back window when she couldn't stand his stinky breath and the tickle of his whiskers, and his pink tongue would loll out of the side of his mouth as he licked up passing scents.

Middletown, Illinois, wasn't anyone's vacation spot. People visited family or settled into small town living where the chill of spring gave way to humid summers and shimmering snow soon covered fall leaves. Despite the miles of agricultural signs and cornstalks, the number of farmers dwindled each year. And yet more people called the once small town home, if the three Mexican restaurants, the crowded parking at the little league soccer fields on Saturday mornings, and the boom in new apartments and townhouses along Highway 150 were any indication. Even though Cara's high school friends dreamed about moving to the big city after college graduation, clearly many had tamed those aspirations.

During Friday night football games at the one and only high school, crowds huddled on the bleachers in blue and orange garb. Once a Bulldog, always a Bulldog. Neighbors met friends, fathers connected with grandfathers, mothers joined daughters. Alumni, basking in the memory of yesteryear's glory, marched along the sidelines, spiriting seniors to a win.

When resident sports fans wanted to stretch their wings, they drove three hours to the big cities of Chicago and St. Louis to take in a baseball game. Middletown divided its loyalty between the Cubs and Cardinals, but during football season, everyone rooted for the Illini. With the roar of the first three letters, I-L-L, the crowd echoed a hearty I-N-I.

Middletown wasn't Mayberry, but friendly people kept track of each other's kids just the same. Year after year, these proud people lined the streets with their kids for Homecoming and July 4th parades, catching candy from floats and waving flags to the high school band's beat. Pastors guided families every Sunday from the pulpits of their twelve churches. The volunteer fire department and the small home-grown police department protected its citizens.

Middletown had been the center of Cara's world for twenty-one years. Despite some long-time citizens ranting to the barber about a shift in the younger generation's traditions and the lack of God on their lips, many hard-working, God-fearing, salt of the earth people believed, like Cara, their hometown to be the best place to live in America.

Most days, nothing big happened in her small town, but for Cara, unlike her high school friends, Middletown had once held every significant dream she'd ever dared to imagine—until that day—the day Ali died. Middletown had a simple energy, but for Cara, it held its own reasons for caution.

Cara's unbound honey brown locks slapped her cheek and wrapped around her neck. Windows rolled down and music turned up, she soared down the sun-beaten two-lane highway. She blasted the eighties music through her speakers to drown out the noise in her head and sang along with the wind rushing through her car. Cara thumped her fist against her thigh to the beat, freeing some of the angst tightening her throat. She was as ready for Middletown as she could be. No matter what it threw her way, she told herself she could handle it.

She felt a little crazy, but not the let-loose, good kind. The potential for a chance encounter with Callum always slipped into her head space. The longer she was in town, the greater the risk was that she would run into him.

Cara imagined seeing Callum again after two years. For several moments, they'd both be struck still, hardly breathing, only recalling. With his gentle demeanor and soft-spoken approach, Callum would say he was sorry, beg her forgiveness, and find her lips.

For crying out loud, cut the melodrama!

Cara put a hard stop to that line of daydreaming and reimagined it. For several moments, they would search each other's eyes and just as Callum would beg her forgiveness, Cara would slap his face and blow past him like he meant nothing to her.

Floating her hand through the warm breeze outside her window, she approached the pig sign, marking a farm to the west that no longer existed. *I'm almost home.* She smiled in reflection.

Ten years ago, the pig on the aged white sign was painted green and the words *THE PIG SIGN* were added in bold letters across the top. At one time or another, every Middletown citizen had used the old, dilapidated, peeling pig sign as a landmark. Its preservation wasn't just for nostalgia. It safeguarded future generations from getting lost. On her first solo drive at sixteen, she'd piddled at forty miles per hour down this fifty-five miles per hour stretch to her friend's house, eyes peeled for the pig image she'd passed thousands of times as a passenger.

Flashing lights interrupted her fond memory, deflating her reminiscing. Her indignation and annoyance simmered when she checked her speedometer.

Ugh! Caught like a novice! I'm a local! I know better than to speed down this highway.

Turning onto a gravel side road, she hoped for a miracle that the squad car's overheads would race past her.

No such luck. She propped her hands on the top of the steering wheel as her dad had taught her, drumming her fingers on the dash and glancing in the rearview mirror at the police car pulling in behind her. She waited for the officer to exit the squad car, probably one of the old timers in her dad's department taking his time running her plates. Suddenly, her pulse quickened, her insides lurched, and the what-ifs hijacked her brain.

Oh, Lord. Please don't let it be him.

She gripped the steering wheel and steadied into her seat. In her rearview mirror, a trim frame sauntered slowly toward her with purposed strides.

Oh no! The odds were against her.

Black boots grazed the asphalt. Oakley sunglasses concealed his eyes. A knock thudded on the rear of her Jeep. Callum signaled his presence.

Paralyzed like a cornered rabbit, fear hijacked her body. Her heartbeat throbbed in her neck, and she willed her panic to subside. She dared not glance out her window.

She grabbed the hairband from around the gearshift and pulled her wind-blown, witchy hair into some kind of submissive ponytail. Agitation needled her nerves that she gave even an ounce of care about her thread-bare black leggings and oldest Swiftie t-shirt.

I'll show him his breakup didn't break me.

When Pat Benatar belted the final chorus of her kick-butt tune, "Hit Me with Your Best Shot" across the airwaves, Cara flipped the volume up, turned toward the window, and bellowed the charged lyrics at Callum.

He pursed his lips and waited in relaxed stillness, not a single fidget until she finished.

Cara muted the radio. Her throat constricted. The pounding in her chest reverberated louder in her head, but she led with her gut and spouted, "Evaluating your options? Go ahead, say what's on your mind."

"I'm not going to fire away at you, Cara." Callum greeted her like he'd just chatted with her yesterday. He propped his elbow on her rearview mirror, glanced into the back seat, and added, "But did you know I clocked you at twenty over the speed limit?"

"Are you sure? Twenty?" She was sure.

The master of control's coolness unnerved her. Cara fiddled with her cross necklace and released it like a hot potato when she realized she'd clasped the gift Callum had given her for her twentieth birthday. She'd grown accustomed to wearing it every day, allowing herself to keep this one small piece of him close.

She glanced back at his composed, tanned face and chiseled chin and caught his knowing smile. An ounce of fury rose in her chest, tapering the unruly desire skipping through her heart. His steady gaze skimmed once again from her cross to her eyes.

Did he just nod? What did that insinuate?

Taking off his glasses, he bent low to her. "Welcome back to Middletown, Cara. I thought I recognized your Wrangler." Her name rolled off his tongue, smooth and soft, almost cradled, and she craved to hear him say it one more time.

The strain of unasked questions surged between them. She'd told herself a million times not to break her promise to herself, to get on with her life, to get over Callum. But not one of those times did she have to face him from three feet away, captured under the stealth of his sunglasses, brave his smile, or answer his questions. Apparently, two years was too short for her heart to forget his grip, his lopsided smile, his cheeky humor, and sideways glance.

Was it the heat or spike in her blood pressure causing the flush on her face and growing nausea?

Her inner demons were working overtime against her. This was the very reason she moved, to get over him. Now she'd walked into the fire like Shadrach or Meshach or Abednego. No matter how committed she was to not be affected by him, she melted inside at the first lick of fire. She wouldn't drive away from these flames unscathed.

I'm not unhappy now. I let go of regret. My tears have dried up. That naive part of me that dreamed impossible dreams has grown up. I am not powerless. Resist his charm.

Sweat soaked her shirt, and her legs stuck to the seat. She twirled her ponytail around her hand and, to move things along, cautiously asked, "Ticket?"

Long, thick, black eyelashes hovered above chocolate brown eyes. His stiff stance and controlled demeanor built a three-foot wall of aloofness between them. She thanked the heavens his professional reserve masked his once unguarded openness with her.

From her angle through the open window, she could see his defined biceps, way more muscular than she recalled. She'd always giggled when he struck a bodybuilder pose, flexed his arms, and bragged, "Check out these guns." They were no laughing matter now, just sheer sexy. Was he taller? Or was staring at him from the discomfort of her seat making her feel small?

Crap. Wipe that lust right out of your head.

Her gut churned. Admittedly, she loved him once, and she thought he had loved her, until…

"What's your hurry?"

His monotone irritated her and thankfully equalized her emotions. "Um," she fought to steady her voice. *You mean besides wanting to magically disappear?* "Gramps is recovering from a ministroke and Nestlé isn't doing well. Do you mind?" she asked, attempting candid indifference toward him to hurry him along.

"I'm sorry to hear that. Lover Boy is the best dog."

Lover Boy. Callum's nickname for Nestlé. He always joked that she prioritized her three favorite things: her dog, ice cream, and then him. Cara pushed away from that thought and grabbed her purse from the passenger seat, scrambling to find her driver's license. "Um, do you need my driver's license?"

"How long are you in town for?"

"Just a few days," Cara said, noticing his focus quickly drop to the pavement.

Was that disappointment on his face?

"I'll let Chief Riley's daughter off with a warning," he said matter-of-factly.

She sat silent and stared through the front windshield, counting to ten while taking slow deep breaths, trying to keep it together. Finally, she fired at him, "Chief Riley's daughter? Seriously? That's who I am to you? Chief Riley's daughter? That's why you're giving me a pass? Not because I'm your friend? Not because I was your sister's best friend? Not because I was your girlfriend? Not because you once promised to love me forever? Not because you're sorry you flipped my entire world upside down? Well, thank you so much, Officer Hall, for your consideration."

Her rant caught him off guard. While she had his attention, she surprised herself and quickly fired again, "And here's my warning for you. Let's steer clear of one another, Officer Hall."

He covered his wide-eyed shock with mirrored lenses. "I'm glad I didn't give you a ticket," he chuckled.

She had always loved their banter and nearly let herself be dragged into a darting dance of words.

"I hope your grandpa is better. Enjoy your visit, Cara." His sincerity eased her ire.

His lips gently caressed her name for a third time. *Lord have mercy.* For a split second, she recognized the man she once loved. Her defenses caved, and she rewound to their dating years. The longing for him she'd squelched for so long broke free. The sense that he still held some ownership over her emotions made her seethe inside, but it would pass. She curled back from the danger of it just in time, slumping her shoulders and pressing back hard against the leather seat.

"Be safe," she offered under her breath.

"Always am," he answered, gripping her window frame. He stalled as if to share something else but then tapped her window frame twice with finality and, with a tight smile, ended their encounter. "Take it easy."

Take it easy? That was anything but easy!

Pinned in her seat, she counted the heartbeats pummeling her chest. From the side mirror, she watched him almost sprint back to his squad car. Once he drove off and cleared her car, she butted her forehead against the steering wheel, slowed her breathing, and found her footing once more.

That was more than awkward. I don't need your warning, Callum. For my safety, I plan to steer WAY clear of you.

TWO

Cara pulled onto the highway once Callum's squad car was out of sight. She clenched the steering wheel, dwelling on her first meeting with Callum in two years. She once believed their love to be lasting and true, and even though she was thankful for the confidence her time away had given her, sadness lingered. She didn't want anything to do with Callum. Sure, she'd been flustered, but he'd caught her off guard. That was all. She refused to let anything close to desire for Callum betray her. Their encounter proved she needed to seal some cracks in her armor. She promised herself she'd tread much more carefully next time.

Cara sped into town, carefully keeping to the speed limit. Word would spread like a forest fire that Callum had pulled over the Chief's daughter. She hoped he took a ribbing for it. She didn't feel sorry for him. The master of calm could hold his own with his fellow officers. He had surely recognized her Jeep. He could have avoided their entire encounter. Why did he pull her over in the first place? To make her squirm? Maybe he'd committed to the traffic stop before he'd realized it was her.

Cara waved at Mr. Herriott on his tractor as she flew by. He greeted every traveler down this road with a long smile and a slow nod.

A new gray-bricked "Welcome to Middletown" sign along the Country Ridge Subdivision grabbed her attention as she slowed to thirty-five miles per hour. Small-town hospitality and big-town spiffy. She liked it. Passing the construction of a new subdivision, she once again realized her nearly two-hundred-year-old village was growing fast. She didn't recall when big city ways invaded Middletown or when the village installed its first traffic light. Her best guess was Middletown now boasted at least six.

Slowing to glance left before the railroad tracks, she glimpsed the church she'd been raised in, a white spire reaching into the blue heavens. Five years ago, after a storm knocked off the old spire, point first into the roof, the congregation voted on this wider, more modern design.

She had felt safe with these people she'd grown up with and this place she'd worshiped in every Sunday. Not anymore. She would need a heavy dose of courage to enter that sanctuary again, to find comfort and healing there.

She didn't trust God. What kind of God takes away your best friend to emphasize His narrative? Spinning in her private orbit, she had taken control of her circumstances and anger and had gotten on with her life, keeping her distance from both God and Callum. But like any renovation, she admitted to being a slow work in progress. Since being on her own, she'd made headway, patching the exhausted walls of her heart and covering the tear-seeping holes after the shock of Ali being torn from her life. She doubted repairing the hole in her heart was ever fully possible. Some wounds dug too deep. Being back home in Callum's presence obviously reminded her she'd have to fortify the walls she built to brace against setbacks.

Rain, wind, and age flecked the gray and white grain elevator that marked her arrival in town. After the train tracks, she turned east at the four-way stop light that ruffled some folks' feathers when it was first installed.

A patrol car crossed traffic in front of her. She sucked in her breath, then quickly chided herself for her fear of running into Callum again. What a nonsensical reaction. She'd made it through that five-minute glitch. If she were in his presence any longer than that, she might be tempted to ask the questions she'd pondered many late nights, trying to understand his choices, but she feared reopening old wounds.

Did answers matter now? Why was she so frustratingly on the fence about whether she wanted answers? She told herself, time and time again, she was fine not understanding Callum's thinking when he broke up with her. What was done is done. Callum's explanation could cool her ire or set it on fire. After her run-in at the pig sign today, did she dare risk the emotional freedom she'd gained after two years for an uncertain closure? Would hearing his thoughts free her or provoke a whirlwind of more nagging doubts?

Passing the police station, she quickly scanned the police cars for her dad's, but didn't see it. He'd told her once, if not a thousand times, being cooped up in the office all day was the worst part of his job. His patrolmen were the luckiest people in the precinct because they got out in the community, among its people. She figured he had ventured out for his usual rounds through the town and had ended up at Jake's Farm to Burger, chewing it up with the locals over lunch.

At the corner of Oak Street and Lombard, she pulled in to get gas, but more importantly, a slushie. In high school, she and Ali had become addicted to Coke slushies, treating themselves after practices and games. Her dad fostered her addiction to the carbonated, crushed-ice goodness, surprising her with a pick-me-up when she prepped for a hard test or finals. Old habits were hard to break, and she needed a treat after the lingering effects of running into Callum.

As she stepped inside, the familiar ding of the door chimed. The tall cashier barely acknowledged her with a side glance and continued counting off coins. She suddenly lifted her eyelids again and cast a wide toothed grin at Cara, racing toward her with arms wide open. "It's our country girl, Cara Bear!" she whooped, spilling the nickname her dad had made popular. She wrapped tight arms around Cara, pulling her into her large bosom. Every eye in the station watched the reunion. "Welcome home!"

"Just for a few days," Cara corrected, her tone laced with overdone warning.

"Head on back. Today's drink is on me!" She pointed at the swirling machines along the wall with her long glossy red nails that matched her lipstick.

Mrs. Kocher had worked the day shift at the gas station for as long as Cara could remember. She said it paid a couple of bills and allowed her to be home with her two boys. Cara had a suspicion it also allowed her to mingle with people and be the first to learn the town gossip.

Cara felt Mrs. K. watching her as she made her way to the fountain drinks. After grabbing the large lid for her usual Coke slushie, she wandered to the checkout line. She placed the exact change on the counter, but Mrs. K. slid it back to her.

"Now listen here, young lady," she said. "You know better than to argue with Mama K."

"I sure do," she said and winked. She stood corrected, slowly retracting her money. "It's good seeing you. I think you're still the sweetest lady in town. Thanks so much for this," she said, raising her drink.

"Think of it as a welcome home gift," Mrs. K. said, squeezing her hand like a hug.

Cara didn't have the heart to reiterate that this trip wasn't her coming home, just another quick visit.

Cara looked hard in the rearview mirror before heading out and knew her struggle for what it was. Distrust. There, she'd admitted it. Distrust that all God's ways were good. She'd not confessed it out loud to anyone, only in her heart, which was as loud as she'd say it among the people that helped grow her faith. Either her choices or Callum's, maybe both, calloused her heart. She once trusted God and believed the Scriptures she'd memorized. But still, under His care, her heart had been crushed, and she continued to trip over its rubble. Cara refused to expose herself to more pain, hoping for Him to patch the wounds into beautiful scars.

Weaving through Lake of the Woods Park, she searched for deer, which had once been a dusk activity for her and Callum. They raced to count who could find the most. At the covered bridge, she stalled to stare into the crevices of the eaves for a brown bat colony. Five years ago, they had flitted over her head while her mom and dad took group prom pictures. She and her friends leapt from the arms of their dates and began running in frantic circles. When Callum caught her, he wrapped her in both of his arms and whispered, "I got you." She had never felt more protected.

On summer mornings, she ran and biked in this park. Summer afternoons were spent boating and basking in the warm glow of the sun on the banks of the river. Summer nights were for parking and fireworks—all with Callum. The onslaught of memories was hard to curb. A honk pushed her on toward the park's exit.

When she turned the corner toward their long lane, she spotted her dad exiting their drive and waved him to a halt.

He jumped from his vehicle and kissed her on the cheek. "Hi, Cara Bear. It's good to have you home. I heard Callum stopped you on your way in," he chortled.

She hit her steering wheel. "I wish that hadn't happened. Small towns! And why is that even funny?"

"Your lead foot ruined your own stealth."

"Glad I could provide you with a laugh."

"I'm not laughing at you. He should've spared you the trouble. He's gonna get teased for that little maneuver— especially from me."

"Good! I sure hope so."

"One of life's unwanted collision courses, I guess," he said.

"Definitely," Cara responded in disgust.

"Can't wait to catch up tonight." He gave a hearty guffaw and drove off.

Collision courses. She pondered that phrase as she gazed down the length of their Cypress lined drive. The crunch of gravel under slow tires welcomed her home.

Mom had decorated the porch for summer. Like clockwork, they depended on Mom to mark the change of season by her porch displays. Her six weeping green fern baskets, fronds cascading down, hung from the eaves across the porch and gave a soft, summery vibe. New tall fern planters flanked the door. The once white swing and rockers had been freshly painted black. The sunshine yellow cushions and teal pillows popped against the darkness.

Cara hadn't helped Mom decorate this pretty porch. She shrugged off feeling left out and thought of pouring a sweet tea and lulling herself to sleep on those thick cushions. Mom's easel chalkboard stood where it always did, to the right of the top step. She'd drawn flowers and left a special note to Cara instead of her usual Scripture verse or funny quote—"We can't wait to hug you, Cara-Bear." The sign invited her in, but she felt sad, like a visitor in her own home.

Nestlé barked a greeting, tail swishing across the hardwood floor.

Cara opened the screen door to a full body wag and hugged him around the neck. "Hi there, sweet boy! Now that's a welcome I love coming home to." She plopped to the floor on a new cream and teal indoor mat. Her furry friend flopped on his back and hoisted all four paws into the air, awaiting a good belly rub.

"Hey, Mom, I'm home," she called from the floor, soaking up all the love and sunshine spilling through the door and from her old pup.

THREE

Cara couldn't wait to take a walk to her pond with Nestlé. She kicked gravel along the trail and smiled at squirrels playing hide-and-seek in hollowed-out trees. Sitting on the bridge near swaying cattails, she let the sunshine warm her skin. Cara petted his sleek fur and reflected on time's impermanence. For so long, she'd taken these jaunts with her loyal sidekick for granted. Today, she sensed she should slow down and savor these fleeting moments.

Making their way back to the house, Cara coaxed as Nestlé slowly waddled along. "Come on, buddy. Just a bit more." Halting at the bottom of the back porch steps and staring at the door, he plopped down in the heat of the sun with a long exhale, lifting his head at the creak of the porch screen door.

"Aaaaa! You're home!" Tori bounded down the steps and grabbed Cara in a fierce bear hug. Still holding on to her, Tori studied Cara. "I love your long bangs. When did you do that?"

"I've been thinking about doing this for a while. I decided one morning to just go for it. A little present to myself for graduation. I can still wear my ponytail with a little flair. I'm getting used to having layers across the top of my eyebrows," Cara said, brushing her bangs to the side. "I think I like it, but the final verdict is still out. I can always grow them out. Right?"

"I like the change. Besides, a little change is perfect to celebrate something big like graduation."

"And a new job," Cara replied, flipping her bangs to the side.

"Ahhhhh." Tori shouted, dancing in a circle. "That's awesome. What is it?" Tori asked, hugging her.

"Working in the school I interned in," Cara explained.

"You loved those kids! You're gonna be just what they need."

"Thanks, Tor."

"Nestlé is panting hard. Did you walk him to the pond?" Tori asked.

"It was slow going, but we made it all the way," Cara said, stooping to pet Nestlé's head.

"He hasn't been willing to make that jaunt in months. He must be as excited as me that you're home," Tori said and hugged her sister again.

"He cuddled next to me on the bridge the whole time. No wandering. No curiosity. Just rested his head on my lap," Cara said, sitting on the bottom step, stroking Nestlé's coarse fur. "I thought he'd give up for good on the way back. I constantly had to wait and coax him."

Tori leaned against the handrail and sympathized, "He rallied all his energy to impress you. He doesn't get out much anymore, except to do his duty, and then sometimes he can't even get outside fast enough for that. When he goes out, we lift him up and down the back steps."

"I can't believe how much he's weakened. The last time I was home…" Cara calculated. In less than six months, Nestlé had aged years. "I can't imagine life without him," Cara voiced through shallow breaths. Her heart raced at the thought of her family without him. Cara massaged his back and legs, and Nestlé thanked her with licks on her hand.

"How was your drive in?" Tori asked.

"You haven't heard? I figured the entire town would know by now."

"Heard what?" Tori questioned.

"Callum pulled me over at the pig sign."

"What? Why? Well, I know you were probably speeding." Tori rose and waved to Cara to follow her. "This I have to hear, but I have to leave for work in five minutes and also eat. Come inside while I make a sandwich. He had to know it was you. I can't believe he didn't recognize your Jeep!"

"That's exactly what I thought. All I can think is he flipped on his lights before he realized it was me. He admitted to recognizing my Wrangler."

Cara planted herself on the stool at the counter and watched Tori make a PB&J sandwich.

"So, he's messing with you? He pulled you over at the pig sign," Tori chuckled. "Did you tell him how appropriate that was?"

"Oh, I so wish I had. I'd take a do-over just to say that!" Cara giggled.

"How did it go?"

"Awk-ward!" she ranted.

"Because?" Tori said, chewing her first mouthful of peanut butter.

"He said he'd let 'Chief Riley's daughter' off with a *warning*," she snarked with air quotes. "I'm no longer Cara, the girl he professed to love. I'm the Chief's daughter. His allegiance is to Dad, his superior."

"I hope you gave him a snarky warning, too!"

"I told Officer Hall he'd better steer clear of me."

"You did not!"

"Oh yes, I did!" Cara said, planting her hands on her hips. "That agitated me to no end."

"Attagirl! How did he seem?"

"I don't give a pig's behind how he seemed."

"Yeah, who wants to hear about that swine's snorts and grunts, anyway?" Tori giggled. "I'm super happy you're home. I'll be back for dinner after my shift, and we'll catch up more. Let's plan some fun together. How long are you here?" Tori stuffed the last bite of her sandwich in her mouth.

"Just five days," Cara said.

Five days and then back to normal life.

Tori tapped Cara on the shoulder to get her attention. Opening her mouth wide, she muffled, "See…food. See…ya," and waved goodbye.

*　＊　＊　＊*

"Do I smell peach cobbler?" Tori yelled from the front door when she returned hours later from work.

"Sure do. Mom's baking up all my favorites."

"Have you been sitting on that stool the entire time I was at work?"

"I ate lunch, took a quick nap, and then visited with Gramps on his porch for quite a while. Mom and I are catching up while she imitates a whirlwind, cooking dinner."

Tori lifted the lid on the pot on the stove. "Spaghetti and meatballs. Yum. Must be bribing her to stay longer, eh, Mom?"

"If only it would work," her mom said under raised eyebrows, coaxing Cara.

"I have a job to get back to, you know."

"Did you tell Mom about your welcome home?" Tori asked, bumping Cara with her hip.

"Of course. I've filled her in on everything. Please, let's not rehash it. It's infuriating," Cara moaned.

"I can't wait to hear what Dad said to Callum." Tori stirred the pot.

"Tori, seriously, let's just let it drop!" Cara emphasized.

"We'll find out sooner than later. Your dad should be here any minute," her mom said.

"I'm right here!" her dad shouted from the hallway.

"Oh," her mom squealed in surprise. "I didn't hear you come in."

"You're late, Dad," Tori called.

"Working on the auction," Dad groaned.

"The auction?" Cara asked.

"Since I'm on the Board, I'm preparing for the Animal Shelter's annual fundraising dinner next weekend. Auction tickets are ten dollars each. You girls want one?"

"What's being auctioned?" Tori asked over the sounds of the refrigerator crushing ice.

"I'll get the list in a minute."

"You had me at animal shelter. No need to see the list. I'll donate twenty dollars. Put my money on whatever two items you think I'll like. I'll set the table, Mom," Cara added, collecting plates and silverware.

"I'm in for one ticket," Tori added.

"I strongly encouraged Callum to stay after his shift and help me get things organized for the fundraiser. He's also agreed to help that Saturday night," Dad informed them.

"Good job, Dad," Tori cheered.

"Invited. Strongly suggested. Highly recommended. Ahem... Commanded. Something like that," her dad said.

Cara and Tori shot glances at one another and broke into laughter at the same time.

"The way I figure it, his actions speak louder than his apology for pulling you over."

"Truth," Cara mumbled under her breath.

"We're ready to eat." Mom pointed everyone to the dinner table.

"Cara, I've got a big favor to ask of you." Her dad's tone switched from jovial to serious.

"You mean besides finagling twenty dollars from your daughter, who has a college loan to pay off?"

Wary, her dad cleared his throat and said, "We'll talk about it after dinner."

"This feels very ominous," Cara joked.

"No, not ominous, but something I know you'll need to give considerable thought to."

They moved to the living room after dinner.

Cara sat in the recliner and clasped her hands together in her lap. "Ok, shoot," she said.

Her dad leaned back, stretched his arm over the back of the couch, and crossed his legs. His forehead wrinkles deepened as he proceeded in a slow, calm voice. "I know your new job starts in August, but as far as summer plans go, I thought you might consider staying here for the summer."

"And?" Cara prodded, when he paused overly long.

He ran his finger over the seam on the knee of his pants, stalling, and then blurted, "I need a police aid to fill in over the summer. Judy's on maternity leave."

"I can't do that. No way."

"I trust you. You're organized—"

"I have a job. They're expecting me," she countered.

"It's only until the end of July."

"Why are you asking me this now?"

"I'm in a bind. The officers rotate filling in, but that solution is not working out. I need someone consistent."

"It's way too complicated."

"I hesitated to ask because I know it might be awkward for you with Callum. But the pay has to be way better than what you're making."

Cara fidgeted, hating to deny her father. He never pleaded with her.

"You're organized and good with people and work well under pressure. I know I'm laying it on thick here, but it dawned on me that you're the best solution."

Her sister leaned against the doorjamb, listening intently.

"I can't."

"Will you take a day and think and pray about your decision? We can talk tomorrow or Sunday. Ask me any questions you need to help make your decision easier, in the meantime."

Cara wrapped both arms around herself but didn't answer.

"What do you think?" her dad asked.

"We'll talk again," she flatly replied, but she already knew her answer.

Tori promptly shot out, "So, you're considering it?"

Cara stopped mid-step on her escape up the stairs to her bedroom, turned to Tori, and flung her a flicker of annoyance.

"If looks could kill…" Tori said under her breath.

* * *

Cara wasn't sure if her mom and Tori were ganging up on her, but they came in a show of force not thirty minutes later.

Cara propped against her headboard, hugging her knees to herself, and waited for one of them to speak.

Her mom sat at the edge of the bed at her hip and held her hand, the way she did when Cara was a kid needing discipline or consolation. Tori stood behind her mom like a sentinel. Cara sensed what was coming and her pulse soared.

"Cara Bear, what Dad asked is hard. We're not here to convince you to take the job."

Cara waited, the word *but* ringing in her head.

"But it's time," her mom said, searching her face.

"Time for what?" Cara asked, deadpan.

"To come home."

"I am home with you guys. And I have a new home in Edwardsville."

"I mean in your heart. To claim this place as yours again and not run from it."

A mist glazed Cara's eyes at her mom's sentiment. Cara couldn't utter a response, or her emotions would spill over. Even though her mom saying she ran away hurt her feelings, her statement hit home.

"More than anything, I want you to remember you are a grown woman—a strong woman. You always have been. Years ago, you broke your rib in a soccer game. Remember that?"

Cara nodded her head but had no idea what that had to do with coming home.

"God designed you to be stubborn and courageous and competitive on purpose. I've known that since you walked—at ten months, no less. You kept running from that moment on."

Cara and Tori both laughed through choked throats.

Her mom's calm soothed her. "When that goliath of a girl clobbered you that day on the field, you got back up. You didn't go after her, even though I almost hopped off the bleachers after her myself. You hobbled to the sidelines. They wrapped your ribs, and you played the rest of the game. I can't imagine the pain you were in. I can't believe I went along with letting you continue to play, but you were adamant."

"I'd have been in pain on the sidelines or in the game. I might as well have played."

"Competitive much?" Tori inserted.

"My point is God also gave you the ability, in here," Mom pointed at Cara's heart, "to get back up from the muck of life. You know the Scripture that says God made woman from the rib of man?"

Cara shook her head yes.

"Well, woman, you've taken some hits, but you can regrow yourself in God. He designed you that way—as a rib. He knew you'd face hard circumstances. Things that would challenge you to stay committed to your community, like coming home after Ali's death and your breakup. But that's why He gave you the ability—a supernatural ability to find the strength He put inside of you to pick yourself up."

Cara rubbed the lines of stitching in the quilt she sat under. Her mom wasn't wrong. Living three hours away, Callum's presence couldn't permeate her newfound strength. Now, she stood on sandy ground, her courage sinking.

"God will give you strength if you decide to stay. You ran away from here to get space from Callum. If it feels like your dad doesn't understand how difficult that was for you by asking you to come home, that's not true."

"I did not run away from home." Cara found her voice.

I ran from Callum—to live without wanting him.

Her mom turned her head in question.

"Think about what I've said while you decide about the summer," her mom said and kissed her on the forehead before leaving her with her thoughts.

"And think of the fun you could have, getting revenge on Callum," Tori whispered in her ear.

FOUR

After everyone left for church, Cara took Gramps his breakfast—Mom's tactic for keeping him healthy. Every day, she fixed him oatmeal with flaxseed and blueberries. Today, she added three oatmeal cookies just to stay on his good side.

Cara attempted to sneak out of the house without Nestlé, but as she bounded down the steps, he waddled from his sunspot on the braided rug, nails clicking down the hallway's hardwood. Refusing to be left behind, he waited nose to screen at the back patio door. Cara pushed it open for him, and her furry slowpoke wagged his tail, beating Cara's calf as he passed. The slamming screen door would cue Gramps to her stroll down the lane to his tiny A-frame.

When she rounded the bend in the gravel road, Gramps waved from his rocker, coffee mug in hand. Since Dad installed the overhead fan several summers ago, Gramps spent most afternoons napping, nestled under the canopy of the old oaks near his porch. He adamantly denied he napped, like it displayed a weakness in his character, admitting only to resting his eyes.

Cara bent over Gramps and gave him a long, tight hug—longer than her usual few seconds—and a couple of extra squeezes to his thin frame for good measure. A wrinkled, age-spotted hand took the bowl from her and balanced it on his lap.

She'd missed their time catching up on his porch. On summer days when she had lived at home, they'd found a rhythm of chatting over a warm cup of creamy coffee after her early morning run or while they watched fireflies propel from the lawn at dusk. She would snap the suspenders he wore every day before releasing him. He would always emit a playful, guttural growl, but he was all bark and no bite.

His bum knee limited his tending to his apple and pear trees, but he nurtured his roses, daylilies, and dahlias with the tenderness of a mother. She'd sneaked up on him once when he was coaxing them to grow. When she'd first caught him talking to his roses four summers ago, she thought he was talking to Grandma, who had recently passed.

Once Cara settled into the rocker to Gramps's right so he could hear her with his one good ear, Nestlé circled and plopped on the cool concrete at her feet. Cara winced at his heavy hind end flop, a bag of bones tossed to the ground. When he was a puppy, she had taught Nestlé to sit or lay as she rocked on the porch. He'd been mostly obedient ever since, except when Callum's truck rolled down the driveway. Her old companion half sighed, half moaned, and then closed his eyes, signaling he knew they'd be there for a long spell.

They rocked and chatted about the arrival of the cicadas until Gramps asked, "Why are you not at church?"

"I'm hanging with you."

His puzzled smirk said he didn't buy her answer.

"Your mom made me stay home and rest this week. Did she make you babysit me?" he accused, handing her a cookie.

Cara munched on his offering and fidgeted in her seat. "Not at all, Gramps. I want to hang with you. I don't want to go to church."

"Hmm." Gramps puzzled.

"Your mom thinks I'll watch church on my TV. Your dad got it all set up for me. I told her I was plenty well to attend church. Best hospital around if anything happens, but here I sit, doing what she insists, refusing to fight a bulldog."

Cara giggled at his contorted grimace.

"You know it's true," he said seriously.

"Oh, I definitely do," Cara admitted, chewing her cookie. Her mom's challenge to her two nights ago, to think through staying for the summer, still worked on her like a pinch to her bum.

"She gets that stubbornness from her mother, you know." Gramps's cheeks lifted in a smile. He included Grandma somehow in nearly every conversation.

"Well, of course, Gramps," she agreed with a wink, "and she gets her docile nature from you."

"Tell me why you aren't at church, kiddo."

"I told you—"

"Don't feed me a line," he interrupted.

She faced Gramps and shared the truth she'd told to no one. "God and I had a kind of break up," Cara admitted. "I can tell Mom's not happy I stayed home, but she's not pushing me either."

"It's not between you and your mom. This is between you and God."

Cara hadn't expected Gramps to defend her choice. He was defending her, wasn't he?

"So, is your breakup with God repairable?"

"I'm angry with Him." The words that came out of her mouth surprised her. "I played by His rules. I checked all the boxes and upheld my end of the bargain. I attended church, read my Bible, prayed, got baptized, went to youth group. Then God stole Ali and Callum. Why? He didn't protect me or Ali. How can I trust His kind of love?"

Gramps rocked and seemed to study his feet. She flushed with worry that she'd been too raw with him.

He handed the bowl of oatmeal back to her and asked, "Will you put that on the counter? I'm not hungry just yet."

"Only if you don't tell Mom I let you eat cookies first."

"They're oatmeal, so they're good for me."

From inside, Cara heard Gramps's chatter. "…Our girl's as pretty as ever, but her heart's aching. You feel it. You always know. She's hurting my heart, skipping church. Seems to me, we all need to be there."

"Who are you talking to, Gramps?" she asked, returning to the porch.

"Our buddy."

"Nestlé or God?"

"I'd say a bit of both," he answered in all seriousness. "Have I told you about the time I asked your grandma to marry me?"

Cara was used to Gramps's hard segues, but this one seemed way off-kilter. No mind if she'd heard it before. He jumped right in on his retelling.

"I asked your grandma to marry me at the end of our senior year in high school."

Cara admired their story of young love and had hoped her first love would be as lasting.

"I love that story. You asked her as you caught up to her in the hallway on your way to English class. She thought you were teasing her because your class was reading Shakespeare. That's why she nicknamed you Romeo. You high school rascal," she said, patting his hand.

"I meant it when I got down on one knee on that hard, tiled floor. When she finally nodded yes, my heart sealed it as gospel that very moment."

I wish Callum and I had gotten that far, him down on one knee with a ring in his hand. I thought we were almost there!

She sighed, remembering. They'd dreamed of building a house one day with enough rooms for three kids.

Cara's eyes misted over, and she smiled like the first time she'd heard the story.

Grandma's rendition included a few more details. She had studied Gramps for sincerity and made him grovel on one knee nearly the entire passing period, enduring all the hoops and hollers from classmates before giving him her answer. She'd once admitted to Cara that she'd known her answer from the start, but felt she was worth more than the little beads of sweat that formed on his forehead.

"I sure miss Grandma." She squeezed Gramps's hand once more and sipped her tea. "She'd hide from today's scorcher." They sat in the quiet, each staring into their own memory of the elegance and grace she embodied even in the heat. Their very own classic icon of style had always worn long-sleeved cotton floral blouses and loose wide-legged pants to shade herself from the sun. Grandma credited Noxzema and staying out of the sun for her flawless skin. Cara prayed it was good genes.

"Three years later, we married."

"Three years?" Cara blurted in surprise. "I didn't realize you were engaged so long."

Gramps chuckled at Cara's dramatic blinking. "This is the part we usually skipped telling. Who likes to dwell on the hard stuff? Folks want you to stick to the good—our church wedding and the together until death do us part." He paused.

The cicadas screamed louder in his silence. She set her hand over his, and he returned from his pondering.

"We broke up before I got that ring on her finger."

"You broke up? I never heard that part of the story!"

"That's why I'm telling ya it now, Little Bear." Gramps was the only one that Cara let get away with still using that pet name. "My dad, your Great Grandpa Moore, died of a massive heart-attack a month after my graduation from high school. Things took a hard turn. My family needed my support. My mom had to find work, and she hadn't worked outside the home my entire growing-up years. As the oldest, I worked two jobs, the grocery store and farming."

"Oh, Gramps, you were so young to carry that load."

"Life got serious, quick. We walked hand in hand to that pond on July third," he said as he pointed down the lane. "About a month after we buried my dad. It was hot enough to scald a lizard. We hung our feet in the water as we sat on the dock, like we had a hundred times before. I let her know all my fears about the future. When your grandma asked what I was going to do, I blew it."

"You blew it? But how?"

"I blurted my fears fast as gunfire at her."

"What fears?"

"Gibberish like, 'I can't start a life with you. I can't have a family. I already got one.'"

"Oh, Gramps—"

"She thought I meant *ever*."

"Did you?" Cara accused, smoothing any sharp edges that might cut into her tone. Gramps could take her bluntness. She meant no disrespect.

"The dark clouds were thick over my head. I couldn't see how I could leave my family. Life was overwhelming. They needed me and any money I could bring in. I just knew I couldn't be a good husband and start a family right then. It's not that I didn't want to. Lord knows, I wanted that more than anything. No way did I want to let her go."

"But you did."

"My confusion sounded like doubt to her. She said she couldn't share a life with someone 'who could so easily set her aside' and she walked away from the pond and me and wouldn't answer my calls. She called me a week later to tell me she was moving to Cheboygan, Michigan, to live with her aunt and uncle the following day. Her uncle found her a good job at the University."

"She left town?" Cara asked, dumbfounded. *I'm in good company.*

Cara felt stronger about her decision to make a start in a new town and, in a strange way, supported by her grandma.

"She could be as stout as a mule if she wanted to," Gramps said, chuckling at his cherished memory as he sipped his coffee.

Grandma had been a gentle giant in Cara's world, but she didn't doubt Grandma's fortitude for one second. She'd seen Grandma stick to her guns plenty of times and admired her indomitable spirit, wrapped in grace. Alongside Gramps, Grandma had worked from dawn to dusk on her family's farm, handed down to her from generations of farmers. She'd worked as hard as the men in the fields, most days longer. Grandma had silenced a room on more than one occasion, speaking her mind only when it was "absolutely necessary." When she prefaced a story of persistence with those two words, she'd look at Cara with a tight-lipped smile and a tip of her head. She was not afraid to raise hackles if she thought decisions needed to be challenged. She'd reiterated her motto over and over to the family: respect people, never drama. That Grandma would stand behind her decision on their engagement, Cara could surely imagine. It was the principle of the thing.

"I was angry at myself for my choices, at the turn my life took. God dangled the life I wanted right in front of my eyes, and then took it all away. I was furious."

Cara knew that feeling. It was a big part of the reason she kept a comfortable distance with God these days.

"When we got back together, Grandma admitted to me that letting me find my own way nearly tore her apart. She'd said it was the hardest part of loving me, trusting I would find my way back to her and God."

Just like Callum shredded my heart.

"How did you?" Cara asked, genuinely interested.

"I never intended for our relationship to end. But when it did, and she moved away so quickly, it hit me like a ton of bricks. Ain't gonna lie that I didn't get rightly mad as a hornet at her about that decision. I couldn't believe she'd done that—and so darn quick. I was stuck in this town and wound tighter than a three-day clock. How was I gonna get her to believe me? After some embarrassing begging, I convinced her dad to give me her aunt and uncle's address. I drove eight hours through the night to land on their doorstep at six in the morning on a Sunday. We sat on their porch and hashed it out."

"It was that easy?" He hadn't talked about how he mended ways with God.

"Easy? Little Bear, her tail was up and stinger out. I slept in my car in front of their house three nights in a row until she showed a hint of giving me a second chance. I almost lost both of my jobs. I mistakenly thought she'd come back with me, and we'd both be back in Middletown that Sunday night. It took quite a bit of convincing."

"I still don't understand. Why did you end things?"

"I didn't. I never stopped loving her. The responsibility of it all twisted my gut. My words came out like I didn't want her, which was the furthest from the truth. I just knew it wasn't the right time to start a new life with her. I had things to overcome. When she left town, it sure seemed like she didn't want to hang around and wait for me to get things together."

"How long before you convinced her to come home?"

"A turn of four seasons and a boatload of prayer. Mostly me yelling, if I'm honest."

Cardinals trilled from the evergreen, a soothing slow rhythm.

"I can't believe I didn't know this part of your story. A whole year? Gramps, that's a long time!"

"My cramped hand would tend to agree with you. I spent many a night writing long letters to her. It's not my most shining moment. I guess that's what I want you to know."

"Gramps, are you defending Callum's actions with your story?"

"Not at all. I can't say what's going on for that young man. I got some words for him." He spit his words like a warning. "I'm defending God. Run hard after Him. He's got good for you, Cara Bear."

Does He really?

Cara doubted that. She didn't want to discuss God right now with Gramps, but she would love to hear what he had to say to Callum.

"Oh, Gramps," she squeezed his arm, as sure he was wrong as he was sure he was right. "Thanks for telling me." Cara forced as much cheer in her voice as she could muster to show that she truly admired his gumption, but his story left her hollowed out inside. Why couldn't Callum have chased her like Gramps did Grandma? She couldn't believe she was envious of her sweet Grandma's good fortune and happy ending.

"Her sticking with me—well, the Good Lord gave me more than I can say grace over. Don't give up on God, Cara. Don't ignore Him. Keep talking to Him. He can take your anger. And if you need to yell, well, then yell. He'll work the anger right out of ya."

Cara laughed at the idea of yelling her way back to God.

"I'm serious. Give it a go."

She'd admit her anger had driven her relationship with God the last two years. Honestly, she wasn't sure what good ignoring God had done her. Keeping her emotions bottled had driven a wedge between her and God, a deep, quiet chasm. Somehow, that felt safer than wrestling for answers.

"I love how you care for me." She stood to leave and kissed Gramps on his forehead.

"We got a couple of days to talk some more before you leave, right?" he asked, like he hadn't quite pressed his point.

Unless I find my courage. Then we'll have all summer.

"Looking forward to them, Gramps. And we'll have more after that. I'm not going away forever."

"In my experience, women can run away as fast as a doe springs into a thicket. Can't take my chances this time, sweet pea."

"Gramps, I'm not running. I'll be three hours away, helping kids in school. I'll be back plenty," she said, hoping he caught the love and not the doubt in her voice. She couldn't give him guarantees, neither could he.

"Well, let's hope, little bird, you fly back, but I'm not holding the little breath I have left." Relaxing his arms on his rocker and resting his head against the back, he gently rocked and soaked up the Sunday morning serenity.

Was he pouring things on thick or had his stroke spurred him to be blunt with the time he had left?

She also worried that a bigger stroke could be around the corner. These were precious moments—soaking up time with Gramps, sharing his life and wisdom.

A hard lump choked her throat, and she hugged his bony shoulders. She might be knee deep in her last chat with him and not know it.

God, don't take Gramps from me, too, she prayed.

Losing Ali had left her breathless at life's briefness.

Losing Callum had left her lost, mistrusting her certainty that love could conquer life's hard trials.

Once upon a time, she believed she'd live happily ever after.

Ali's death obliterated the *ever after.*

Callum's exit obliterated *happily.*

What will losing Gramps do to me?

✳ ✳ ✳

Cara sat alone on the front porch swing, biting her bottom lip and deliberating with herself. Middletown was Callum's home, but it was her hometown, too. The place she'd never expected to leave. She missed being with her family. Was she ready, like Mom said, to challenge herself? Taking the job was one way to find out, to put herself to the test.

Gramps had helped her find her courage and didn't even know it. She wanted to be the strong woman her mom and Gramps saw in her.

The minute her family stepped from the car, she called them into the living room to share her decision. Her dad clasped his hands together under his chin as if a prayer had been answered.

"How about free room and board and peach cobbler?" Cara maneuvered, having learned to negotiate a deal by watching her dad.

"Deal! Peach cobbler, *if* you start tomorrow," her dad countered. "We'll throw in free lunches, too. Won't we honey? Whatever you find in the fridge." The heaviness in his voice from earlier had dissipated, replaced with playfulness.

"Absolutely! And spaghetti and meatballs once a week," her mom chimed in.

"I'm so happy. We'll be together for the summer before my final year of college!" Tori flung herself into Cara's lap and hugged her, giddy with anticipation.

Nestlé joined the excitement with a loud, deep bark.

Tori flitted from Cara's lap like a dragonfly among pond rocks to sit on the floor and pat Nestlé, elated at the turn of events.

Shaking her dad's hand to seal the deal, Cara said, "Things change quickly around here. Looks like I'm home for the summer."

Her mom popped up from the couch with a spring in her step and kissed her cheek. "Oh, I'm so happy you're home, baby girl," she said.

FIVE

Cara felt the eyes of every officer in the room zero in on her, questioning her presence at roll call. Many were just getting off patrol, but the Chief had asked them to attend the briefing. Standing beside her dad at the podium, Cara worried fainting was a real possibility if weak knees and waves of nausea were symptoms. Could she forget to breathe and pass out? It certainly felt plausible. That last time she was this nervous, she almost peed her pants at her fourth-grade talent show.

Push through. She gave herself a pep talk. *You're stronger than you think.*

She looked out at the officers with a soft, plastered smile, avoiding Callum sitting in the corner. But seconds later, like magnets, their eyes locked, and she didn't hear one thing her father said about her after that. Callum's eyes bore into her. His expression was heavy. He didn't smile in politeness or arrogance or surprise. She couldn't read this controlled connection he made with her, but one thing she knew, he was trying hard, too hard, not to give anything away.

Cara concentrated like she had when she was the captain of her soccer team. She drew from the quotes she'd often used with her teammates to push through to a win.

You're strong even if you don't feel like it. It's a team effort—just do your part.

Boisterous hoopla suddenly erupted, breaking their connection, and Cara's eyes turned to the safety of her dad's smile when he placed his arm around her and pulled her to his side. They gave her a standing ovation, clapping and cheering at the news of her hiring. Their warm welcome helped settle her nerves.

She glanced at the corner. Standing there with the same neutral expression, Callum offered a composed clap and a hint of a smile.

"She's Miss Riley to all of you. But she's my daughter—remember that!" he cheerfully warned and scanned the officers, landing on Callum. A round of jeering broke out, and she offered them a nervous grin.

Give it your best effort today.

Chief Riley turned the briefing over to his sergeant, and they exited along with the off-duty officers. "You made it through two o'clock roll call and almost through day one," he said, hugging her close. "What do you think? Are you going to make it this summer?"

"So far, so good," she answered, when she really wanted to say *too soon to tell.*

Callum caught Cara's eye as he exited the department after roll call. Neither said a word. Her stare didn't waver. Since he looked away first, she counted herself the winner. All she could think was *win, don't let him rattle you.*

Working with that member of the team worried her. He was dangerous to her heart. She couldn't avoid him entirely. What's that saying about keeping friends close but enemies closer? She'd keep him in her sights alright…to ward against his natural charm.

Teamwork? How exhausting!

That Cara was nervous was an understatement. She reminded herself she was the golden child, at least for this first day. Her dad depended on her to run the show. Whatever that was. She might have to remind him more often as the weeks went by, or when mistakes happened, that she'd rescued him from his officers' irritation over working the desk.

Winners aren't people who never fail, but people who don't quit.

It helped that she'd spent most of her first day sheltered in her dad's office, shadowing him, meeting personnel, getting oriented with her responsibilities. She'd negotiated a Monday through Friday, eight to four schedule with her dad, who she now had to call Chief around the department.

✳ ✳ ✳

Callum slammed out the back doors of the department and breathed a sigh of relief when the fresh air hit him.

One more minute of watching men ogle Cara at the podium and he'd have lost it. The eager smiles from men who didn't know the real Cara twisted his gut. Pretending they had no history had made him physically nauseous. He wanted to sweep her away, find a place for just the two of them, kiss her senseless, and beg her to come back to him. But for two years, he'd done nothing about his desire. He bent over and steadied his breathing. He was happy for her and darn sick of himself.

"Hey, wait up," Dylan called from the door, exiting close behind him. "Are we still on for the range?"

"Yeah, how about in an hour?" Callum answered and beelined toward his truck.

Dylan hustled to catch up with Callum. "Yeah, that'll give me enough time to grab my gear and uniforms from the dry-cleaner." A little out of breath, he continued, "Did you meet the Chief's daughter? I just introduced myself. The guys lined up to shake her hand and thank her for filling in. Everyone's going to love her."

"No, I had to process a report really quick. But we've met."

"Oh, right, you pulled her over. You could have officially introduced yourself, paint yourself in a good light and all. Something as simple as, 'Welcome, Cara. How is your first day going?'"

"I will, Mr. Manners," Callum insisted. "I didn't avoid Cara," he countered with a hardened face. "Just waiting for a better time to approach her."

"Was that your suave approach today? That's how you make the girls want you? You ignore and resist them, and they come running. I haven't tried that method before, but I'm glad I got a head start on you with Cara."

The competition between them was never ending, but it was a friendly rivalry built on respect. Their friendship made them better officers and, more importantly, inspired them to be better men. Callum's reliance upon God was the only subject Dylan never challenged, and Callum didn't push Dylan's reticence to talk about his faith.

"I'm not trying to make her want me," Callum urged a tad too loudly, but nothing could be further from his truth. That's exactly what he wanted—Cara to want him.

"She's good looking. I wasn't the only one checking her out." The cat-like eagerness in Dylan's eyes set Callum's jealousy on edge. "The Chief knew exactly what we all were thinking."

"No doubt," Callum grumbled in agreement. He'd certainly been looking. Her long, silky hair had hidden her face from him, but every mannerism of her veiled discomfort registered like a punch to his gut, and he desired to free her. Take her away. "Close your gaping mouth and wipe the disgusting drool from your chin," Callum said, already exasperated by Dylan.

"Sounds like the Chief's daughter has gotten under your skin, too. Are you thinking of asking her out? I am. I'm putting every guy in the department on notice, including you—if you snooze, you lose."

"May the best man win," Callum retorted, swiping his fingers through his hair. "We didn't exactly start off on a good foot, but I plan to change that," he cockily added, even as doubt swept across his face.

Dylan burst out, "Wait? What? Do you mean you're gonna ask out the Chief's daughter? You better bone up on your manners then. You missed your first opportunity back there. I may just beat you to her," Dylan said, punching Callum playfully in the arm.

Callum had missed two years' worth of opportunities. Opportunities he was pretty sure Cara didn't want him to take. Dylan kept jabbering, annoying the heck out of Callum's occupied thoughts. Turning to leave, Dylan's words hit him like a bullet.

"…her jeans. She fills them out just right," Dylan said.

"Knock it off!" Callum elbowed Dylan.

"So protective. Don't act like you didn't notice."

"Believe me…" Callum stalled and his gaze turned downward when he muttered, "I noticed!" *Always have. Always will.*

The back door clanged open, and Dylan clamped his mouth shut at seeing perky Cara bound toward them.

Saved by Cara.

The hope of reuniting with Cara had been saving Callum for over a year now. Not that she knew that. He'd not reached out to her. Yet. He'd been stymied by the regret of how he'd navigated Ali's death. Fear that she'd moved on and no longer dreamed of them kept him from acting on what his heart longed for—to beg her to forgive him and convince her that it will always be her for him. Coward. His fragile hopes would shatter like glass if she denied him, so he hid behind regret. Double Coward.

Cara being back in town, in his space, was a sign he couldn't ignore. He'd prayed for God to give him the desires of his heart. To be stronger and braver. And God's answer was now headed directly toward him.

Something told him he'd have to spend a whole lot more time in prayer, asking God to reveal how to gain Cara's trust.

Cara called out, "Hey, Officer Bright."

"See, she's already asking for me." The slightest attention from Cara had so easily turned Dylan's head.

Callum growled.

"I hoped I could catch you. You left your hat on my desk." She waved it at Dylan and avoided glancing at Callum.

"On purpose," Callum scratched out under his breath.

"Thanks for the rescue," Dylan voiced as syrupy sweet as any self-respecting man could get away with.

If Callum's gritted teeth and cautious glower were any indication, Dylan might need to be rescued from Callum's grip.

"How was your first day on the job, Ma'am?" Dylan quickly jumped into polite conversation as she made her way to them.

"Great. Everyone was so welcoming. And don't you dare call me ma'am." Cara flashed a facetious smile between the two of them, and then scowled, eyebrows arched, at Callum.

Dylan cleared his throat, and with a hard stare, cued Callum to give a shot at niceties.

"It's been a crazy day. Well, you probably know that. I had two arrests, both outstanding warrants. Lots of riffraff passing through town lately," Callum offered, not meeting Cara's eyes, afraid of the indifference he might see in them. Dylan stood between them like an awkward referee.

"Yep. I helped process those," Cara responded coldly.

As Dylan retreated to his black Charger, he nodded at Callum and said, "I gotta run, but I'll catch you at the range in an hour. Want me to pick up Jimmy Johns?"

"Sure," Callum answered, deadpan.

Just before ducking in his car, Dylan once again addressed Cara, "This was my week for desk duty. Thank you for coming to work at our zoo at just the right time to take that grind off my plate. I owe you, big time."

"It won't be that bad. At least I don't have to clean the cages," she teased back.

"Just don't take any crap from anyone," he warned and started the engine.

Callum shot quick daggers at Dylan without Cara noticing.

"Oh, I won't. No worries there," she smirked. Dylan laughed and waved at Cara before shooting off the lot.

Cara gaped as Callum hopped in a shiny new black Ford F150 without stepping on the runners. He had replaced his old truck—the one he'd owned since learning to drive. It held stories of them together. Cara had snuggled close to Callum from the middle seat. Nestlé slobbered on the windows and leather seats. They set lawn chairs in the bed and watched baseball games and fireworks. Her eyes darted to the rearview mirror. The cross necklace she gave him for Valentine's Day no longer dangled there. He'd parted with his prized "second best girl," as he called his truck.

Resting his arm on the door, he attempted a casual conversation with Cara for the first time today. "How's Nestlé?" Talk of Nestlé was common ground.

Cara wrapped her arms around herself, gripping her elbows. "It's hard to watch the end. I try to keep him from following me to the pond, but you know how persistent that chocolate lab can be."

"It's good to be with him at the end, though." Callum avoided her eyes and fidgeted with the rearview mirror. Being alone with her, he wouldn't be able to hide his longing. Anyone with eyes would see his attraction. "Thanks for taking the position. All the patrolmen are glad you're here. Chief Riley has someone he can depend on." Sincerity laced his words.

"He'll probably lighten up on everyone now, and return to his old, grumpy self," she joked in a familiar way.

"Everyone will thank you for that. He's been juggling a lot. If you need any help, let me know." His truck purred to a start.

"You got a new truck." Cara stated the obvious like an accusation.

"The old one had a lot of miles and..." he explained, waiting uneasy seconds before finishing his thought, "too many memories." He had thousands of words to describe his treasured memories of them in his old truck. The silence between them thickened as he tapped the steering wheel.

He was making a bumbling idiot of himself. He didn't know how to do this with Cara. To have her this close. To have this opportunity. To want her. But also to respect her desire for distance between them.

"Well, I guess we both need to get some things done. Have a good night," he conceded to end the awkwardness.

"You too," she rotely offered, heading for the back door and her duties.

"Cara," he called to her and waited until she turned to him. "I'm trying to do what you asked—steer clear—as much as possible, considering…" He stopped there, letting his thought hang in the air. "Nevermind. See you tomorrow," he said, instead of pleading with her for what he really wanted—a second chance.

SIX

"Pill-ow fiiiiiight!" Cara screamed down the hallway and charged at Tori, whacking her upside her shoulder.

Tori clasped a throw pillow from the couch and dodged out of Cara's reach. "That was weak. Give me your best shot," Tori egged Cara on.

Cara jumped from the floor onto the couch and whapped Tori again. The force of the swing set Cara tumbling back to the floor.

Tori squealed with delight and retaliated with a strong wallop to Cara's backside.

"Swing and a miss," Cara giggled when Tori tried to strike a second blow.

As Tori hopped to the floor, Cara pummeled her midflight. Tori dramatically sprawled across the rug in fake defeat, hugging her sides in laughter.

Cara joined her, exhilarated.

"I sure needed that." Cara had made it through her first week on the job with little incident and with as little professional exchange with Callum as possible. All she wanted to do was hide away from the needs of officers and run-ins with Callum.

"You get the movie ready, and I'll grab our chocolate chip Blizzards," Cara directed.

Anything to get work out of my head.

"Did you get Dad one?" Tori asked as Cara made her way to the kitchen.

"He's working on auction stuff tonight," Cara reminded Tori. "He wouldn't like our rom-com marathon."

"But he'd love a Blizzard." Tori settled into the oversized chair and crossed her legs on the ottoman. "Speaking of rom-coms. How's your revenge going?"

"Revenge?" Cara asked, handing Tori a Blizzard and a spoon.

"Agitating Callum?"

"I steer clear of him. As little interaction as possible."

"Looking at him in uniform is nice eye candy, though."

Cara worked hard to manage her blush. "People make such a big deal about a man in uniform. He does look good. I'll give him that. But his best—" Cara stopped herself from imagining Callum.

"Come on, Cara. Every girl knows a guy in uniform is the best look," she chuckled. "And if Callum in uniform doesn't get the heart palpitating, then patting you down for an arrest will."

"He didn't arrest me. He gave me a warning. I didn't even get out of the vehicle," she protested.

He arrested my heart for a second, but I'm over that.

"I wasn't talking about you specifically."

Cara walked right into that one. "I think Levi's and a Henley are his best look," she said with a wistful smile, "or a black tux, or a tight t-shirt and running shorts or a…"

"Or in anything," Tori agreed. "Me, you, and every girl in town are one hundred percent in agreement."

Cara blushed, thinking about Middletown's entire female population ogling Callum. Her chagrin sobered. He belonged more to them than to her. "Oh, stop!" Cara begged and popped Tori upside the head with her pillow. "Let's get the movie rolling."

"I know you don't want anything to do with him, but it's surprising you guys can avoid one another so well at work."

"We stay out of one another's way."

"I just figured eventually you two would have to talk."

"About?" Cara asked.

"About the breakup."

"No reason to look in the rearview mirror," Cara said, her voice lacking any hint of emotion. He'd carved his heart out of her chest two years ago.

"I thought since you two were once in love, you might strike up some…"

"Some?"

"I don't know."

These days, Cara associated love with suffering. If one more person quoted the trite expression about there being no love without suffering, or that to avoid suffering, you avoid love, she just might hurl.

"Apparently, I was the only one madly in love," Cara offered. "Mad for believing him, that's for sure." She petted Nestlé who settled at their feet.

"You both had it bad. You might not want to bring up the past, but you know it's true."

Cara wondered if her sister, who had never given her heart to another, was wiser about love. She swiped the air with her hand, vanishing her lonely-hearts-club thoughts. They dissipated like smoke in the air, but a bit of the wanting lingered, hovering around her heart.

"Are you okay?" her sister asked, apparently expecting no answer as she quickly moved on. "Don't try rewriting history. I saw the boxes of cards from Callum you saved on your closet shelf."

"You went through my stuff?"

"You said I could take anything you left."

"Clothes. I meant clothes, Tor." Cara frowned.

"Did you keep every single note he gave you?"

"I forgot to throw them out," Cara lied.

"You mean you couldn't throw them out," Tori pushed.

"Stating the obvious doesn't help," Cara admitted, frustration building at her mistake. She'd throw them out once she got upstairs to her room.

"How many times have you reread them?"

"They've been collecting dust," she said, not admitting the bit of setback she'd experienced when she stayed up all night reading them during Christmas break.

"Always," Tori paused and surveyed her sister's face.

"Always?" Cara asked.

"Callum signed every letter, every note, every scrap of paper with that word."

"You read them?" Cara shrieked and flushed at the exposure of Callum's sentiments. "What happened to respecting someone's privacy?"

"I didn't mean to. I peeked in, thinking you had shoes in them. What's AHAW?" Tori pronounced it like it was a word.

"Always have, always will." Cara stirred her Blizzard.

"Sounds like he meant forever to me," Tori added.

"Apparently, always is a very short timeframe for Callum."

"Well, God's given you a new beginning. Looks like He's created a fresh future for you," Tori exclaimed.

"Precisely. I'm super excited about this fall. Thank the Lord I left town. If He's orchestrating things, I'm loving the door He opened." Cara wondered if Tori meant a new beginning in life or with Callum, but she led the conversation in the direction she wanted.

"But with your history, do you still feel connected to Callum in some weird way? I'm just wondering. I've never been in love like you."

Cara might have gotten whiplash as fast as she swung her head to glare at Tori. "I do not. I don't think about him anymore," she lied through the knot in her throat. Tori hit a nerve, and the pain shot like lightning through her entire body. "I'm fine with things now." She picked at the pills on the pillow fabric.

The silence between them gave credence to Cara's nerves, and Tori pushed a bit more. "Sis, you don't seem fine. You seem…" Tori hesitated for the right word.

"Furious!" Cara responded.

Tori wouldn't stop their heart to heart any more than Nestlé would lay down a bone. Cara thought she might go mad dredging up emotions over Callum. Either that or she just might shatter like a glass vase into a million pieces.

"Pissed?" Cara asked, rhetorically.

That word, from Cara's mouth, shocked Tori. "Yes and—"

"Done," Cara signified with raised eyebrows, hoping Tori would get her hint.

"And—"

"I'm done with this conversation," Cara insisted, grabbing the remote.

"Oh, right." Tori finally clued in. "I still think you're missing an opportunity. A little revenge doesn't hurt.

Does it?" Tori asked, wrinkling her nose, knowing full well revenge was not a dish they should serve.

"I'm over him. Happy without him. Let's move on," Cara repeated deadpan, clicking buttons on the remote.

"But harmless fun is good fun," Tori teased.

"Have you been plotting ideas?" Cara asked, devouring an extra-large spoonful of Blizzard.

"Slashing tires?" Tori blurted out.

"Tsk. Tsk. Not harmless, Tor."

"Limburger cheese in the vents of his truck?" Tori laughed at her own idea.

Cara bobbed her head and flicked both eyebrows up. "Not bad," she conceded.

"Sign him up for Good Housekeeping Magazine?"

"I'm not spending a dime on him."

"Good point," Tori admitted.

"How about ignore him like I've been doing," Cara simply suggested.

"Maybe watching *How to Lose a Guy in Ten Days* will get our juices flowing."

"Hmm." Cara spooned another large chunk of chocolate into her mouth. The movie wasn't going to help. Cara's thoughts about Callum flowed way more than she wanted them to this evening.

SEVEN

Surprised by the tight pattern on his target, Dylan plopped his ear protection on the bench and celebrated. "Well, would you look at that? There's a first time for everything. Should I mark the calendar as the first time this city stud from St. Louis beat the country bumpkin from Small Town, USA?"

"Dude, the last time you lived in the big city was when you were nine."

"It's my lucky day! I'm headed straight to Mrs. Kocher at the Circle K to buy a lottery ticket after I pack up here!" Dylan teased.

Weeks ago, Callum set up this range session to hang out with Dylan to start their days off before shift change. It had sounded like a perfect plan, but after leaving Cara in the parking lot, he needed to be alone. To regroup. To pray for guidance and a surefire way to win her back.

As much as he wanted God's clear answer right then in his truck, he got crickets. An answer would come, though, he was sure. He'd wrestled with God through his grief, and he knew that waiting on God was best. He just hoped it would come soon. He was on borrowed time with Cara.

He wasn't in the mood for company, just the pop, pop, pop of rounds being fired. But if anyone was going to put up with his gloom, his best friend would.

Hired on the same day by Middletown's Police Department, Callum and Dylan had become fast friends. They'd competed neck and neck in class standing, in physical fitness scores, and at the range at the police training institute.

Callum and Dylan's frequent trips to the shooting range always evolved into a competition. Dylan had beaten Callum a time or two in physical training, but he never came close to besting the top gun in their class. Not once had he beaten Callum at the shooting range—until today.

Callum removed the magazine from his Glock 22 and stared down the lane at his target. Dylan couldn't read the flat expression on Callum's profile. Frustration?

"Your shot pattern sucks. Are those ripples on the lake or a figure eight?" Dylan ribbed, studying Callum's stiff stance, waiting for him to crack a won't-happen-again-wise-guy challenge.

"Hmm," Callum responded without arguing or mocking, his train of thought clearly not on Dylan.

Callum's insipid response put Dylan off his comeback game. He'd expected a death glare. Dylan almost felt sorry for him. Almost.

"Well, I've got a date with the tooth fairy tonight. Can I borrow your new truck?"

"Sure." Callum's empty delivery was as automated as his loading of the magazine, and Dylan knew for sure he wasn't listening.

Callum slammed his magazine in his gun, keeping his eyes on his poor shot pattern. He racked his slide, aligned the sights on his target, and stalled. In a rare move, he reholstered his Glock and backed away from the shooting line to steady himself. Rolling his shoulders backwards and forwards, he loosened the tension between his shoulder blades and unclenched his jaw. He cracked his neck, tipping it side to side, and said, "Not enough sleep again last night, I guess." He stared blankly at the bullet holes speckled across the eights and nines of the target.

Dylan harrumphed at Callum's excuse for the scattered pockmarks. "Sure. Lack of sleep," he said in total disbelief. "You'll figure this out." He waited for Callum's rebuttal.

Instead, Callum stepped back up to the firing line, readying himself to shoot.

"Hey man, step back. Tell me what's eating at you." Dylan tapped Callum's shoulder. "Did you hear what I just said to you?" he asked, concern and irritation permeating his tone.

"I'm listening," Callum defended without looking his way.

"Hardly. Your head is not in the game. You didn't even flinch when I told you I had a date with the tooth fairy!"

Callum holstered his pistol again and backed away from the bench, blowing out an exhaustive exhale. "Maybe I had no reaction to that bit of news because 'I have a date' has fallen from your lips quite a bit. If it moves, you'd date it."

"Harsh," Dylan uttered, staring at him in disbelief.

"Are you going to give me a chance to defend my shot or what?" Callum asked, diverting Dylan's attention from dating. Nodding toward the line, he proposed, "How about fifteen more chances to get it tight? If I don't best you, the bait's on me next time we fish."

"You're on." Dylan never backed down from Callum's challenges, no matter the winnings.

Callum released a long, slow breath, exhaling thoughts of Cara from his mind. When he aligned his sights, Cara slipped back into view. Her soft smile, her wind-blown hair, her fierce determination, and then those seething song lyrics she sang when he pulled her over.

Dylan did a double take at his buddy's hesitation.

Callum resettled into his stance at the firing line, extended his arms, both hands firmly on the grip, lined up his sights, and positioned his finger on the trigger. When he stalled again on squeezing the trigger, Dylan opened his mouth, but Callum refocused, applied steady pressure, and shot a solidly tight group over the ten ring, putting his buddy's ridicule to shame.

Dylan emptied his magazine and compared their two targets. Removing his ear protection, he smiled at Callum's typical tight pattern. "No doubt there, man. I'm up for the bait next time."

"No doubt?" Callum glanced narrow-eyed at his buddy. "Since when are you happy to lose?" Callum asked, shaking his head.

Dylan holstered his pistol after reloading. Turning to Callum with a wide stance, he clapped his hands once and then rubbed them together like he was getting down and dirty tough. Fists on his hips and elbows wide, he said, "A blind man on a galloping horse could tell something's troubling ya. You got lost at the line for a moment."

"You know. By now, the whole department knows I pulled over the Chief's daughter."

"Yeah?" Dylan questioned, leading him. "Is the ribbing all that bad? Seemed kind of mild to me."

Callum grimaced at Dylan's meddling, but only because he knew Dylan would make him spill it.

"Like I said, I just need some sleep," Callum said, shutting Dylan down.

"Well, get some sleep before qualifications next week. But something else is eating at you." Dylan prodded, calling Callum's bluff.

Callum shrugged resignedly and stepped up to the firing line. "Just keep shooting, will ya?" Clapping his earmuffs back on, they shot without chatting until they had finished for the day.

Callum checked his watch, hoping in the fifteen minutes it would take to clean his gun that Dylan would keep his chatter to a minimum—or at least away from Cara.

Dylan stepped up to the counter across from Callum to clean his pistol and asked straightaway, "So, are you going to tell me what really has you all fired up, or am I going to keep guessing?"

Callum ignored Dylan's question until the silence between them rose to an irritating crescendo. He scanned Dylan's calm and patient face.

"You know, it might help to talk about it. Not keep it all bottled up inside," Dylan said.

"Talking about it is futile. Staying busy keeps my mind from unraveling."

"Are you going to come clean about Cara? I figured out there's history. She's got you wound tight."

Callum shrugged his shoulders and fought to make sense of what was going on for him, to admit the emotional turmoil created by his encounter with Cara.

"What's this mean?" Dylan imitated Callum's shrug.

"She's angry," Callum admitted, running the bore-brush back and forth through the barrel of his gun.

"Because?" Dylan inquired.

Callum shrugged his shoulders again and shook his head. Guilt piled up. Guilt for the way he'd ended things with Cara. Guilt over pushing her away. Distance and counseling helped him realize his knee-jerk break-up was because of his guilt and anger. Leaving her soccer scholarship at the University of Illinois and moving out of town without a word to him was an obvious gesture; she wanted nothing to do with him.

Now she was back, and he was desperate for a new start.

"Start at the beginning?" Dylan prompted and sat down, indicating he expected the entire story.

"She's the one girl I'll always love. That's the beginning and the end," Callum said with an air of determination.

While Callum put his gun back together, he found more words. "Cara was my sister's best friend. We dated for two years, going on forever. She's the one," he said and then clarified, "was the one."

"She broke your heart?" Dylan said, treading lightly.

"I broke hers," he admitted, "and mine."

Callum slumped down hard on a metal chair and nearly toppled off balance to the floor. He glared into the scuff-marked black and white checked tile as he recalled the day his world flipped upside down.

"Why didn't we wear helmets that day?" Callum thought out loud. Things might have been different, even though doctors told him it wouldn't have made any difference with Ali's injuries. Callum backed up. "We decided to ride our ATVs, Cara and I on one and Ali on the other. I suggested a race to the back of our property. Cara yelled, 'Last one there is a rotten egg.' In our hurry to win, not one of us put on a helmet. Ali detoured from the usual route and took a narrow path through two trees at full speed." Callum hung his head and rested his forearms on his thighs, holding himself from the weight of that day. "There was a ditch—"

"No," Dylan said under his breath.

"Ali flipped and flew into a tree."

He couldn't coax any more words from his dry throat after relaying that image. He hadn't seen it happen. He and Cara had been too far ahead. At the same time, they'd realized they only heard the whir of their own engine.

Pain etched Callum's face. He stood and packed away his cleaning kit. There was much more to tell Dylan to make him understand. Already exhausted, he'd get it out and leave.

"Some of that day is a blank in my memory. When I think of that day, my heart still races like it did when I flew back to her on that ATV. She lay at such an odd angle against the tree. I knew. I just knew," he stuttered, unable to say the words.

"It's okay," Dylan reached out to him.

"The weight of her in my arms. Cara screaming and running to the house. I wailed. Sirens wailed."

"I wanted to forget it was real, but nothing about the days after that would let me. I soldiered on, but that only made me a ticking time bomb inside. My self-loathing was intense. I didn't know where to direct my anger. I felt alone. I knew I wasn't, but at the same time I wanted to be left alone to explode."

"Grief and trauma do weird things to us," Dylan attempted to comfort him.

"I remember my dad wore a soccer tie to her funeral. When I first saw it, I was mad. It seemed irreverent. But then God showed me how Ali would have looked at him.

She would have run to Dad and given his tie a tug and said, 'Oh, Dad!'"

Dylan offered a slight smile.

"That would be all Ali would have to say and Dad would have known it meant, 'You're my hero. I love you. I love it. Thanks for being my bold cheerleader.'"

Dylan's focus never left his friend. Callum had never been this troubled, this desperate, this raw in front of him.

"It was exhausting holding things together that first week, up to her funeral. Every step felt heavy. I tried to be strong to support my parents and everyone else. I kept going until the day we buried Ali."

He sat silent for minutes, remembering.

"And then I couldn't."

"Understandable," Dylan said.

"I broke things off with Cara at the funeral."

"At the funeral?" Dylan's shock was tangible.

Callum nodded his head, and his voice cracked as he said, "I broke her heart."

"But maybe not for good." Dylan voiced hope for his friend.

"Being near Cara kept the accident close, over and over." Callum looked intently at Dylan. "I blamed us for Ali's death."

Dylan's jaw dropped in disbelief. He set his hand to Callum's shoulder in support. "You know that's not true, right?"

"I do. But knowing that logically and acting out in pain aren't contrary. I felt responsible for Ali's death, and that made Cara responsible, too. It wasn't our fault. I know better. I am better…now. But I've already hurt her in ways I promised I never would."

"She can forgive—"

"I betrayed her faith in me. I pushed away the only person I want to love."

"But now?" Dylan pushed him.

"She's doing a fabulous acting job in the office, but her attitude and disdain gutted me when I pulled her over at the pig sign. From what I can tell, she doesn't want anything to do with me. I can't say I blame her."

"I had no idea, man. I'm sorry for ribbing you about her."

Anger flared inside Callum at how he'd destroyed her trust in him. "She needed me, needed us to be together, but I couldn't be with her, carry on with our life together as if Ali wasn't ripped from us, leaving a gaping hole. Life, as usual, didn't exist. It didn't seem possible for us to go on together without Ali."

"You never went after Cara?"

Callum reached for his water bottle and took a large gulp. He picked at the label while he explained his cowardice. "It took unbelievably long to break through the haze, the anger. When I mentally got to the spot where I wanted to beg her to forgive me, I didn't think I deserved her. My pastor says that's the lie of shame and regret."

"What do you want?"

"I want the accident to have never happened and the three of us together," Callum vented.

"Yeah, I get that but—"

"But reality bites, right? I want her. I want us. I want what we promised one another—forever."

Callum stood and tossed his gear bag over his shoulder, and they walked to the exit.

"Explaining to her what happened for me may never be good enough to win her back, but I'm praying. She tolerates me at work, but I don't think she wants a heart-to-heart.

I'm not gonna lie. Most days, I still think I should just leave her the heck alone."

Dylan grabbed Callum's arm, stopping him. "Then you have no choice," he said decidedly. Callum puzzled at Dylan's contemplative pause. "You have to get her back! And give it your best shot!" Dylan blurted.

As Callum's truck rumbled off the lot, he strategized his next tactical maneuver—the biggest one of his life. Spurred on by Dylan's words, he would beg Cara's forgiveness and win her back.

EIGHT

Callum woke on the first Saturday he'd had off in a while in a foul mood with a racing pulse. He checked his watch. It was his chance to sleep in, but he wasn't able to relax back into sleep on that dark morning. He laced on his shoes for a long run, attempting to rid his body of perturbing effects of the dream. He might just get in the best shape of his life if he couldn't stop the dreams.

His dream had screamed at him. Or rather, dream Cara had. He answered a knock on his front door, and there she stood. Through the doorway, he saw Ali, leaning against her car, arms folded across her chest, agony plastered on her face. He smiled and waved for her to come in, but instead, she walked around the car to the driver's side without acknowledging him. Cara shrugged her shoulders at him and bounded down the steps to the car, yelling at him to make a decision.

Three dreams of Cara in the past week had messed with Callum's sleep. At the steady pounding on the pavement and the regular rhythm of his breathing, his thoughts ambled back around to the dream that woke him early this morning.

Dream Cara gutted him. Her normally soothing voice ranted high-pitched assaults and pounded death strikes.

In one dream, angry words spewed from Cara's lips. "It's your fault I've missed being with my family for two years. But I haven't missed you. You did me a favor that day at the cemetery. What kind of man blames the person he claims to love for something out of their control?" When he reached for her, she backed away from him and spurned him with words that burned into his soul, "Don't touch me. You know nothing about love. You say you're a Christian, but you don't love like one. Grief is no excuse for not keeping your promises. You can't be trusted. The best thing I did is run from your toxic inability to communicate."

His dreams of Cara weren't always nightmares. In a dream he'd had two days ago, her touch electrified him. Cara laid her head on his shoulder and caressed his leg as they glided in his boat over a lake. When he'd begged her to come home, she confessed, "I miss you. I don't want to be apart any longer." When he kissed her tender lips, she begged for more. Dream Cara had vaporized the second his eyes opened to the light of day. He'd clung to her presence, soaking up her essence. The desire to be near her had remained throughout the day, discombobulating his emotions and thoughts, especially when he had to face her in real life at work.

He missed Cara, plain and simple. He worked hard to forget that gnawing agony. She didn't miss him. That much was evident from their meeting at the pig sign.

He should have talked to her two years ago, but he let her choice to leave town be their final chapter. Letting things stand between them as they were now, pretending to be cordial, pretending neither was angry, created too much tension.

They needed to hash things out, to push through Cara's resistance and make things right. He owed her that much.

The weight of being around her and not engaging with her was a lie gaining speed, a true hell on earth torture. He couldn't keep his distance much longer. He wanted to touch her, to hold her, to tell her he loved her. Always had. Always will.

Callum never gave much credence to dreams, but Cara's interruption of his slumber had him asking questions. He was pretty sure God had included Ali in his most recent dream to get his attention. He'd been acting like a coward. He had a strong suspicion of what he had to do.

He'd covered only two miles before he gave up and returned home. His run had been useless in staving off the haunting remnants of angry dream Cara and Ali. Callum headed for a shower, tugging his shirt over his head, and considered his long to-do list for his day off when a banging at his door abruptly halted his plans.

"Keep your shirt on!" Callum yelled at the incessant pounding. Pulling on a pair of sweatpants, he raced to the window, peeking through the curtains before opening the door to his sister's frowning face.

Raelee scrutinized her younger brother's inside-out sweatpants, lack of shirt, and bare feet as she stomped across wooden planks into his house. Before he could speak, she walloped him with her greeting, "You should keep *your* shirt on."

"Hilarious."

"I'm sorry. Did I wake you? I thought you'd be up by now." Her blazing-red dress warned him she was on her way to work, and this was no casual visit.

Her gaze surveyed his meticulous quarters. Two throw pillows were tossed at each end of a cozy leather couch. A carefully folded deep blue cover was positioned over one arm. A glass coffee table—without a beverage or book or fingerprint—highlighted the design of the inky colors of the rug. End tables displayed cork coasters, a stack of books, a family photo framed in silver, and a close-up of him and Ali at her last Thanksgiving dinner.

"It's my day off except I'm working the Animal Shelter auction for a couple of hours tonight."

"Well, you don't look so good."

"I had trouble sleeping, so I went for an early run. I was jumping in the shower," Callum explained, pulling his shirt back on.

"I have a house showing in an hour." She glanced at her wristwatch. "Got a minute?"

"The crazy life of a real estate agent. I always have time for you. Want a cup of coffee?" he offered, grabbing a mug blindly from the cabinet.

"No, thanks. I can't be here long. This might seem like an ambush. I don't want it to be, but it's long overdue." She gestured for him to begin his morning routine and sat on the stool at his counter while he worked. "I came to say," but she stopped mid-sentence, perplexed and distracted, as she peered at his spotless kitchen, not a smudge on any of the stainless-steel appliances. "Do you even live here?"

"You came to ask about my place?" he asked. He tapped the counter, waiting for the coffee to drip and Raelee to explain. "I work a ton. There's no time to make a mess when I'm gone for ten hours a day, sometimes longer."

Raelee forged ahead through a clenched jaw. "Callum, I love you and I miss you."

"I've been around," he defended.

With a finger to her lips, she shushed him. "Let me get this out. Yes, you have shown up—not as much as we'd all like," she added as a polite aside.

"But?"

"But I'm worried that when you are home, all of you is not really showing up."

"Meaning?"

"Mom and I had a little chat a while back. She's really worried about you. Well, a lot worried. She cried and said she's lost a bit of you." He whipped around and stared into his sister's eyes, glistening with tears. "We all have. Those are her words. And we want you back. This is me fighting for you."

Only the most callous of men made their moms cry, and now he faced the hard truth that he was one of them. His emotions locked in his throat. Knowing his mom's heavy heartache strangled his throat dry, and he gripped his cup.

"I'm not here to make you feel guilty. Really!"

"Well, I do anyway," he said and gulped his coffee, needing caffeine.

"Please, hear my heart. We all miss the you from before the accident. The one that was open and vulnerable with us. I know we're all different now. Losing Ali did that to us. There are parts of our family that we can never get back. Heck, we may never be able to find our way back to the family we were before, but…"

"But?"

"Our family can't just go through the motions each time we get together. Ali's death broke us open. We're molding ourselves back together. We want the Callum that wants to be home, who wasn't afraid to stay and share his struggles, who let us help when he felt weak."

Callum sat on the stool next to Raelee, saddened by his sister's honest truth.

"Dad suppresses his grief to appear strong for everyone. He can't express what he misses. He just says he misses you. And he'll never tell you that. You take after Dad, you know? It's like you're hiding in plain sight, sometimes. Pretending accentuates the farce."

"Hmm," Callum agreed, taking in every word Raelee said. "I don't know that I'll ever get over Ali not being with us. More days than not, I cope okay with that reality. Some days anger overwhelms me. I'm sad to admit that being home triggers those days." He looked into Raelee's eyes, begging her to understand. "I don't want it to, and it's not every time, but some moments I'm knocked off balance and afraid of unraveling. Just when I think I'm in a good spot, the rawness of missing her hits. Family will always do that, I guess."

"Grab on to us. Ali is part of each of us. You hold on to her when you hold on to us. When you hold on to Mom, you hold Ali's strong faith. When you hold on to Dad, you feel her gentleness." Raelee clasped Callum's arm. "Hold on to me, and I'll remind you of her persistence."

"I want to do better," he bowed his head in regret. "Pastor Caleb has encouraged me to truly deal with things, not just avoid them." His explanation rang trite in his own ears after Raelee's sincere openness.

"I'm glad you have someone to talk to. But we're here to talk, too. It's hard having Ali's seat empty at our family dinners. It's that much harder every time your seat is empty." Raelee hugged him hard.

Raelee continued, "Sundays have always been sacred to our family. Church. Dinner. Games. Movies—whatever we did, it was together. Come play with your niece and nephew! With your schedule, we don't expect you to be there every Sunday, but you don't have to handle life alone. We have each other. Just let us in a little more—right here." She patted him over the heart.

"I'll do better," he promised, confident he could step up. Sunday dinners had been the hallmark of his family since he was little. Callum hadn't attended them as often as he could over the past two years, but his sister wasn't talking about the number of times he'd shown up. She was talking about *how* he showed up, and Callum knew it.

"Christmas was the last time you stayed for the whole day. You're part of our healing, and even though it's hard, we're part of your healing. I'm pleading for all our sakes. Grief grips us all in the weirdest ways. But don't let it change your ability to love."

He wrapped his arm around his older sister in a side hug and walked with her, coffee in hand, to the front door. "Starting this Sunday. I'll be there—for a long time. Promise."

"Mom won't complain because she knows your life is stressful, and she doesn't want to add to your stress. She said it's not her place, but it is. She's your mom. You're one of the most loving men I know. Dad needs someone to talk to. Mom just needs to see your reassuring face, see you smile at her, share what's going on, have you wrap your arms around her. We're all missing Ali so much, but missing her is even worse when we're also missing you."

Callum wasn't convinced he had much to give, but he'd try.

Raelee grabbed the doorknob and then stalled, turning to encourage him one last time. "Come home and be truly home," she begged and wiped her misty eyes.

"I'm not always much comfort to anyone these days," he gently said, cupping her shoulder.

She hugged him tightly to her. "Everyone being together will be a comfort for us all."

"I'll see you Sunday," he whispered to her. "I promise."

She studied him for several long seconds. Her face tightened and brow creased, and she bear-hugged him again. "I refuse to lose you, too."

"I love you," he whispered, planting a quick peck to her cheek as he followed her, barefoot, onto the stoop.

Just before she ducked into her car, she pointed at him and called out, "Love you!"

He waved goodbye, sipped his coffee, and watched her drive down the street. He turned to go back into his house and suddenly stopped in his tracks. Every muscle in his body tensed at the mug in his hand. Cara had given it to him as a reminder of the first time he'd told her he loved her.

On a hot afternoon in August at the edge of the dock, Callum had lifted Cara over his shoulder, playfully threatening to throw her in the pond. He had fumbled with her, pretended to lose his balance, and then purposefully plunged into the water. He stopped her squealing with a kiss. When they parted for air, he whispered against her lips, "I'm in love with you, Cara."

His heart had soared when she whispered back, "And I love you."

She'd bought him the I CAN DEADLIFT YOU mug to mark their milestone.

Callum's chest grew heavy like his heart was sinking.

Time to make changes.

NINE

Callum hugged the curb, cut the engine, and studied the traditional two-story gray cape cod he'd grown up in. Three dormers, one for each kid, jutted from the steep, black-shingled roof, studying him like the eyes of a wary alien prepared to repel invaders. Raelee and Callum's bedrooms bookended Ali's dormer in the center of the house. In so many ways, his life still rotated around Ali.

Sun rays beamed off Ali's bedroom window. Callum couldn't help but think her curtains resembled eyelids, closed to the light of the world. Behind those curtains, Ali had once begged Callum to help her paint a sky-blue ceiling and wispy clouds. Splatters of white paint had sporadically plopped onto Ali's face and arms. When Ali had realized they weren't accidental, she burst into a roar of laughter. Callum had smirked at her just as she brushed a white mustache above his lip. He then whirled and rolled a line of blue down Ali's back as she dipped her brush. Eventually, they were covered head to toe and their sides ached from laughter, so they called a truce.

When he'd rented a small house in the village at the end of his sophomore year in college, he found the quiet surprisingly agitating. He'd missed Ali's incessant singing at the top of her lungs and jazzy funk dancing to Lauren Daigle songs. Every day, he still missed her joy and enthusiasm. He even missed her pitching dirty clothes at him when he got on her nerves, especially for shouting at her to turn down her music. If he could have her back, he'd gladly let her fling her entire wardrobe at him. Heck, he'd sing out loud with her, or maybe not, but he'd be happy to hear her belt out off-key lyrics.

Callum grabbed the large bouquet of white daisies, his mom's favorite, from the passenger seat, and hopped out of his truck to join his family. He had called the Village Garden Shoppe on Saturday minutes before closing, but Connie insisted she'd have something lovely arranged for him in fifteen minutes. Thank goodness for Connie's kindness.

His niece and nephew's laughter carried through the screen door. He stood outside for a minute and listened to his brother-in-law relay a story about his recent fishing trip. Callum needed to take one of those fishing trips with him again soon.

Callum asked the same thing of God every time he came back home, back to where Ali's contagious joy had filled every room. "Give me Your strength," he reiterated his shortest prayer ever, gulped a deep breath, and rapped his signature knock—three hard, followed by two light taps. His chest tightened. Coming home did this to him every time.

The house grew quiet. Seconds later, he heard light steps on the hardwood pick up their pace to a near run down the long hallway. His mom clasped her hands together, resting them on her lips in a delighted thank-the-heavens prayer.

"Hey, Ma. I made it," he said with possibly overdone cheer, raising the flowers in the air.

She opened the door and squealed, "Get in here."

Callum pulled his mom in for a tight hug, enveloping the petite woman. Closing his eyes, he absorbed the warmth of her soft cheek against his chest. This woman he adored had endured twenty hours of labor to birth him and his twin sister, Ali, coached him through junior high scuffles with a bully, prayed him through endless antics, and endured his distance since his sister's death.

His dad's strong arms wrapped tightly around them both. "It's good to see you, son. We set a plate for you at the table and made way too much food, as always. Can you stay for a bit?" Callum heard the hope in his dad's question.

"Sure can. I'm off duty for the day," he said, patting his dad's back in affirmation.

He bowed and handed the bouquet to his mom with mock formality, a minor gift compared to his presence. She thanked him with a kiss on his cheek and quickly handed the flowers off to his dad. Clasping her hands around his arm, she walked with him to the dining room.

As he rounded the hallway into the floral wallpapered dining room, a fork dropped hard on a plate, a chair scraped the floor, and his sister rose from her seat to hug him, whispering *thank you* in his ear. His brother-in-law stood and extended a handshake across the table. Just as he sat down, his squealing five-year-old niece, Niah, and three-year-old nephew, Jace, jumped onto his lap like puppies and hugged him around the neck.

He joined their Sunday table banter, participating in the battle to convince Niah and Jace to finish eating as he relayed the animal shelter's fundraiser results from the night before. Somewhere between the kids' fight over whose soccer game he should attend next and his dad's recap of

Pastor Caleb's prayer requests, he zoned out. He glanced across the table at Ali's empty chair. During times like this when the family chatter grew mundane, he and Ali had rescued one another by engaging in secret communication across the table. That secret language was useless now. No one knew it anymore—except for Cara, who'd translated it better than anyone else. But she wasn't here anymore either.

Callum helped clean up, drying the pots and pans Raelee washed, while his mom loaded dishes in the dishwasher. Afterward, he refilled his raspberry sweet tea and followed his family to the screened-in porch at the back of the house.

He stalled for a slight moment before opening the screen door. Like every visit before, he searched far down the property line for the two trees, the trees of their nightmares, trees that had left his family heartbroken and the place where he pulled Ali's pinned body from her ATV. There was the trunk that had fractured her neck and their hearts. He had a powerful urge to run down the lane and cut the suckers to the ground just as they had struck down Ali's future. Rational or not, he hated those sycamores and hoped the visible gash eventually killed the tree that killed Ali.

Callum plopped down on a rocker and refocused. His niece and nephew squealed from the jungle gym. Cardinals competed at the feeder and chirped from the pine trees lining the property. The highest limbs swayed under the sun as a faint breeze rolled across his skin.

"It feels good to relax," his dad said.

Callum couldn't agree. His childhood home had become the hardest place to find rest.

"It feels good to have you here," his mom added. She reached to squeeze his hand, a firm grip for such a little woman. The real strength of her hands, he knew, came when she pressed them together in prayer.

He pointed past the open space of the newly mowed lawn to the trees and confessed, "Seeing that is always hard." A sudden knot choked his throat. Wood squeaked against wood as the chairs rocked. He couldn't cohesively access his feelings or thoughts, until his mom's voice spoke his name and pulled him back into the fold.

"I know," she agreed and rested her small hand on his. "We all know." When he was little, her words reassured him. She could magically make things better. With the falter in her voice, he knew she joined him in his sadness.

Her understanding offered him a retreat from sharing anything further and eased his efforts at working on being honest with his feelings and not shutting people out. He owed his mom that, and he wanted somehow to soften her ache.

Before the accident, Sundays with his family had been a weekly retreat, a respite from the crazy, a refuge of love and acceptance despite his faults and fears, the stuff that built the backbone of the powerful man that he showed the world. How could he tell his parents that what they'd built for him as the safest of places had become the hardest place for him?

Callum voiced to no one in particular, "I'm missing a part of me. No matter how many times I come home, being here without her feels like I'm betraying her."

"She loved every moment we spent as a family," his mom said with a slight smile as she traced the grain on the arm of her rocker. "But she treasured our Sundays together most of all. That's why being here without her feels wrong."

His dad stopped rocking and leaned over to grab Callum's arm. "But son, let me tell you, that's exactly why all of us being here together is right. She'd want us to continue the tradition. Do you see what I mean?" He surveyed Callum's face for understanding. "We do it especially for her now."

Callum hung his head and propped his elbows on his knees. "I have flashbacks, sleepless nights, reruns of her last day in my head, wishing we hadn't ridden on those ATVs." He shook his head and continued in a hoarse voice, "I want more days with her. More time to show her I loved her."

His dad rested his palm on the back of Callum's head, trying to soothe his pain like he did when he was a child. "She knew you loved her, but we're right there with you, son. We understand everything you're going through." His dad paused. He was all too familiar with the grief, the insomnia, the anger, the endless dialogues with Ali even though she wouldn't hear them. He continued, "Some days, the desperate urge to change the outcome almost crushes me."

Callum wiped emerging tears from his eyes and cradled his face in the palm of his hands.

His mom caressed his back as Callum shared his story. "For longer than I care to admit, I couldn't call out to God or read His Word. I went through the motions each day. I forced myself to get out of bed. I told myself work was the reason to run, to get dressed, to act civil. One difficult morning, I cried out to God. To be honest, I yelled at Him. He told me He knew I was angry at Him, but that He wasn't going anywhere. He'd always be there with me, so I didn't have to be afraid of all my feelings. It was okay to be angry and sad and confused and question Him. He said someday He'd answer all my questions when we sat together in Heaven, but until I got there, He was taking care of Ali." He swiped both hands through his hair and sat up against the back of the rocker. "He asked me to trust that He knew the answers I needed the most right now. And that's what I'm still doing, day by day, trusting in His promise."

"Things won't ever be the same again," Raelee said. Unshed tears glazed her eyes. "We're finding our new normal—together." Her scratchy voice broke. Six years older, Raelee had loved on him and championed his academic and athletic efforts his entire life. He endearingly nicknamed her M2, short for Mom Number Two, for all the times she'd doted on him. Her desire to carry his pain was evident in her plea, "I love you, Cal." The words she didn't say conveyed as loudly as those she did—*we need you here to help us pick up the pieces.*

"We all need each other," his mom quietly added, resting her other hand on Raelee.

"Everything shifted and broke without her," he admitted, swiping his palms across his eyes. He couldn't keep his tears from flowing.

His dad pointed to each person on the porch. His steady voice turned urgent, "In this house, we can be broken, be a mess, be lost, be confused." He squeezed Callum's hand. "We'll find our way together because we have love."

"Thanks for being my strength these last two years when I should have been yours. I'm sorry for not showing up in the way you all needed, but I'm working on using my words." He chuckled and found his sister's sympathetic smile. "Does that make me sound like a pouty five-year-old?"

"No! It makes you sound human. To celebrate, the next Sunday you're not working, it's pineapple-upside-down cake for you," his dad cheered. "Just let us know."

"Uncle Cal, Uncle Cal? Can you push me on the swing? Please?" Jace's smile beamed from the jungle gym.

"Sure, buddy," Callum answered, finding a sliver of joy he didn't know he had. He kissed his parents' cheeks and whispered into his mom's ear, "I promise not to hide anymore, Mom."

He pestered his sister with an overbearingly tight hug and declared, "I promise you too, M2. And if I don't keep my word, you can kick my butt."

She pushed out of his bear hug, giving herself enough room to look in his face. "You know I will," she warned with good humor.

"Don't I know it!" he laughed.

TEN

Cara felt good about her first week on the job. In just one week, she'd gotten the hang of the department and was accomplishing way more than rescuing the officers from the burden of extra clerical duties. Her freshly brewed morning coffee lifted the first-shift patrolmen's spirits. She'd scheduled all the police vehicles to be washed, manned the front desk, and fielded questions from calls for the Chief when he stepped out. Chief Riley's riotous laughter and backslapping good cheer had returned. The entire place was more jocular, thanks to her efficiency and her let-me-help-with-that spirit.

Cara had fallen into an easy routine of driving to work with her dad, using those ten minutes to talk about their day. Today, she barely got a word in as her dad's exuberance about the success of Saturday night's auction bubbled over.

On their walk into the department, Cara brushed his arm and warned, "Careful, Dad, they'll ask you to be in charge again next year. I guess Tori and I didn't win since you didn't bring anything home."

"Guess not. But you're still a winner to me. I'm looking forward to watching what the Queen of the Station accomplishes this week. Go get 'em, Cara," Chief Riley encouraged, opening the door for her.

Cara sighed and waved her hand in dismissal at his praise. "Dad, let's ease into my second Monday, okay? It will take all morning just to tie up loose ends from the weekend," she mock-complained, making a face. "You better watch out, though," she called to her dad, following him into his office. "Rumor has it the patrolmen are already petitioning for a raise for me, just for manning that horrid phone system!" she teased.

Cara rounded the corner and stopped in her tracks at the sight on her desk—a stunning bouquet of tall sunflowers.

It better not be from him.

She approached the bouquet like it was enemy territory. Glancing around for spies, she quickly snatched the card from the vase and peeked at the note.

You brighten every day here.
Have a great second week.—Cal

No! He did not.

Cara looked around for a trash can big enough to hide the bouquet, but better judgment assailed her—darn her sensible side. She planted them on the tall filing cabinet behind her chair and jammed the card deep in her purse.

She sped into the workroom to freshen the coffee, flummoxed by Callum's gift. She flung the door open, and her perfunctory response vanished when she came face to face with a tired Callum at the copier.

Confusion scrunched his forehead. He stared at her, and she stared back, not wavering. When his stare broke into a smile, Cara nodded impassively and nearly sprinted, head down, to the coffee machine for her daily barista duty.

Note to self—tell Dad to purchase a Keurig to make her life easier.

Cara realized within a minute that her clanging was the only noise in the room. No rhythmic whir and whoosh of the copier. No clicks of footsteps. She dared not look, but the thick blanket of silence piqued her curiosity. Nosy Cara couldn't help herself. She turned and surveyed the situation he was in.

Callum stood paralyzed at the copier. His jaw tensed in frustration. He started pressing buttons like he was playing whack-a-mole and suddenly the copier began working.

She tidied up her coffee supplies and nearly escaped when the copier jolted to a sharp halt, blinking bright red.

"Don't give me that crap paper jam message again!" he spurted.

Cara giggled. Callum turned and met the maybe-you-deserve-this arch of her brow. Cara giggled again, covering her mouth when she couldn't stop.

Don't get involved. It's not your circus, she urged herself.

Staying far away from Callum's business was her first inclination. Not helping someone in need went against her own convictions. But this was Callum, and he made everything trickier.

He won't ask for help. I just know it.

Callum worked through the step-by-step instructions on the screen. Cara halted for a second, already well versed after one week with this touchy machine.

"UGHHH," Callum growled when his attempt didn't restore the copier to life.

Every impulse to rescue him barred her from bolting out the door. Cara opened her mouth, but, on second thought, quickly pinched her lips shut. She stared at the close-trimmed hair at the back of his neck. She'd touched there a thousand times, pulling him to her for a kiss. His broad shoulders slumped over the copier were so familiar.

He turned to her, scrunched his eyebrows, and asked, "Is there a trick to this thing I'm not aware of?"

He's asking for help!

She took the risk and remained in the room, melting into her attraction.

Cara saddled up beside him and read the machine's instructions over his shoulder. It's what she'd done for another officer last week.

At this close distance, they were magnets. The traitorous beating of her heart ramped up.

Oh heart, never forget. His charms have no power if you don't surrender to him.

"Thanks for the help."

She glanced sideways, caught his eyes, and his sincerity spiraled through her senses.

Don't read too much into my offer to help, Callum, she thought to herself.

He sighed an admission of defeat and waved her into his vacated spot, escaping the madness of the machine. When he lightly brushed his fingertips along her forearm, the space between them shrunk. Every one of his little touches over the years overwhelmed her with memories.

Stay steady, girl!

Cara leaned over the screen and concentrated on gathering her wits. Following the instructions, she opened and closed the top drawer, finding nothing to clear. Callum leaned in closer, nearly hip to hip. Her body was utterly aware that he focused his attention entirely on her.

She attacked the copier malfunction with the same determination she had approached her opponent on the field, a play-by-play, drawer by drawer, single-minded determination. She needed to remove herself from Callum—and fast.

When she chanced a quick glance at him, sheer admiration spread across his face.

Flashes of alarm and panic bolted through her body at the immediate grin his smile put on her face.

Kneeling, she opened the drawer to the inside drum, and her hair fell to the side, exposing a small tattoo at the base of her neck. *Phil 4:8 Ali.* Ali's name and favorite verse, both in her own handwriting.

"Aha," she said, releasing the culprit, a small torn piece of paper. "Next time, ask for help sooner," she commanded. She pressed the button to finish his copies.

"Next time, I'll ask for help, for sure. Lesson learned!" he echoed, but the weight of his admission included way more than his copier lesson.

Cara batted the copies solidly against his chest. A zing of electricity sparked through her at the mere touch of him.

He cupped her hand, and she froze, her hand resting over his heart.

In slow-motion, he slid the papers from her fingers. "Thanks," he struggled to say, his voice weak and scratchy.

"Sure thing," she politely offered, weak-kneed. Being around him both infuriated and thrilled her. And that frustrated her.

"I'd probably still be in the same spot if you hadn't shown up."

And now I can't seem to move from the spot I'm in.

"It's doing that more and more. I'll call someone to come and look at it. If it happens again, just come get me."

"You saved me. I owe ya," he said and patted her shoulder. The warmth of his words and his hand rested seconds too long.

She stared at his fingers, alien objects landing on her.

I WON'T let him charm me.

"Nope, you don't owe me anything," she responded with the same civil courtesy in her voice she would use with any other officer. "It's all part of my job. Take it easy! Let me know if the machine bites again."

"Wait," he called as she started to leave. When he reached to cup her face, she thought he'd try to kiss her, but instead, he rubbed her chin with his thumb.

Cara startled at his touch, jerking her head back.

"You had a smudge of ink there."

Her jaw clenched, and she swiped at the spot, trying to wipe away his touch.

"And I hope you like the flowers," he said with a smile in his voice.

"I set them where everyone will enjoy them," she answered and hurried to the door.

ELEVEN

A white envelope with the animal shelter's logo, a puppy cuddled next to a kitten, and Cara's name written in all caps sat in the middle of her desk.

Starting my Tuesday with a win! Woo-hoo!

Cara ripped the end and pulled out three identical tickets. This entitles CARA RILEY one date with CALLUM HALL.

Wait! What? Nooooooo!

Cara tossed her winnings across her desk like she held a live grenade, but they fell like confetti at her feet. She sprang two steps back, keeping her eyes on them, disoriented and shell-shocked. She scanned the office, checking to see if this was someone's cruel joke.

Picking them up from beneath her chair, she read the fine print at the bottom of the ticket:

Upload a picture of each date to our website. Don't forget to tag us. #raffleforanimals.

"I won Callum?" she hollered, unwittingly, and plopped onto her chair, pretending to hit her head against her desk. "This ticks me off!" She pounded the desk with her fist.

Surely, my dad didn't know!

"You won Callum?" Cara jumped at Kim's cheerful voice. "You lucky duck." Kim was the school resource officer for a reason. She had great conversational skills, which was code for being a gossip and an expert at enhancing a story.

She hurried to hide the tickets in her lap, but one flew to the floor at Kim's foot.

Cara scooted in her rolling chair to grab it, but Kim scooped up the ticket. "Wow, you did win a man!" Kim yelped as she read. "And a hot one at that," she added with a wink.

"His good looks just irritate me," she mumbled, snatching the ticket out of Kim's hand.

"What! Can't hurt," Kim said, confused.

Want to bet?

By the time she made it to her dad's office to ask him if he knew about this charade, the entire department would know of her winnings.

"He's so sweet." She stole the ticket right back from Cara and read it again in disbelief.

"Yep. Lucky me." She smiled in mock cheer, tapping her nails on her desk.

"Have a great time," Kim squealed, hugging the ticket to her chest. "I can't wait to check out the pictures you post. When's your first date?"

"I just found the envelope on my desk. No arrangements have been made." She plucked the ticket from Kim's hands and tucked all three into her back pocket.

"There won't be any dates," she unconsciously blurted. Her dad had some explaining to do. A chewing out was in order.

"What do you mean? I'm sure you can figure something out. I bet he's already decided where you two will go for each one. He's very intentional, if you haven't noticed."

"Intense, you mean," Cara muttered under her breath.

"Well, that too," Kim agreed and winked, nudging Cara's elbow. "But mark my words, you'll be wishing you had more dates with him when these three are over."

"I don't want the first three," Cara grumbled.

A pang of relief washed over Cara when she remembered the steer clear message she'd given Callum. He might graciously back out once he discovered she was the ticket holder.

"Don't be a Debbie Downer."

"Here! You take these and see how far you can get with him," Cara said. She pulled the tickets from her pocket and slapped them into Kim's hand, a smidge reticent to relinquish them.

"Oh no, you don't," Kim said and tried to give the tickets back to Cara like they were dirty money. "I'm not explaining the switch to Callum." Kim studied one of the tickets as if she were entertaining the idea for a minute. "See, I can't take these. It says down at the bottom that he will contact you. Apparently, the organizers notify him of the winner's name."

"I don't think he'd mind the switch. I simply donated money for the animals, and he donated himself," she laughed and scrunched her face. "That's just weird. What does that say about him? Oversized ego, if you ask me."

"It says he knows he'll bring in lots of money for the doggies."

"Well, he's barking up the wrong tree if he thinks I care."

"Geez. You sound like a girl who's been burnt bad. Dare to share?"

She rolled her eyes and ignored Kim's request. "It won't matter who Callum takes. The doggies got their money."

"Even if Callum doesn't mind the switch, my boyfriend surely will," Kim said, setting the tickets in the middle of

Cara's desk. "Don't get your knickers in a twist. You didn't win a man. You simply won some dates. To win that man, you'll have to work a lot harder. Relax and enjoy three free dates."

"I don't want to win dates with him," she refuted with more vehemence than Kim understood. "I donated to help the animal shelter. And I definitely won't share how my dates go. This isn't *The Bachelor*."

"But it says at the bottom to upload photos of the date. That sure sounds like show and tell. Don't leave us out of the fun," Kim teased with a giggle. "Imagine how much fun you would have if the ticket said he had to do whatever you told him to do?" Kim flashed arched eyebrows and hip checked Cara so hard, she swiveled in her chair like she was on a carnival ride.

"That would be a miracle. He seems to do what he wants," Cara said, ignoring Kim's insinuation.

"Ooh. I can't wait to hear about what he wants to do," Kim lightly scratched her finger down Cara's arm.

Cara swiped Kim's hand away. "Get your mind out of the gutter. You know I didn't mean anything like that."

Kim laughed. "Women around here go gaga for him. Watch this." Kim grabbed a ticket and stepped toward the evidence room. "Hey, Kathy!" she yelled, waving her tickets in the air. "Come see what Cara won!"

When the clicks on the tile grew closer, Kim flashed a hand signal for Cara to twatch Kathy's facial reaction.

"You hit the jackpot!" Kathy shrieked at Cara, clapping her hands together.

There was a day I thought that.

She couldn't quite make out what Kathy whispered to Kim between giggles. She wasn't sure she wanted to know.

"I wouldn't say that," Cara said. The ladies knew nothing of the hurdles that Cara and Callum would have to overcome to be at ease with one another.

"This is so much better than a dating app," Kim advised. "At least you know what you're getting into."

That's the problem, Cara thought, tight-lipped.

"The big deal is that I didn't choose this. I had no idea when I donated money for an auction that I might win dates. Winning a gift card to Filippo's Pizza was more what I had hoped for."

"Don't look a gift horse in the mouth. You get three free dates. You can go to Filippo's on one of them. There's no pressure. He's a good guy. I can't figure out why someone hasn't snatched him up, other than he doesn't want to be, apparently," Kim answered.

"Well, I'm certainly not snatching him," Cara asserted.

"What is it they say? 'The lady doth protest too much, me thinks,'" Kim prodded.

Kathy's smile beamed from ear to ear with an idea. "Make him take you someplace expensive. You should wear a fancy dress. Get your hair done. My hairdresser at TK Salon will make you look fabulous."

"Go to Silvercreek. It's quaint and classy," Kim suggested.

"Stop, ladies!" Cara pleaded. "I'm not planning any of the dates," she added, fearing any emotional investment.

But Tori's ideas about revenge popped into her head.

If getting all made up didn't sound so exhausting, spending his money would be a good start toward that goal.

Cara grinned like the Cheshire cat. "Do you know him very well, Kim?" Cara asked. The last place Callum would choose was a restaurant with white tablecloths and fine china.

"Do you?" Kim asked.

Not as well as I thought.

"Um. Just a bit," she said shyly, to keep Kim and Kathy in the dark.

"You two would be a cute couple," Kim inserted, inspecting Cara head to toe.

All right, that's it. This conversation needs to be over.

"Well, imagine the three dates all you want," Cara said, raising up out of her seat and plucking the tickets from Kim's hand. Cara slid them back into the envelope and tossed it in the top desk drawer. "This lucky girl has to get back to work," she said flippantly and plopped back down in her chair. She clasped her hands in her lap and arched her brows, waiting for the ladies to scurry back to their places, but they continued to stand around her desk, brainstorming fantasy dates for her as if she weren't there.

The competitive side of her wanted to accept the tickets to get back at Callum, but she honestly didn't know how to make him miserable without some harsh revenge and that was so out of character. She tried to reframe the concept of revenge in her mind. Fight back. Settle up. Have a little fun. Those sounded much better. When the word *reckoning* came to her, she gave a sinister laugh. Oh, that is perfect. Cara—the reckoning.

And yet, a large part of her, the size of the southern hemisphere, worried she'd be wrecked by the end of their time together. That cautious side knew the danger she would put herself in if she weren't careful. She'd be setting herself up to endure more rejection from him if she didn't resist wanting him back. She felt strong enough to survive this. She had a whole new life ahead in a few short weeks that she was absolutely thrilled about. Three dates weren't going to change that.

I could go out with him and prove to Callum how strong I am now. I can show everyone I'm fine living without him.

Maybe.

Maybe not.

I'm making too much out of this prize.

Realizing Kathy and Kim were still mooning over various dates scenarios, she shooed them away with a polite shuffle of her hands just as the heavy metal back door slammed shut. All three ladies' heads turned. Callum and Chief Riley, in a seemingly serious discussion, turned the corner. They halted in unison as if under attack from the wide-eyed, frozen faces staring back at them. Callum's attention darted between their paralyzed stares.

"Everything alright?" Chief Riley asked.

"Definitely. Just clarifying some things," Cara inserted without hesitation. Her loud pronouncement jarred everyone's attention. All heads turned toward Cara, whose bugged eyes and nodding head begged them to keep their conversation secret.

"Well, uh, good," her dad responded with perplexed scrutiny, following the tennis match of odd expressions volleying between the ladies.

Callum stealthily ducked into the locker room.

"An uneventful start to the day is what we like," Chief Riley pronounced, still glancing between them as if looking for answers.

At that, they broke their awkward pauses and scurried back to their desks.

"Cara, can I see you, please?" the Chief asked as he walked away.

"Most definitely," she answered and sprang from her seat, following him into his office.

TWELVE

Cara barged into her dad's office, shut the door, and leaned her back against it.

"Dad, what did you do?" She issued her question like a warning.

Pulling the envelope from her back pocket and tossing it onto his large mahogany desk, Cara pointed and dialed back her angst. "Did you set this up?"

"Have a seat, Cara Bear," her dad said without glancing at the tickets. He motioned her to the reception chair in front of his desk.

Cara didn't budge. She clasped her hands behind her back and waited for his explanation.

"I'm too flustered to sit," she replied, recognizing his polite directive as a restrained tactic to calm her down.

"Please sit, Cara," he said, more demand than request.

She stumbled back into the chair and plopped like a petulant child. Gripping the arms of the chair, she watched him read the tickets and waited for his response.

"Go ahead," she said with more edge to her voice than she'd intended.

"First off, I arranged nothing."

Her jaw jutted stubbornly. "But you took my twenty dollars and—"

"Wait," he interrupted and leaned forward, intent and firm, and then clasped his hands together on top of his piles of work. He looked her in the eye and deliberated. "I—" he started but stopped, reframing his words.

Cara waited, impatiently tapping the arm of her chair.

He propelled his large frame from his seat and perched on the front of his desk. Toe to toe, he locked his gaze on hers. "I did not arrange that."

"But you knew about it?" she said, relieved that her dad had not schemed behind her back, but still fuming inside.

Chief Riley's brows creased, and frown lines grooved into the corners of his mouth.

"But?" she guardedly asked, her agitated leg movements urging him to expedite his explanation.

The quiet in the room was palpable. The Chief didn't twitch, cough, smile, or release a single muscle. He was studying her responses.

She crossed her arms and glared back at him. Her nails dug into her skin.

"But I have to confess," he paused, and every second ticked away like an hour, "I didn't *not* arrange it either."

"Oh, Dad!"

He cleared his throat and adjusted the family photo on his desk. She seethed, certain crushing something, anything, would make her feel considerably more in control, but she resisted.

"You gave me twenty dollars, which bought two raffle tickets toward any item."

"And you couldn't find anything I'd enjoy winning more?" she pressed with all the control of a professional interrogator.

"Maybe," he said, ignoring her caged ire.

"What aren't you telling me?"

"I handed your tickets to Callum and told him to place them on something you'd like."

Her eyes bugged out. "Callum arranged this?" Cara yelped, pointing at the tickets. She slapped the arms of the chair and bolted out of it. "After what he did and after all I've done to move on from him. The tears. The prayers. The talks. The isolation. The move. I asked him to steer clear!"

Her dad hesitated and then ran ahead with his thought. "Maybe this will ease some of the tension? Anyone in a room with you two feels it."

"Dad? Really? What good is this?" Cara paced in front of his desk, exhausted by the turn of events. She massaged the tight band squeezing her temple. "This comes off as creepy. Callum auctioned himself to an unknown person for money. Does this border on illegal? You are the police chief, for goodness' sake, and you knowingly bought a date for your daughter."

"Well, technically, you did. I didn't drop your tickets in his bucket, he did. He's not selling himself. He donated his time for a good cause and worked the entire auction on his Saturday night off. He was probably as surprised as you that your ticket was pulled. He had a bucket full of tickets."

"And Cara for the win!" she mocked, rolling her eyes.

"Maybe your time together will give you two a chance to work things out."

"Work things out?" she echoed with sarcasm, clenching her jaw. "So now it's an opportunity for therapy? Are you positive you didn't arrange this?" She eyed him speculatively. "What about me, Dad? Did you think about me? You know how things ended between us. This isn't what I want. We've both moved on. I have balance again in my life. I'm headed to my new job in just a few weeks," she rapid-fired.

"I'm always thinking of you, Cara." His calm reassured her. "If you don't want to go, then tell Callum that. I was as shocked as you when he told me on the way from the parking lot."

"I can't believe he told you before me!"

"He seemed a little anxious about it."

The idea of a nervous Callum appealed to her, suddenly inciting a foolish notion. *Bring on Cara's reckoning.* A small smile lit up her face.

"He must really want you to agree to go," her dad pondered out loud.

"Well, you know what they say, 'hope springs eternal,'" she quipped, jetting air through her tight lips.

"Wounds fester if you ignore them," he pointed out.

"He dumped me!"

"You're both living in the shadow of one day."

She wasn't sure why his words hurt, but they choked her speechless. Tears flooded her eyes.

He rose and pulled her to him, wrapping her heavy limbs in a bear hug, a Cara Bear hug, the reassuring kind he said he'd never stop giving no matter how old she got. He pushed strands of her hair that had fallen across her face behind her ear.

"Callum asked me if you'd seen the envelope yet. He thinks there's a good chance you'll refuse to hang out with him. I told him he would have to talk to you. I was staying out of it."

"Oh, I see. He was asking for your help with me."

"Slow your jets. He did no such thing. He just tested the water to see how I thought you might react."

"Tested the water? Is that what this little chat is? Whose side are you on?"

"You know I'm on your side," he corrected her.

"He was hoping for your help," she muttered under her breath.

Silence landed between them.

"The ball is in your court. As the winner, accept or not," he said, cutting to the chase.

"Thanks for the heads up. What else did he ask you?" Cara stood to leave.

"What makes you think he asked anything else?"

"History, Dad, history! I know Callum. Come clean."

"He wanted to know the best way to ask you, and I told him to just ask."

"So, he did ask for your help," she knowingly smirked and plopped her hands on her hips, copping a defensive attitude.

"No, he's trying to be respectful of where you are."

"He thinks I'm scared to be around him? I'm angry with him, Dad, not a coward!" Her folly gained momentum. "It's a perfect chance to exact a little revenge."

"Revenge?" her dad asked, worried.

She hadn't meant to audibly express that last line. "Not literally, Dad." *Unless it's all in fun.* "Just prove to him things are over between us." *And maybe to myself.* "We can't go back. But I'm strong enough to navigate this hiccup," Cara said. She grabbed the doorknob and halted, thinking of the complications that could arise.

"You are," her dad encouraged. His tone was careful as he added, "Cara, I'm getting a little whiplash. I honestly can't tell if you want to go on the date or not."

These dates could be trouble or freedom. Fear and desire wound around Cara's heart. What if being close to Callum made her long for what they once had? Her pain would escalate one hundredfold. She'd made the hard decision and let her hopes of him go. It was best for her. For two years, she forced herself not to want him. For two years, she avoided him. She'd fought hard to trust her own emotions and decisions.

Could she be in his presence now and not hope for him to love her? Melodramatic as it sounded, she felt deep inside that he could break her again. Uncertainty caused her to second guess the strength she'd found to resist that longing.

Being so emotional about a decision that revolved around Callum agitated her. He was taking up too much space in her head and heart, and she swore she'd never make that mistake again.

Callum's words to her under the hickory tree at Ali's funeral replayed in her head. Her frustration escalated, and suddenly, she stubbornly wanted to prove to herself a few dates couldn't break her.

"You two can work this out."

Can we?

She wondered what he'd meant—the dates or closure, but discussing Callum with her dad had already become too intimate.

"This could give you a chance to catch up with one another since you—" he broke off.

"Since I what?" she snapped and stepped back into the room.

"Since you went away."

"You were going to accuse me of running away."

"I made no such accu-"

"I hear what you're not saying," she interjected, contemplating for a couple of seconds what to confess.

"There's truth in it. I'm not ashamed to say I ran away from him. It was a smart move. I gained perspective about the breakup. I quit suffocating under the dream of me and Callum growing old together."

Her dad offered a knowing half-grin and patted her shoulder. "I'm proud of you. I'm due for roll call in two minutes, but I'll catch up with you later to see what you decide. Until then, say a prayer. Ask for guidance on what's best for you."

I definitely need input.

"I could just go on the first one and be done."

Her dad swung around, shocked. "Callum's auction was for one date."

"No, Dad, there were three prize tickets in that envelope."

"Clever move on his part." Her dad shook his head and chuckled heartily as he walked away.

"Manipulative ploy is more like it," she yelled, heading for her desk.

* * *

Her dad's suggestion that their getting together could be a way forward hadn't been lost on her but was eclipsed by Callum's deception with the tickets. It would serve Callum right if she issued an adamant *no*. It would also be an easy way out of her confusion. In the name of fair play, she could take the high road and fulfill just one date. Callum didn't need to know her intentions up front. More wisely, or not so wisely, she could continue the dates until she'd settled the score to her heart's content.

Had she even given God more than one-sided, cursory prayers since Ali's death? She'd certainly not asked for His guidance. She'd run headstrong with her plans without seeking God's wisdom, or her parents' for that matter, for the last two years.

She needed to have a real talk with God, too, but right now wasn't the time. She was too flustered. God was probably up there passing judgment on her thoughts of exacting revenge. Or maybe right now was as good as any to say a few quick words, giving Him an opportunity to prove He still worked for her good.

Lord, I'm coming to You for help. I need discernment about these dates. To be honest, I have more doubt than anything when it comes to relying on You for answers. You're probably shocked to even hear from me. I'm not sure why I'm bringing my concerns to You now, but I need help with this choice. Is there something to gain from us being together like my dad suggests, besides the fun of making Callum squirm?

She sat down at her desk and stared at the leather blotter as if she'd find her answer written there. A pang of guilt over her selfish hope that He would solve all her problems hit her.

Cara shot from her chair for a quick cup of coffee to settle her nerves and added a few more words. *I'm still angry with Callum. I'm sure You don't like that. I want to avoid him, but then I don't. I feel like a traitor, expecting answers when I've been ignoring You, when I'm still angry with You. I'm so tired of being angry. I miss You.*

Her prayer had felt like she had been talking to herself. No writing appeared on the wall. No audible voice from the heavens responded. No parting of waters directed her path.

When Cara rounded her desk, Callum was down the hallway, headed her way.

"Lord, help me be strong," slipped from her lips. Every step he took toward her felt too close.

"Hey, there." Nervous restraint splayed across his face. She cleared her dry throat, but her attempt at lightheartedness came out scratchy. "What's up? You're doing that thing you do when you have a question." Cara retreated behind her desk and back to her chair.

"That thing I do?" Confused, he checked himself.

"Go ahead and ask," she said, blinking away the clouds in her head and jutting out her chin in pert attention.

With a slight shuffle of his feet, he rested into an obviously well-rehearsed invitation. "Did you get the envelope I set on your desk?"

"I did," she politely answered, poker-faced.

"I would like to invite you for our first date this Thursday night. Assuming you'd like to go, that is."

Dragging in a deep breath, she held it for a second before letting it slowly release. "I'm not sure," she drew out the words *not sure,* stalling for that answer she asked God for.

"Not sure?" He mimicked her drawn-out speech. "Not sure you *want* to go on a date or not sure if you already have plans?"

She fidgeted to pull her phone from her pocket. Her twisted nerves made the simple task difficult. After clicking through her phone, she glanced at him. "I'm open," she answered. A simply stated, kindly spoken answer exercised the wisdom she had sought from her prayer.

"And will you go?" he asked again. Doubt and the need for clarity warred for her answer.

Cara, with this last chance to back out, was tempted to offer her regrets, but then "Yes" spurted from her mouth, clearly and confidently and gently.

Where did that come from?

Could she blame her swift change of heart on the upside-down wisdom of God? Had He heard her prayer?

"If you're sure," he said, studying her.

Did he notice the fierce uncertainty rolling through her insides?

"My dad told me you weren't sure I'd accept," she said, curious.

"I was one hundred percent unsure. Who knew asking for a first date could be this hard?" Callum asked, wiping sweat from his brow.

"This was hard for you?" Cara's candid question popped from her mouth.

"You betcha!" Callum fisted a soft thump on her desk, staring hard into her eyes. "And thanks for—" Callum stalled. She'd watched his hesitation enough to know he was filtering through a mountain of thoughts. When they dated, she'd learned to draw out his thoughts with patient questions.

She shuffled the papers on her desk to hide from the awkwardness between them. When he didn't immediately finish his thought, she completed their exchange for him. "Thursday it is," she said, aligning the stack of papers with a hard bang on the desk.

Callum double tapped her desk and turned to exit. She watched him saunter down the corridor.

Cara knew she'd have to double tap into God to get her through the first date with Callum.

THIRTEEN

Cara couldn't decide if the last two days were the longest two days of her life or the shortest. She dreaded and anticipated this date with Callum.

Cara had tied her hair into a loose ponytail and tucked it under a ball cap. Silver hoop earrings dangled against her neck. Wearing her ankle boots with jean shorts and her white blouse was a little casual, but comfort on the outside might compensate for her jitters on the inside.

Nestlé instantly rose from the floor, hearing the rumble down the driveway, and mustered a tiny pounce to the door. As he pressed his nose to the screen, his thick tail, swinging in excited circles, nearly knocked Cara off balance.

Dad closed his recliner, but Cara shot him a look that settled him right back into his seat with the News-Gazette. She waited in the shadow of the screen door, enjoying a balmy summer evening breeze. A cloud of dust followed Callum's pickup truck down the gravel drive.

Nestlé's paws pranced in place. He released two bellowing barks when he recognized Callum in the driver's seat, his elbow propped on the window. Cara rubbed her dog's noggin and whispered, "Don't get used to his visits, buddy." She propped the door open and said, "Go for it," patting Nestlé on the head as he waddled out onto the porch, searching for Callum's ear rubs.

Callum jumped from his truck, hurriedly tucking his charcoal t-shirt into his jeans. When the screen-door slammed shut behind Cara, he froze in place at the bottom of the steps, eyes locked on her.

Nestlé whined and begged for Callum's touch. For a split second, she saw herself skip down the steps, jump into his arms, bury her face in his neck, and hold on for dear life. Nestlé barked again and drew her gaze away from Callum, rescuing her from her awkward thoughts.

"Hey," Cara greeted Callum coolly, keeping her attention on Nestlé. "You better put him out of his misery," she suggested, patting Nestlé. "Getting down there is the last thing he wants to do, but he'll try it for you."

Callum bent to tie his unlaced boots and angled his focus up the steps, swelling Nestlé's eagerness with sweet talk. The more Callum called to him, the harder his tail beat against Cara's leg, and the weaker Cara's knees became. When he sprang up the six steps and balanced toe to toe before Cara, she edged back a step, hoping the heat flushing through her body hadn't reached her face. When Callum squatted at her feet, wooing Nestlé with a full body massage, Nestlé grunted in blissful approval, and Cara tensed at Callum's closeness.

"Want to come in for some sweet tea, Callum?" Chief Riley called from just inside the screen door.

Callum stood to his full six-foot two stature, and she swore heat radiated from his body two feet away. His gaze shot from her to the screen door and back to her, seeking an answer to the dilemma etched on his face.

He read her body language and politely declined into the darkness beyond the screen. "Thanks for the offer, but maybe another time, Chief," he answered, heading down the stairs at full throttle. She'd never been so thankful for his retreat, giving her a second to regain her cool.

Nestlé whined in protest and pawed at the porch for Callum's continued touch. Callum obliged, hopping back up the steps to give him another whole-body rub and sweet whispers in his ear.

He wrapped his hands around Nestlé's muzzle and kissed his forehead. "You're a good boy, but I gotta go for now." Nestlé whined to ride shotgun. "Aww. Not this time, Lover Boy." Callum offered his hand to Cara, as if she needed help down her own front stairs. The deed of a gentleman. The snapshot of their dating years.

Letting his hand wrap around hers just this once would be so easy, so comfortable, a familiar tenderness and strength. She quickly scolded herself for the momentary craving.

"I'm good," she fired back and turned resolutely from him, bounding down the steps with staunch confidence.

Her insides trembled. Nausea washed through her. She was hardly good. With one simple offer, she'd nearly betrayed her rules for being in Callum's presence. Rules she'd created and rehearsed out loud to herself ten minutes ago, pointing a warning finger at herself in her full-length mirror.

Callum Rules:

Don't touch him.

Don't let him touch you.

Don't be fooled by all the ways he touches you without touching you.

She had to fling the itch for him far from her brain and body. One detour could be her unraveling. Even his friendly protectiveness there on the steps had plunged her into a false sense of togetherness. If she let herself think differently for one second, she might wind up tangled in her longing for him. She had no choice but to follow her rules or she'd come apart once again.

"Yep, you always are," he responded and bounced down the steps two at a time after her.

"Wise guy, I know you set up this entire scenario. First of all, you rigged my winning. Go ahead and admit it," she challenged, crossing her arms in front of her chest.

"And you said yes," he responded, imitating her defensive stance.

Ignoring his lame attempt at teasing, she asked, "Only one date with you was supposed to be auctioned off. Is that true?"

A sly, pleased smile beamed across his face at her tenacious interrogation. He eased his arms to his side and complied with her command. "Yes."

She pointed her finger at him. "*You* changed my winnings to three dates?"

"Yes," he said, drawing out his voice as if she'd finally had all the clues to comprehend the case on her own.

"At any point, did you tell my dad about your little manipulation?"

"This morning on our way into the department I told him about your winning. That's all. Nothing else. I promise."

"You promise?" She raised her voice in dismay. "Hmm. Is your promise supposed to be reassuring?"

He lowered his head for several seconds. When his gaze finally rose to meet hers, he took slow steps toward her and raised both hands in surrender to calm the fire burning in her eyes. "Okay, okay, I admit I set all this up to get some time alone with you. That was truly my sole objective."

Cara pursed her lips. *Tell me something I don't know.*

It didn't do her any good to continue to discuss his little scheme, especially since they were already on the date, but confronting him and setting the record straight gave her confidence and control.

"You manipulated me," she pointed at him again, staring him down. "You do know what they say about paybacks?"

"That one good deed deserves another?" he said with a hint of relief and sarcasm.

"Just remember, no good deed goes unpunished," she warned.

Eager to put some distance between them, she stutter-stepped on the concrete walk and recovered without falling on her face and, more importantly, without taking the hand Callum extended to steady her.

"Walk much?" he teased lightly, like the Callum before Ali died.

Cara chronicled Callum's behavior and all events in her life by Ali's death. There was her life before Callum's cut and run, BC, and the life she forged after Ali's death, AD.

"Tease much?" she jabbed back at him, making a face. She was rarely clumsy and refused to play the shy, awkward female needing a man's rescue.

I'll rescue myself. Thank you very much!

"Can't miss the opportunity to see your nose scrunch like that," he said, wrinkling his nose to mimic her. When they were a 'we,' Callum's demeanor softened when they teased and poked fun and laughed together.

"A little of your lip goes a long way," she threw back at him, empowered, until she heard the double meaning in her own words and practically choked. She'd pitched him an easy fast ball instead of a curve ball.

"Glad you brought your grit tonight. You'll need it. We're going axe throwing. Ever been?" Callum asked.

Rounding the hood of his truck, she stopped sharply, transfixed by the six letters, FOR ALI, on his specialty police memorial plate.

The grip around her throat strangled her words. Unable to move, lest she stumble to her knees, the burn behind her eyes blurred the license plate and the world beyond it. The wretched wound in her chest opened at unexpected moments.

Would it ever heal? Why now?

She bent low before the plate, and her pointer finger lumbered to trace the A-L-I, as if hoisting a ten-pound weight. The heaviness of losing Ali flooded through her body.

Callum stepped close behind her and followed each tense movement.

God, could you have given me one more day with my friend? One more hug. One more proper goodbye with words between us.

When she stood and tore her focus from the plate, he didn't deflect her pain, but acknowledged it with a nod of understanding.

She paused before mounting the running board to swipe away any mascara smudged under her eyes. He reached for her hand as he had when they dated, but she trembled too badly to take it.

Not now, she thought.

She held onto the grab bar and hoisted herself onto the leather seat, determined to disguise her discomfort.

Don't endear yourself to me. Any tremor of kindness from you and I might melt into this seat and erupt into a blithering, clinging mess.

Each second passed like an hour. She buckled her seat belt and swiped the trail of tears from her cheeks, waiting for her throat to loosen enough to speak. She cleared the lump in her throat, but her breath still scratched as she rasped, "What did you ask?"

"Have you ever been axe throwing?" Callum asked again.

"Nope. But I've wanted to try," she answered with forced enthusiasm.

"Me, too. We can each experience our first time… together." They turned to one another at the same time and then quickly turned away.

Silence reigned as they drove into town, trading glances at one another. Cara hadn't realized how tense she was until her body relaxed when they parked in front of The Bad Axe.

"Let's go throw down for an hour," Callum hyped as he slammed his door shut.

She smelled competition, and it invigorated her.

"Me with an axe. Me with an axe next to you. Muahahaha. That's either a very brave or very naive move on your part," Cara cautioned with a sinister laugh, hopping from the truck.

"It's not my best move, is it—being anywhere near you with an axe in your hand?" Callum grimaced and crossed his fingers. "Let's hope you're in a good mood."

"I can't be responsible if it hits you," she teased.

An employee guided them through the safety rules and throwing strategies, iterating the golden rule—throw together, retrieve together. He supervised as they practiced throwing at their adjacent targets, then took their drink order, and promised to check on their throwing progress.

"Wine, huh?" Callum laced his question with insinuation.

She stared him down. "And what's your problem?"

"I've just never seen you drink." Callum took a shot at the board. "Crap," he muttered, frustrated that his axe flew off the wood, hitting the side wall.

Fixing her hand on her hip, she gave him some attitude. "Have I hit some new low in your opinion?"

"As long as you don't order six. We *are* hurling axes."

She turned from him, focused on her next shot, and hurled her response, "Only you'd cause me to drink that many." Cara flashed Callum a smug smirk, satisfied with her comeback and hitting the four ring on her first shot and a bullseye on her second.

"I'm glad to see I still affect you."

"Like heartburn."

Callum's mouth dropped in a gape, and he fought for his response. "Ouch."

"This really is great for relieving some angst." Her axe hit the bullseye with a loud thud.

"Or increasing it." Callum wasn't used to facing her wrath or being bested.

Even after great concentration, his axe flew off the board.

In a dramatic show of one-upmanship, she set her axe down and sauntered to his side. "You have to loosen up. Here let me help you." Cara walked behind him and hugged her arm around him, running it slowly over his biceps and down his forearm. She wrapped her hand over his, covering his grip on the axe.

Callum growled low in his throat, and she smiled in self-satisfaction.

First lowering of Cara's reckoning ball. Revenge is indeed sweet.

Cara leaned her chest solidly against his back and pulled his arm into position just past his ear. "Place your thumb here on the handle under mine."

He blew out air in concentration, but more likely primal frustration.

"Keep your eyes on the target," she teased, tapping him lightly on the temple. In her best husky voice, she breathed into his ear, "Steady now. Lock your wrist and elbow." Wrapping her fingers into his belt loop, she tugged him back into her. "On your release, let it fly in front of you, not too high or too low, like you're throwing in a soccer ball."

Cara stepped away and felt the disappointing loss of his heat.

Callum exhaled and turned around to her, eyeing her with as much restraint as he could summon. "You're killing me."

"No good deed…" she pertly reminded him and picked up her axe, hitting the four mark again.

Cara returned to her Callum rules after purposefully pushing his buttons, pleased with the distress she'd clearly caused him, but her little lesson was dangerous. Touching him, even just to instruct, whirled her body and mind from manageable indifference into an influx of want.

Adrenaline and anxiety pumped through her. She quit bantering and settled into the rhythm of hold and release, rallying her self-control once again.

Their scores were neck and neck when Callum instigated a challenge for their final five throws. "Double or nothing?"

"You're on," she said.

"Are you sure?"

"I'm not afraid to take chances," Cara retorted.

"I love that about you. I'm counting on that!" Callum said.

The way he said that set Cara's nerves on edge.

"Let's take a quick selfie for the animal shelter website before I beat you," Callum said, grabbing his phone.

Cara plastered an expression of grim frustration on her face and positioned her axe over his head like she was going to hack him.

FOURTEEN

Riding triumphant from her win at The Bad Axe, Cara turned up the country music on the radio and basked in her private glory of managing Callum and their first date. When Callum turned onto Highway 150, Cara's insides deflated. She clasped her hands together, pressing them hard into her lap. Her body went rigid. It wasn't the mid-summer heat causing her to sweat. The tires' roar, Tim McGraw's crooning, and the quiet between them magnified in her ears. They rounded the bend in the road and Cara held her breath, seeing the entrance to the cemetery Ali rested in. Private, unspoken thoughts plopped down heavily like a third passenger between them.

Cara hated that cemetery.

She'd visited Ali only once since the funeral, to say goodbye on her way out of town. She'd promised to visit when she came home. She hadn't. Couldn't. Not once. Ali wasn't there, and Cara refused to honor the ground that buried her friend as if it were holy.

She did talk to Ali when she sat at the bridge over the pond where they'd spent endless days swimming and sharing secrets. Cara had visited the bleachers of the high school soccer field where Ali's memories haunted. Ali had been everywhere in their church where they'd grown up together. But so was God. And it suffocated her. He felt more silent than Ali. And just as absent.

Callum flipped his turn signal on, heading for the one place she'd absolutely refused to go. Dread creeped up her neck. Her chest tightened. Rebellion coursed through her. The anger that she'd let lapse during their competition flooded over her once again.

"I don't go here," she blurted the warning as he parked in the shade of the hickory tree.

Callum turned to her and nearly begged, "Just this once?"

She felt the air being sucked from the truck and gasped. "I can't believe you brought me here!" she snapped, holding her stomach. Fear and sadness crushed her. "I can't get air."

He gently touched her arm, and she flinched like he'd burned her. In her head, she bolted from the truck in escape. In her heart, she quickly restored her guard.

"I need air."

"Where's your asthma inhaler?" He hurried to open her door. She stared at him, zombie-like, and stepped out.

"I can't stand with you under this tree." Her voice collapsed and her resolve to stay strong began to crumble.

Callum didn't look behind him at the hickory tree. He knew what that tree meant to her, to him. "Let's take a little walk and talk."

Cara hadn't intended to walk, just step out to end her hunger for breath. While concentrating on inhaling air into her lungs, she followed closely on his heels and watched the grass swallow his shoes.

He stopped still.

Cara adamantly disagreed with whoever said cemeteries were peaceful places. As much as she wanted to, she didn't run away from this moment. Instead, her glance fixed on the flat bronze plaque installed on granite at his feet. Ali's faithfully worn birthstone her parents had given her on her sixteenth birthday was now glued into her headstone beside her name. Cara muscled against tears. Memories rushed in: begging God to bring Ali back, to open Ali's eyes, to make things good again.

Callum cleared his throat and startled her. He turned to her and their eyes bore into each other's, each asking, needing something from the other. "Cara, I'm sorry. It's too little, too late, but I need to say how deeply sorry I am for blaming us for Ali's death. I was so wrong."

His words broke her heart.

My heart was so much safer numbed.

"How could you bring me here when you—"

"I need to confess this to you. Here, in front of Ali. She's here with us." His calm unnerved her. Callum bent low, closer to the marker, closer to the etching of Alison Rose Hall. "Forgive me," he blurted out. Then he lifted his gaze to Cara. "Forgive me." Cara saw the world through his dark, liquid eyes. "I don't deserve it. I was a jerk. I understand if you won't, but I'm asking, anyway," he pleaded.

The chains around Cara's heart loosened a bit with his apology. It didn't end the churning in her stomach or her shortness of breath. She wasn't sure she could give him what he needed.

"I'm working on it," she lied, knowing full well she hadn't even considered forgiveness. Her anger toward him and at God for taking Ali had grabbed hold, and relinquishing it was difficult.

"I replay the accident in my mind over and over. When we'd made it back to that tree, and I knelt next to her, I knew her heart had stopped. Maybe in some ways, so had mine."

"Mine, too," she whispered.

"For the longest time, I felt guilty. My insides were a raging storm," Callum continued.

Cara nodded her head in agreement. "Same," she said, barely audible.

Callum stood and faced her. "After the accident, I felt the weight of letting everyone down. Ali. My family. You. Questions haunted me for so long. Why hadn't I used my head and said no to the race? I berated myself. I should have made us wear helmets. If I'd done things differently that day, Ali wouldn't have died."

"I asked myself the same question." Cara echoed his loneliness.

"But I shouldn't have blamed us. I was wrong." He shook his bowed head and repeated under his breath, "So wrong. I was never in control."

She was close enough to touch him, but she couldn't bring herself to reach out to soothe his turmoil. She had no words for him. He was wrong to blame her.

"I struggled with misplaced anger. It was maddening." He gave a mirthless laugh and stood. "I even got mad at Ali. I blamed her for not fighting hard enough to live. She had always been such a fierce fighter, determined to make a difference. I felt cheated," he confessed. The memory rolled across his face like a cloud eclipsing the sun. "I'm here with a full life ahead of me. She should have that. I felt guilty for being alive. I wanted to trade my life for hers."

"Don't say that!" Cara cried, grabbing his arm. Losing Ali was hard enough. She couldn't imagine losing Callum.

"Ali wouldn't let you anyway," Cara consoled herself out loud and released him.

"No, she wouldn't. Stubborn girl," Callum agreed.

Her heart melted a little, witnessing his hint of a playful smile at remembering his sister.

"I've made peace with my regrets, but it took a long time to forgive myself. I still have bad days and torment myself with guilt."

"I thought Ali and I would share college graduation, weddings, babies…" Her voice trailed off. "I want one more day with her," she nearly yelled to the heavens. "Who am I kidding? I want one more lifetime with her. Every day, I never really get over how she's not here, how she's not ever coming back to me."

Cara stopped talking for a second, then rushed on, before the pain of remembering could overwhelm her. "She won't ever hop in my Jeep again. We won't text to make plans. Life goes on as normal for everyone. I even cursed the Schwann man. I swore I wouldn't eat their ice cream again without her. I couldn't find normal for so long. Everyone danced around my anger, unsure of my next move."

She slowed her words to catch her breath and continued, "If only stomping tantrums worked with God. I was so angry with Him." She paused. "So many times, even now, I want to call her. It's getting better, but I still get ambushed at the strangest moments. There's no place in my world that she hasn't touched." With each word confessed to Callum, Cara released tension she didn't know she held.

A hint of a grin spilled across his face.

"What was that? I share my heart with you, and you smile at my pain?" Cara asked.

"I'm not grinning about that. You described my pain so well. It's oddly comforting."

Cara offered him a faint smile and stepped up to Ali's marker. The soothing summer screech of cicadas echoed through the trees.

"I still stumble through grief, too. I'm better today thanks to a lot of soul searching and counseling," Callum said.

Cara had refused counseling when her parents persisted. She'd regretted it a time or two. No amount of talking would bring Ali back. She figured her crisis couldn't be solved by analyzing it, so Cara staggered on to regain order in her own way. She didn't want to mourn with someone who didn't know Ali or Callum. She knew perfectly well what she'd lost. She forged ahead with life in a new school and a new town.

"I didn't just lose her that day," Callum said, his eyes begging her to understand. "I lose her every day." He wrestled with his words. "I'm learning to live without her, but so many things remind me of what I'll miss without her for the rest of my life." He gripped his bowed head with both hands.

The light played with the world and danced through the branches of the hickory tree, throwing moving shadows across Ali's gravestone. She heard her dad's words in her head. *You live in the shadow of one day.*

Callum tugged on her finger, and she caught his sad brown eyes when he nodded for them to head back to the truck.

Cara whispered what she couldn't say at this spot two years ago, "Goodbye, Ali."

She lost the dauntless edge of assertiveness she'd gained at the axe game and melted into an unsteady, vulnerable fragility. When Callum pulled her to his side, she didn't pull back but let herself lean against him for the short walk.

"I prayed for a day like this—a day you'd share what was going on for you. But it didn't come. So, I gave up hope that God answered prayers. I gave up any hope for you and me," Cara confessed.

Callum opened the door for her, and as she ducked in, he said, "Please, don't give up hope. Be angry with me, but don't stay angry with God."

Cara popped out of his truck like a Jack-in-the-box. "I am angry at both of you! Don't ask me not to be!"

"Wait. Hold on." Callum stepped back and raised his hands as if deflecting a punch. "I know you are angry with me. And with good reason. But God can make things good even though I can't. That's all I'm saying."

"All you're saying is forget all my heartache, stop wallowing in the past," Cara exploded.

"I am not saying that. I was mad at God, too. Her death broke me, so I broke us. I pushed you away." He paused and took a few deep breaths.

The shock of his confession spread like a consuming fire through her.

"I hate this tension between us," Callum said. "I hate myself for how I handled things. Now that you're willing to sit in the same space with me, I want to share what was going on with me before you disappear again." He glanced into her watery eyes, waiting for permission to continue.

Cara climbed back into the truck. Callum rounded the front and jumped in. She stared straight into his tender, vulnerable face. Goosebumps crawled across her skin.

"I couldn't explain or even name my feelings and actions back then," he said, still needing to rid himself of guilt. "My soul was torn from my chest. I was numb. My job was the only tangible thing I held onto. I gave it the little physical and mental focus I possessed. Grief kicked my butt. Understanding it was a slow rise from the ashes. My anger, my doubts, and my insecurities blinded me to seeing your pain. They consumed me. Until I heard myself relay things in counseling, I didn't realize just how selfish I was and how awful I treated you."

Cara screamed inside. It didn't have to be like that if he had let her in. Talking about this now wouldn't undo how he'd hurt her, but not talking left her in weary limbo, begrudgingly trying to accept what she did not understand. It was time to travel down this road, no matter how hard she railed against hearing his explanation. Then maybe she could put the past truly in the past.

"I thought letting you go was best for you," he explained.

She froze at his admission, and she couldn't filter her thoughts through kindness. "For me? You broke up for me?" she argued, exasperated, as if he'd flung red-hot embers on her.

"I want to ex—"

"Say it right!" Cara hit the dash. "You didn't break up for me." Cara's mouth flattened into a tight line. "How could you know what was best for me or how I felt? You never once asked me. You decided your life would be less complicated without me. You left me out. You did that for you."

She faced the window and swiped at pooled tears before they flowed fully down her cheeks. If only she could brush away the inexplicable wound from that day as easily.

She turned back to him, cleared the thickness in her throat, and continued, "You blindsided me. I didn't know when you walked toward me that day that it would be the last smile of yours directed my way. We both were in horrible pain. You don't think I blamed myself for my best friend's death?" She shook her head as if shaking off the bitterness that took root at the hickory tree. "I thought you would turn *to* me—and me *to* you." The emptiness of standing alone that day hollowed her chest afresh and warm tears flowed like lava down her cheek.

"I crawled inside myself and couldn't find my way out," he said, clenching the steering wheel.

"You changed everything, every plan, every dream, and erased every day between us."

"I'm so sorry," he whispered, hanging his head.

"Sorry?" she asked.

"And I know my words are not enough," Callum quickly added. "I can't change what I did. I am sorry for not knowing how to grieve. I thought I knew so many things, but when my sister died, I didn't have those survival skills."

"You gave up on me, Callum," she cried.

"I didn't give up on you. I gave up on myself."

She didn't trust his words.

"I spent my days trying not to think of you, avoiding you and your family, feeling sick every time I saw you, and wondering why I wasn't enough."

"I wanted to be with you, but I lost faith…in everything. It took me so long to see that God's promises are true, that He is good and near to us, to the brokenhearted." Callum took her hand in his. "I'm so sorry for abandoning you."

She rallied her waning strength. "Well, I'm fine now! You were doing what you had to," she quipped. Her throat stung at her cringe-worthy barb. "When you broke up with me, I not only lost Ali, but I lost you when I needed you most. You were the one person who could best understand my pain." And with that last sentence, more tears spilled down her cheeks and betrayed the cool sentiment she attempted.

He moved closer to her and leaned shoulder against shoulder. They stared at the hickory tree, at a past they couldn't alter, and at the twists and turns of life. A heaviness hung in the silence between them.

"If I could have the past back—"

"That's a dangerous proposal." She cut him off. She'd wished that dream a thousand times.

"We'd be together," he pondered.

"Would we?" she doubted under her breath.

They rode home in silence, letting the words they'd spoken settle between them.

FIFTEEN

After Callum's truck rolled away from her house, Cara grabbed her quilt and ended her evening rocking on the porch under the stars. Their date to the cemetery and the battle with their history left Cara weepy, and she gave into her grief, reliving that day that taught her the transformative power of a moment.

Two years ago

If Cara allowed the first tear to fall, it would start a messy unraveling of her hard-fought composure. Deep in her pocket, she clutched a tissue in her fist and pushed her nails into her palm, the pain oddly centering. She squeezed her trembling legs together for balance.

Cara jumped at the dull thump of Pastor Brent's Bible closing and caught the end of his gentle recitation, "and the God of all comfort, who comforts us in all our troubles…"

The God of all comfort?

Ali's casket was slowly swallowed by the earth. Cara wasn't comforted. When would solace wash over her? She squeezed Callum's hand as her eyes welled with tears. He mustered a brave face and gave her a slight glance through sad eyes. Cradled tears spilled down her cheeks, and a choked sob ruptured her throat. Agony nearly wrenched her to the ground, but she thanked the heavens she and Callum had each other for support.

When a desperate cry from Ali's mom pierced the thick stillness, Callum stiffened and released Cara's hand. Cara felt alone, sitting mere inches from him. The scales of Cara's fragile balance tipped, and her insides constricted into a tight ball, crushing her under an unbearable heaviness. The pain was more than she could hold in her chest. She bent like a willow tree to her knees and smothered her mouth with a ball of tissues, muffling her own shivering wail.

The flag clapped in the wind, startling Cara. She peered into the grave as the pastor attempted his final words of comfort. Fighting back another outburst, Cara kept her mouth masked with tissues and slowed the rhythm of her breathing.

She watched the pastor peer at the sky as if searching the blue heavens for his words. "We ask that You give our precious girl, gone from us too soon, Your eternal peace. Shine Your eternal light on Ali while she's away from us." Cara sniffled and choked on the lump in her throat as the pastor concluded. "We will miss you, Ali."

Those words caused an avalanche to pour from her heart.

God, I don't want to get through life without Ali. Why did You take her from us?

Cara stepped up to the open grave that held the friend she planned to have for life. She never figured life could be so short. Her shaking hand tenderly dropped her last letter to Ali on top of the spray of white roses splayed across the rich mahogany. Words, so many words between them—

spoken, signaled, written, texted—had knit them together morning, noon, and night. Without their exchange, she clung to her thoughts, hiding them deep inside.

In silence, friends and mourners filtered through tombstones to the solace of their cars. The scratch of slow tires on gravel echoed through the air. Her parents, she knew, hung around somewhere nearby, waiting to let her fall into their arms. Cara pressed the tissue harder against her compressed lips as tears rolled faster down her cheeks, blurring the unfathomable sight of her best friend's coffin leveled underground.

When Cara sought the comfort of Callum, he had wrapped his arms around his mom and dad. His mom clutched his black suit coat. When he turned to her, Cara's weary eyes, glistening with tears, searched his for refuge, finding none in their emptiness.

Cara followed Callum from a distance as he escorted his parents to the shelter of the limousine. Kissing his mom's cheek, he motioned he would return. He buttoned his suit coat as he crossed the street to Cara, his eyes trained on each slow press of his brogues into the manicured green grass. He stopped before her but didn't meet her red-rimmed eyes. He wrapped his hand around hers and, without a word, led her to the shade of the nearby hickory tree.

Callum's grip on her hand tightened when he propped himself against the solid hickory, pulling her with him. She waited for what seemed like minutes for him to speak, unsure how to proceed with the mountain of grief they bore. His lips parted without emitting the slightest of sounds.

She'd fallen into him, wrapping her arms around his waist, and his fingers clung to her, a desperate grasp for stability until a nearly imperceptible slip signified his letting go. Callum wiped his eyes. Her hands fell to her sides, and a lonely chasm opened between them.

Clearing his throat after what felt like an eternity, he lifted his head, and his spiritless eyes bore a warning she couldn't decipher.

"Ali has always been the other part of me," he scratched from his throat.

The warm, late June breeze swept across Cara's exposed arms. Caressing his cheek, she whispered in his ear, "I know you hurt like crazy. Your bond was beautiful. She loved you so much. You loved her so well—like only twins do."

She wrapped her hand around his head, pulling him to her, and he leaned on her shoulder. When his body shook, she willed her arms to be the balm he needed. It wouldn't be enough, she knew that, but his closeness soothed the ache growing in the pit of her stomach.

"Her death has changed everything for me," he started and hesitated, struggling to put his thoughts into words. "Even us," he finally murmured under his breath.

Every part of her stilled. His last two words, *even us*, rang like a death knell.

He leaned back against the tree, avoiding her eyes, and Cara shivered at the space between them.

She cocked her head to one side, questioning his thoughts.

And then, with a single sentence, clouded with remorse, he crushed her.

"We killed her." His empty eyes darted to the mourners climbing in cars. "I can't go on together."

Feeling dizzy, she gasped for little breaths of air. His blame struck her heart like a dagger. His sharp, absolute words cut through her veins, paralyzing her with fear. Cara hugged herself instead—little comfort that provided. She could barely hold up her own weight. As much as she wanted to argue with his thinking, to rail at him to fight for their love, she instinctively knew that nothing mattered to him but losing his twin.

Sorrow dripped from his face.

"I don't un—" Her words fell dead on her lips when he gripped her fingers. His pained face begged her not to expect more.

She inhaled sharply, hoping he would not let her go, but he feather-kissed her forehead and whispered against her skin, "I gotta go."

SIXTEEN

The morning after the disturbing end of their first date, she found a pile of her favorite candies in the middle of her desk: Payday bars, Whoppers, and Peanut M&Ms. There was no note, but the strategy was textbook Callum. Callum had often pandered to her sweet tooth. He was sweetening her up to say yes to a second date.

Later in the day, he texted her "Happy Friday," along with an apology. "Sorry, the end of our date was a whopper. Thanks for sharing your feelings and for listening to mine." This first text from him in years felt intimate, and she caught herself reading it over and over. The amount of space she allowed him in her head after one date gave her major trepidation about going on a second. The text changed their boundaries, and she'd have to process how she felt about that.

After work, Cara retreated to the pond, her quiet space. On the way, she dropped off a sandwich for Gramps and found him sitting on his porch. Her sidekick settled on the cool patio slab, propping his head on top of her shoes.

"Nestlé sure took his good old time getting here," Gramps cautioned. Two ears perked up at the mention of his name.

Cara massaged his ears and said, "Yeah, we're taking things slow these days. We're headed to sit on the dock. We'll see if he makes it that far. I brought your favorite snack, Gramps. Peanut butter, so thick it seals your mouth shut, with a bit of Manuka honey."

Gramps took the sandwich out of the baggie and Nestlé raised his head, laying it back down when Gramps shooed him, dashing his hopes for a handout.

Nestlé's ribs rose and fell in short, quick breaths, and Cara grimaced. "I didn't want him to come, but his begging eyes won. Why not let him limp around at this point in his life if he wants to?"

"Getting old ain't for sissies. Squirrel chases are a thing of his dreams. Might as well give him free rein over his waking hours."

"Whatever makes him happy. He's still got spirit."

"And what about you, my dear?"

"Me?"

"How's your spirit? Looks to me, you've got concern set between those brows."

"There's a lot on my mind. I'm worried about Nestlé," Cara said, and his tail thumped when she looked his way.

"Is that all?" he nudged.

"I'm a little stressed about my new job as a social worker in the Edwardsville schools, but it's good stress," she deflected, avoiding the issue of Callum.

"Change is a challenge," Gramps warned. "But you could straighten out the most twisted river, given the chance."

"Ahh. Thanks, Gramps, for believing in me." Cara stood and gave him a hug, signifying the end of her visit.

"Sit back down there, bug," Gramps commanded, pointing to the rocker she'd vacated.

Cara did exactly as she was told, surprised by his firmness.

"What's up?"

"I've been in jail long enough, and I want to go to church."

Cara giggled at his using her as a jailbreak. "Mom knows you're ready to be sprung. She already mentioned it."

"I want you to take me," he insisted.

Cara hemmed and hawed a bit before responding. She'd managed three weeks of not attending. But how could she say no to her favorite guy?

"Sure. I'll drive you."

As if he'd read her mind, he added, "And I want to sit next to you. It's time." Gramps took a large bite of his peanut butter sandwich, licking honey off his fingers. "You can't outrun Him, sweet pea," he garbled with peanut butter still clinging to the roof of his mouth.

"I'm not," Cara responded dishonestly.

Gramps knew it and left her in silence to swallow her obvious lie. His half smile questioned her without words. And with the skill of a magician, he pulled the truth from her.

"Well, I guess I have kept my distance," Cara admitted, rubbing at a mosquito bite on her forearm.

As a kid, she loved being in the warm cocoon of church, learning about God's love. She'd trusted His promises, but not so much anymore. She'd once believed His plans were good. That was before death invaded her life, and her faith shriveled.

"He has a way of getting our attention, especially when we work so hard to run from Him."

She didn't want to discuss her relationship with God, or lack of it.

"I'm serious here," he cautioned, steady and earnest. He reached for her. His rough, age-spotted hand clung to hers. "I'd like to be in church with you."

She felt trapped. Funny how she'd been able to tell God no, but she couldn't speak those words to Gramps.

"Don't hold grudges against God. They're about as useless as tits on a bore."

Cara choked on her own spit. "Gramps, I can't believe you just said that."

"Well, fear and doubt lead us down a rabbit hole of heartbreak and lies. That's why I won't sugarcoat what I have to say. Someone's got to be a straight shooter with you."

Cara did not doubt her heart had broken, but she'd picked up the pieces and gotten on with her life.

"Heartbreak is like heartburn. It hangs around and causes all kinds of trouble," he said, like a man languishing in the discomfort of a memory.

Cara stared at her frugal grandfather, who saved advice like he did pennies and spent every last cent when it was necessary. She noticed the tremor in his hands and made a mental note to ask her mom about it.

"I'm going to quote the Bible to you. I know you young ones don't like that but give me one second. Do you know the part about the iniquities of the father passing down to the next generation?"

Why do I feel like a little girl getting a swat on the bum?

"Yeah, I've heard that one," she cautiously answered, and began rocking nervously back and forth.

"Maybe they skip a generation cause your mother is as steady as a nailed down deck. Can't say I'm a Bible scholar, but this could be my fault."

"What could be your fault? I'm honored you passed me something," she teased to ease his concern.

"You don't wanna wear this badge. That's why I need you here. I'm helping you examine your motives."

"Oh my, what did I do?"

He patted her knees. "Nothing to feel guilty about. Just listen to the drip of this old man's honey." Gramps joined her rocking and began, "By the time you were eleven, you were waking yourself at dawn, packing your own lunches, and hooking your own worms when we fished. You rowed yourself to the center of that pond and waited out the fish even when your skin melted right off ya."

"I loved the quiet mornings of just you and me and the pond."

"Maybe too well," he muttered under his voice and took the last bite of his sandwich.

"By fifteen, you were doing more sunbathing than fishing." He grabbed her knee and her attention. "Maybe your common sense got fried." He laughed at his own joke.

"Remember how you taught me to identify fox dens and use the tractor to mow the tall grass? I loved sitting on that tractor. Mowing is relaxing."

"You caught a fever for soccer and ran the grass fields like a wildfire burned in your soul. It took your time and attention until…"

"Until?" she asked.

"Until one special guy buzzed into your nest and stung you more fiercely than that yellow jacket got you under the eye."

"Callum," she faintly admitted, unconsciously swiping the spot under her eye. "Gramps, it's over between us."

Ugh. Why does this have to come around to Callum?

"That may be, but it's not over between you and God."

"Meaning?" she asked, her quizzical tone a bit more defensive than she'd intended.

"When you lived here, you escaped to the pond to tune out the chaos, but these last two years you escaped town and tuned out the pond. Sometimes independence isn't such a good thing. Trusting your own understanding too much creates crooked paths."

Cara still didn't connect his points.

"Forgiveness is like mortar. It holds the bricks and builds trust. Skip the mortar and things shift and crumble." He paused, then continued. "When your grandma moved to Michigan, I was furious, but I forgave her."

"You forgave her? Sounds like you were the one that was in the wrong, Gramps."

"We both had to forgive—that's the way of things. That's what I'm telling you. You can't clean out someone else's teeth, only your own."

Cara laughed at his figure of speech. "No offense, Gramps, but I'm not really buying this."

"Seems to me you tuned out God. It all started over that boy. Don't you think it's time to be honest with Him and yourself? You're making this fresh start. Make a change with God, too. The best way I know how is to start where you are. Tell Him all your fears and worries. If you don't get what I'm yakking about, ask God to show you your heart. Start with forgiving God for what you're blaming Him for."

"God doesn't need my forgiveness," Cara corrected, miffed by that truth. The belief that God needed her had once been a comfort.

"I agree with you. He doesn't need you." He patted her hand as he added, "He wants you to need Him. And getting straight with Him is the fast lane to help you forgive others. You haven't forgiven that young man, so you keep living out of the hurt he put you through. Ain't no future in that."

"It's water under the bridge."

"Not yet, it ain't. You've dammed up the river and stored up the water."

Cara shot him an I-don't-even-know-what-that-means face.

"You forgive others for your own sake. It's like you let a fish off the hook you didn't want to catch. You get your line back. Unforgiveness festers, makes your heart—" he grabbed and jiggled her knee and added, "bitter."

"I am angry, Gramps!"

"I see that. I was fire-ant angry, too. I jumped into my truck one day and hightailed myself up to Cheboygan in eight hours, fully expecting your grandma to jump in my arms." Gramps started into the part of his story she was now hearing for the second time this summer. He was showing signs of his age.

"No such luck?" she giggled, going along with his retelling as if she were hearing his story for the first time.

"Her eyes shot daggers. If she weren't a lady with oodles of grace, I'm sure she would have spit in my face and turned around without a word. My heart couldn't take missing her anymore."

"How did you fix things?"

"Sleeping in my truck—or not sleeping being more like it—set my thick skull to realizing I needed to ask for her forgiveness."

"Sometimes it takes a little pain to push us," she said.

"Funny thing was—she beat me to it." He paused in a haze of memory. "By the third day of me living out of my truck at the curb, her aunt told her to do something about me. She marched down the sidewalk first thing that morning and apologized. That knocked the soles right from my boots," he reminisced.

"What did she apologize for?" Cara asked, shocked at the turn in the story.

"She asked for my forgiveness for reacting to my stubborn streak and not seeing my heart. 'I'm sorry' always rolled off her tongue easier than mine. Those two words relieved some of my pain and hers, like rubbing Ben Gay into sore muscles. They soothe the soul and let forgiveness do its work." Gramps laughed and added, "But she warned she planned to pray the rest of her life for my thick skull."

Cara caught the double dog dare in his eyes. "You need to search your heart. Sometimes, that's easier in church. Sometimes not. You'll figure it out. Let some of that clogged water flow downstream. If you get my drift." He gently squeezed her arm and belly laughed at his play on words.

Before Cara headed to the bridge to mull over his advice, she committed to going with him to church. "I'll pick you up for our date on Sunday."

"Perfect." He clapped and shot her two thumbs up.

SEVENTEEN

After Gramps's request for her to attend church, she needed to escape to her special place at the pond's bridge, her cure for anxious overthinking.

In the past, when something had thrown her off balance, she deserted everyone but Ali, her closest confidant who knew when to speak and when to sit in silence with her, and Nestlé, who listened without judgment behind his droopy eyes and erect ears and offered a compassionate paw.

When she was a young girl, she felt guilty for avoiding her mom and dad, sister, and Gramps. She'd craved silence, not advice, questions, or ramblings. Carving out a bit of relaxation in the fresh air became her reset.

At age nine, her parents finally allowed her the freedom to walk the lane alone but only as far as the bridge—always with a lecture and a promise not to get in the water. She'd pop off her shoes, dangle her feet over the still water, and watch ducks waddle out of sight down a finger of the pond. She had no idea when she sauntered along by herself, thinking she was big stuff, that her parents had alerted Gramps to keep a close eye on her. On a couple of occasions, Gramps joined her, sitting on the bridge, legs sprawled under the railing, swinging his wrinkly bare feet in time with hers. The years and his imbalance made that effort impossible now.

She didn't welcome his watchful eye when she'd dated Callum. A mass of poplar trees thankfully hindered his view of the finger and the furthest point of the pond where she and Callum had hunkered down for long afternoons at the dock. Surrounded by the cover of cattails and the soundscape of red-winged blackbirds and marsh wrens, they engaged in long, sweet, secret-hideout kissing sessions.

On her way today, Cara cautiously tunneled like a deer through her troubles and through the tall grasses of the pasture to her waterside hideout. She waved a willow branch like a scythe. Summer thistle pricked her legs. Mosquitoes nibbled at her limbs.

Sitting on the bridge, watching the fish, the frogs, and the fireflies, she released the confusion that clogged her mind. Her quiet place by the water steadied her. In the stillness, she shed the week's hustle and sorted her worries about Callum and God. Going to church didn't have to be the colossal issue she'd built it up to be.

***

Before Ali's death, worshiping at Sangamon Valley Christian Center on Sunday had offered a weekly respite, much like sitting on the bridge. Despite the hundred other people in the sanctuary, God's presence had wrapped her in peace. The worries of her world, the concerns she let fill her mind, had fallen away at the feet of Jesus. She'd always left encouraged and grateful.

She had entered the double doors of the church she'd grown up in precisely two times since Ali's Celebration of Life service. Those two crowded Christmas Eve Services, with as many strangers as attendees, were perfect for hiding.

Today, the pond's peace disappeared the moment she pulled into the parking lot for Sunday service. Memories had Cara reticent to exit the car.

Like an excited kid, Gramps slow-stepped toward the church, cane in hand, her mom's one requirement if he insisted on doing things himself.

Once she finally stepped out, she held onto the open door and took in her surroundings. The sun blazed its claim across the cloudless, celestial skies. Kids squealed and chased each other on the lush lawn until parents called them inside. This was the promising kind of summer day when churchgoers flooded in with smiles and lifted spirits, knowing after service, they'd extend Sunday as long as possible with porch lunches, picnics, walks in the park, and bike rides.

An unexpected cool breeze blew her sundress between her legs and brushed goosebumps across her skin. Panic tightened her throat at remembering Ali's Celebration of Life taking place under a similarly cerulean sky. She smoothed the goosebumps, clutching her arms across her body. Her knuckles white, she willed herself to hold it together.

Back then, only three steps inside the foyer, Cara's entire body had grown heavy. Her feet had cemented to the floor. When she had teetered, a church elder steadied her and guided her to the sanctuary.

It had been the beginning. The beginning of the end.

She'd peered inside the sanctuary. Ali lay thirty feet away, tucked into a box, her hair bathed in warm hues that filtered through stained-glass sunlight. If Cara's breath had not caught in her throat, her whimper might have been a scream. All week, she'd been reliving the nightmare of the odd angle of Ali's neck at the base of the tree. Her chest had constricted even at the glimpse from afar of a gray and lifeless Ali. Cara couldn't bring herself to stand beside her friend and let Ali's still form, made to look at peace with death, embed as a memory.

Callum and his family had sat motionless in the front row holding hands. She'd frozen in place, wanting to reach out to him, to be pulled in, to be shielded from the pain assaulting her chest. Callum had lifted his chin toward her as a tear ran down his face. He'd patted the empty seat next to him. She could barely put one foot in front of the other, but had managed to flump into the chair he'd offered.

"Today we will take all the time we need to say a difficult goodbye. Many of you will share stories of our Ali's determination, loyalty, friendship, and love," said Pastor Brent. He'd retired, but he'd been Ali's pastor since she was born and had baptized her.

Cara's chest had ached like it might split open from being torn in two directions, a sweet look back at joy and strength and goodness, and a bitter glance forward to a world without Ali, a world in which her heart crumbled into pieces.

She had needed more moments with Ali. This would be all she'd get. Cara bowed her head and spoke to Ali through spirit and space, and the minister's instructions muted to a low moaning monotone.

I won't say goodbye to you, Ali. I just can't. I know I'm supposed to, but you know being told to do something because I'm supposed to aggravates me if I don't understand why. And honestly, I don't know why you had to die. This is all wrong. Why do I have to say goodbye? If I utter those words, it means you're gone. Saying goodbye pushes you away. You can't be gone. There's still too much of you here with me. I can feel you. I will miss you forever.

Tears had spilled onto her lap.

Soft voices had sung piercingly beautiful words of Ali's favorite childhood song, "As the deer panteth for the water, so my soul longeth after Thee…"

She couldn't sing amidst the cruel reality of the day. Not to God, not to herself. Dry thirst and sorrow had coated her throat. The God that was supposed to be near had seemed far from her.

Longing to be near an alive Ali had gripped her heart like a vice. Anger had flooded her soul, and she'd wanted nothing to do with suppressed emotions or delicate sighs or displays of polite composure and fortitude. What she'd wanted was to wail at the world for her loss.

"Don't let sorrow carve paths so deep that grief is forever hardened into your heart." At Pastor Brent's words, the silence in the room had been palpable, as if all five hundred congregants had taken a collective breath.

A nearby moan had morphed to a steady wail, spilling pain throughout the sanctuary and quieting the pastor's next line. Ali's mom had raised a banner of loss.

It had struck Cara as the most honest response. Mrs. Hall's pain had given credence to the stifled emotions in the room. A flash mob of mournful cries, sniffles, and tears had joined her in weeping, the most truthful tunes of the day.

Gripped in the clutch of grief, they had succumbed to their sorrow.

Too late, Pastor Brent. It's eloquent but...

As if he'd agreed with her thoughts, Callum had clasped her hand as a lifeline and settled their hands on his thigh, both of them scared to be present to this moment, yet not wanting to be anywhere else. Where else could they go with their grief when this sanctuary had been their safe place?

Ali's life—celebrated only in memories.

She had contemplated fleeing. The problem, she had concluded, was that she'd had a simple life growing up, until this moment. Her supportive parents had raised her in a loving family. As far as she remembered, she'd never wanted for anything. She hadn't thought of herself as rich, but neither had she considered herself poor. Her family had the support of a praying church community. She'd worked hard to be an excellent student, to win a soccer scholarship at the University of Illinois, and to gain a degree in social work. She'd been healthy, and she called the shots in her life. And God had honored her efforts.

Until the accident.

She'd grown up with her best friend since preschool, two peas in a pod. Always together. They'd planned their future together. With Ali's death, God had gotten something horribly wrong. She'd never encountered death, except her grandma's when she was ten, and she'd remembered only the feeling of sadness. Tragedies were horrible things that happened to other people. The reasons for her prayers. She had lived as a bystander to other people's trauma, praying for God to bring peace to the wreckage in their lives. Until the accident when God had jerked her hands from the steering wheel and pulled her from the driver's seat of her own life.

A tree trunk had shattered her well-ordered life. God promised not to give her more than she could handle. His still, small voice hadn't comforted her. When would His peace that passes all understanding fall on her? Cara hadn't felt God's presence in the church as the pastor claimed, only the violent ripping of Ali from her life.

"Cara-Bear, are you coming?" Gramps called and pulled her from her memory and away from the car. "I'll meet you at our seats."

She hustled to his side. "Let's not hurry. Besides, you wanted me to come with you, remember?"

The earth had made two full revolutions around the sun, and Ali's death still haunted her. Ahead of her, the double glass doors, etched with crosses, led into the last place she'd seen Ali's face. She took her time approaching.

A door flew open, and a well-dressed Callum greeted them. "Good morning, Mr. Moore. Good to see you. And you too, Cara."

"Nice to see a new greeter at the door, young man," Gramps said, making his way inside.

Callum locked eyes with Cara. "You look very nice today."

"You mean a dress instead of khaki pants? Someone's unusually chipper this morning," Cara said.

"I mean all of you," he suggested, still holding her gaze.

If Cara could speed Gramps through the doors, she'd escape this dramatic entrance and Callum's scrutiny. Her chest tightened. She ran through her Callum Rules.

Don't touch him.

Don't let him touch you.

Don't be fooled by all the ways he touches you without touching you.

"I saw you coming and thought I'd grab the door for you."

Callum could not have possibly seen them coming unless he was purposefully peering out the double glass doors.

As she passed Callum, he leaned in close to her and his shoulder brushed hers. His fingers lightly grazed hers for a millisecond, and her breath skipped. His lashes butterfly-kissed her cheek when he whispered in her ear, "You'll be alright. I know how hard this is for you. I got you."

And darn if she didn't trip on the threshold.

Callum hugged her waist to steady her. "See what I mean?" he teased.

She wriggled from his grasp and hastened into the foyer after Gramps.

Their elder, Tom Dewitt, seemed grayer than he was the last time he'd greeted her at church. He hugged her inside the door, pulling Callum from her attention. "Good morning, Cara. It's nice to see you."

The low buzz of conversation filled the foyer. She rubbed her arms, the chill of the air conditioner noticeable. She ducked her head and wiped a nonexistent crumb from the front of her dress, a subconscious need to escape Callum's proximity. On her march to the much-needed coffee station, she glanced into the sanctuary, quickly searching for her parents.

Callum found her pouring creamer into her cup of coffee.

"I figured you'd hit the leaded station first," he said, startling her.

"Not sure why they even make unleaded. Nasty stuff," she said.

"Excuse me," he said and leaned into her space to grab a cup.

His closeness disoriented her. She busied her hands swirling her creamy concoction, determined to exude self-possession and effectively maneuver small talk with Callum.

When she glanced his way, Callum was staring at her. His caramel eyes drilled deep into her very soul. Voices around her muted. Afraid to blink and let more memories rush in, she tethered herself to him, gaze for gaze.

The strength of what poured from him was too excessive for her to skip to a polite smile. Anger should grip her and force her to ignore his intense perusal here in church, but anger had abandoned her. Every moment he'd milled in her space at work minutes too long, every hint of a smile he'd offered for no reason, every chance he'd taken for idle chit-chat, every reminder of how he'd remembered her had chipped away at the anger she harbored.

Her paralysis, surrounded by the church's onlookers, should have been uncomfortable, awkward even, but for some unfathomable reason, he summoned her attention without a single word or deed, and she responded in kind. Her body's unexpected response was traitorous. She wanted to cuddle against him, hide in his arms—the one place that she'd always felt safe.

Until that day she hadn't.

A red-light warning, *don't cave to his charms,* signaled her to refuse Callum, but a contest of wills raged between her mind and her conflicted heart. Lashing out at him wasn't the catharsis she'd thought it would be. Clinging to anger that had motivated and sustained her after their breakup exhausted her now. She'd been angry with Callum for so long. Was that the way she thought she should exist with him? Was her heart ready to give up the fight? His apology had stripped back calloused layers, leaving her raw and wanting more from him. She didn't know which to trust to win the war, her heart or her head.

She pushed the lid onto her cup, and it slipped under her pressure. Brown liquid spilled across the bar, dripping down onto the floor. Cara jumped back.

Callum jumped in. "I got it," he said and grabbed paper towels from the cabinet.

"Thanks for the help. I'll just go find a seat. That should be safe." She left the mess for Callum to clean up. Attempting this reunion with her church community, being here with Callum, it felt suddenly tortuous.

Lord, help me now. Her spontaneous plea surprised her.

On her way to her seat, several people stopped her to talk, but she finally hustled to the far side of the sanctuary and to the safety of her seat in the section her parents occupied every Sunday since she was nine. Her eyes skipped down the row to the seat her Gramps had saved for her. She gasped when she spotted Callum in the seat in front of hers, whispering into his niece's ear, making her giggle.

You have a rousing sense of humor. Is this a test of perseverance, God?

Out of the two hundred seats in this sanctuary, the five seats her family selected had to be behind the seven Callum's family occupied. Driving separately had backfired on her. This morning, arriving at the last minute with Gramps had seemed like such a good idea. She traipsed to the end of the row, took a deep cleansing breath, and bumped her sister's shoulder, nodding for her to scoot down.

Tori glared wide-eyed at Cara with a slight nod to the seat Callum occupied, acknowledging Cara's pain. When Cara collapsed onto the maroon fabric of the chair between her and Gramps, Tori gave her knee a commiserating pat.

Gramps tapped his cane against her leg to garner her attention and leaned close. "Everything will be alright. You're in His house now."

Cara offered him a masked smile. "Thanks, Gramps," she said, but she didn't believe a word he said.

Callum turned around and handed her a cup of coffee. "No need to play it safe around me. I made you a cup. The lid is secure." He smiled and dared to wink at her.

How could Cara refuse him?

They stood at the call to worship and Cara caught the corner of Tori's mouth turned up in a smile. Band members began the first worship song, but the thoughts pounding in her head drowned them out.

Standing behind Callum, Cara had a difficult time paying attention. With her eyes, she traced the swirl of the cowlick along his hairline. His cologne saturated her senses, and she stepped back, holding on to the edge of the chair. His baby blue button-up pulled taut against his shoulders revealed the lines of his undershirt. She wanted to smooth her hand across his back.

Naughty girl! In church, of all places!

She plastered her gaze on the screen, but Callum turned to steady his nephew standing on his chair and stole a glance her way. She held it for seconds longer than safe. When the corner of his lip turned up in a knowing smile, her breath hitched, and she covered her mouth. Bowing her head and closing her eyes was the only way to avoid him, so she did just that.

Tori tapped her on the arm. When Cara shook her head, refusing to open her eyes to look her way, Tori leaned against her shoulder and whispered in her ear, "I think I see fireworks." Tori giggled. "And they're absolutely stunning."

After the song ended, Pastor Caleb said, "The title of my message today is 'It's Time for a Comeback: A Lesson from the Prodigal Son.'"

Seriously, God? Not very subtle.

Wriggling in her seat, she clasped her fingers tightly around her paper coffee cup and closed her eyes to block out everything but the sermon.

Cara had never looked at herself as a prodigal. She'd never considered herself wayward or selfish or reckless. She hadn't been wasteful with her time, foolish with her money, demanding of her parents.

But today, she felt an inkling that she might be as lost as the prodigal's older brother, the one who was selfish with his forgiveness. God had let her down, and she'd shut Him out. She'd held on to feeling wronged by Callum, too. For a while, it was self-preservation, but what about now that Callum had apologized? Was holding on to her pain holding a grudge, a grudge she used like a shield against risking, against fully feeling her feelings? Was God hinting for her to hear Him out, too?

EIGHTEEN

"Cara," her mom's whisper beckoned, obliterating her dream about Callum and her hiking in the mountains with Nestlé. She squinted at her mom's wrinkled brows and gentle hand nudging her awake.

"Callum's here to see you."

"Huh?" she asked, calculating if she was still dreaming.

"Callum's on the porch. Are you okay to come down, or do you want me to tell him you're napping?"

Callum's presence forced her to join the normal rhythm of life once again. *Not now* was her honest thought. She wasn't sure she had the strength for Callum today, but she mustered a groggy, "I'll be right down."

Cara was too drained to go to work. She felt like she'd endured days since Sunday night, since returning from a visit with Gramps and a jaunt to the pond. Last night, Nestlé had stared her down the lane and retreated to the house, too weary to follow her. When she'd returned, she made it two steps onto the back porch in the shadows of the moonlight and froze. Nestlé lay curled at the door. Cara had sensed his stillness. Her breath had hitched, and tears welled in her eyes. He was gone. His droopy eyes had blinked their last goodnight, and his doggy days had run out.

She had cuddled next to him, stroking his fur. Loneliness welled within her. Her gut wrenched at the familiar ache of loss. After a late-night family burial, Cara had succumbed to her grief and cried herself to sleep.

On this first morning without Nestlé, Cara's energy flowed at the rate of cold molasses, and so did her desire to tackle work duties and the needs of personnel. Her world dulled without her four-legged friend—the day's sunshine wasn't warm, the clouds stretched across skies more gray than blue.

Cara rarely took naps, but while swiping through pictures of Nestlé on her phone, she had laid her head on her pillow and faded to sleep, emotionally exhausted. Three hours later, here she was dragging herself from under her comforter, dangling her pink polished toenails above the hard-wood floor, and halting for a couple of seconds to gather her senses. She half-expected a furry bundle to be resting on the floor at her feet. Time would help her mind get this straight. She winced at the bright rays spilling through the window and plopped back down on the bed.

She had sat frozen in place too long. Her mom poked her head in again and called through her haze, "I'll tell Callum you're napping."

"I'm coming," she said, her voice flat. She forced her feet to the floor. Cocooning herself in her teal quilt, she headed for the porch, catching her bed head and tears mixed with mascara in the mirror. *I don't care*, she told herself. Looking presentable wasn't a priority.

Glancing out the dormer window, Callum's new black truck reminded her of when he'd used his truck and a ladder to sneak into her room. Just a few weeks after they had started going steady, he'd knocked on her window.

Split second visions of Jason movies had her scared to pieces, but she'd yanked back the curtains to a grinning Callum. He'd handed her sunflowers, her favorites. She thanked him with a kiss and told him to knock on the front door if he dared disturb her dad while he watched the late news. He'd opted for calling her in the morning and quietly dismounted from the roof. She'd felt bad to see him go as he waved from his truck window, but not nearly as bad as she'd feel if she got caught letting him in. That mischievous Callum had transformed into a dutiful, disciplined Callum, and she felt sorry that others at the department didn't see more of the playful part of him she missed.

Through the front door's long windowpane, she glimpsed Callum's short, thick, brown hair and the slight stubble developing on the pronounced curve of his jawline. He looked at home in the rocker, legs extended and crossed in front of him. He held a drink in each hand, resting on the chair's arms. He gazed down the lane as if in search of Nestlé. Her mind and heart mellowed to a time when they had no walls between them.

"Are you planning to talk to him through the window?" Her mom pushed her to action.

Cinching the cover more tightly, she exhaled a deep cleansing breath and opened the screen door to Callum.

When the screen door creaked, he set the cups on the porch and stood to greet her. He wrapped her in his arms, drawing her solidly into him. She relaxed in his strength. His cheek rested against hers and he softly offered, "I'm so sorry to hear about Lover Boy."

And still he held her, and still she let him.

"I know I can't make your hurt better, but I figured a mocha latte might be some comfort," he said.

"Yeah," she agreed, basking in being held by him in her grief.

He pulled back enough to study her face, still holding her in his arms.

"Your arms are the best comfort," she said as he handed her a cup, catching her words too late. "I mean you are so sweet…for the mocha…well and the hug…" Cara fumbled through her words. Callum had the decency not to smirk or tease about her flub.

Rocking with him on the porch in silence soothed her sadness. She tried to reject that realization, regretting the very thought she'd been balking at—needing him.

Curling her legs into the rocker, she tucked the quilt around her feet, cold from the wooden planks, and sipped the warm chocolate. She cupped her chin in her palm and leaned against the arm of the chair, gazing beyond Callum into the tree line across the field. She'd played fetch there with Nestlé in that green field and trained him to listen, to stay, to sit, and to ignore bunnies and deer on command.

Callum studied her languid eyes and followed them beyond the line of hanging baskets of ferns into the distance. "It's a hard day. I miss him." The gentle touch of his muted voice caressed her heart, and she swiped at the tears that blurred her eyes.

"I found him at the back door when I returned from the pond last night," she explained, not looking him in the eye. If she did, the floodgates would break under his gentle sympathy.

One date with Callum had wrecked her emotions more than she'd expected. After her chat with Gramps and the message at church, she needed a late Sunday night stroll to the pond under the moonlight to get honest with God and herself about Callum.

When she had returned home, she wholeheartedly trusted her decision that the safest way through the weeks ahead was to keep her distance from Callum and not dredge up her angst over their past. But Callum, offering apologies, sitting inches from her on the porch, bringing her favorite coffee, and lending a patient ear, felt safe—the more solid kind of safe of being truly seen and understood. Her heart had heard his apology and wanted to believe it. Why then was she so set on a dire need for caution?

"He was waiting for you?" His warm whisper spilled from his lips like a gentle wave washing over the shore.

Cara had gotten lost in her thoughts, and it took her a second to catch up to what he had asked. She took a sip and looked him in the eye. "Yeah. He was curled up on the outside rug. So still. I instantly knew he was gone. I bent down to pet him and kiss him goodbye on his big ol' noggin."

Callum listened as she shared her heart.

"I shouldn't be shocked, but I am," she scratched out. "Looking back over this last week, if I'm honest, I watched his energy level and interest in food wane and his breathing grow more labored. But I didn't want to believe he was this close to the end. It doesn't feel real that he isn't lying in his sunspot or settling at my feet here on the porch. I keep expecting him to be coming around the corner."

"Grief is hard." He stared into the far field with her. "And complicated, especially when it is sudden," he added as an afterthought.

"When I came home this summer, I knew he didn't have long. But understanding that in my head doesn't make this easier."

"When our hearts are broken, we can't always hear what our heads tell us."

"Now that he's gone, it's still a shock. I feel his absence in every room of the house. They feel empty without the jingle of his tags and his scratching to come in at the back door." She drew her legs up closer to her chest and rested her chin on her knee.

"Every time I go home, it's still hard to see photos of Ali, walk past her room, see her things, and not wish she was with me." Callum brandished a half-smile, more pain than pleasure. "Nestlé was your best bud. You have great memories with him. I know that's no comfort right now, but one day, they will help you find your way through the hard days."

She grasped the honesty of his words. Living without Ali, he understood the ebb and flow of grief.

"I knew something was up when I stopped by the department and didn't see you in your spot barking orders," he said and winked.

"Barking?" she winced. "Is that how people see me at work?"

"Not at all. I'm sorry. That was a clumsy attempt to lighten your mood. Purring?"

"That's better." She nodded in approval. "I just didn't have it in me today to pretend to be okay."

"Chief told me Nestlé's buried under the dogwood tree." He reached for the arm of her rocker, and she thought he'd reached for her hand and loosened her grip on the cup to reflexively hold his. Instead, he rested his hand inches from her elbow, and she gripped her warm cup tighter.

"He had boundless energy just a couple of years ago. He would run down the lane to meet your truck, howling at your arrival before we could see you. Before you could close your door, he jumped in your seat like he could drive.

He'd let you push him to the middle, but getting him out, he sure put up a stubborn fight. He knew you were a softie. You would never kick him out. How many times did he fall asleep in your seat waiting for a ride? He knew you'd drive him somewhere, even if it was just down the lane and back. He sure loved you."

Callum nodded with a smile. "The best feeling in the world was turning onto that long drive, seeing you two waiting for me on the top step," Callum said.

Funny how some memories didn't fade, and right now she was glad they hadn't. One of her best feelings in the world had been gently rocking next to Callum on this porch. Resting against his chest under the moonlight, sealing secrets and stealing kisses, the cares of the day fell away. Little things he'd said and done meant so much, like bringing her coffee today. Those unexpected moments had become her favorite memories.

Right now, exchanging stories with him felt like healing. She wouldn't have guessed it could be. She wouldn't have thought she needed him with her until this moment. *Needed? Wanted. Both.* She missed him. His thoughtfulness. His quiet strength. The calm in her when he was near.

"I won't hold my big furry guy any longer," she said, her chin trembling.

And I won't be holding you either.

"He loved you, and you gave him fourteen great doggy years," Callum consoled.

"We buried him in his quilted blanket that matches mine," Cara said like the ten-year-old girl who first cuddled Nestlé as a pup. She wrapped the blanket even tighter around herself. A tear burned its way down her cheek. She let the quilt catch it. There was no reason to hide her pain.

"We tucked in that nappy toy fox he slept with every night." She sighed. "These last few weeks when he laid on the porch, he would sit and stare at the sky. Do you think God calls to dogs?" She wiped away another stray tear.

Cara had a faraway look in her eye. She wanted just one more pond sit with him. She supposed that was the way of death—loved ones left behind, desperate for one more moment. If the heavens would have allowed it, she'd have looked into his old loyal eyes and said, "You're my sweet dog, such a good dog!" Nothing was more endearing than watching his little gray eyebrows move up and down as she talked to him, except maybe the feel of his salt-and-pepper snoot rubbing against her hand, begging to be pet.

"In school, they taught us so many things, but never how to lose someone. You know?" she wondered aloud.

Callum nodded in agreement and leaned forward, resting his arms on his knees.

"No one talks about how to grieve," Cara explained with a faraway look of remembrance. "They taught us to read and analyze literature, to write and do math. They hammered all the bones and the organs of the body into our heads. They made us study history so we wouldn't repeat the mistakes of the past. But no one explained how to handle grief."

She paused, searching his eyes for understanding. Under his empathetic gaze, she continued. "Even in church, I counted off the Ten Commandments, recited John 3:16, and memorized the books of the Bible in order. I learned to pray, study, fast, worship, serve, and love. But I don't know how to endure loss, wanting what will never be."

His hand clutched the wooden arm of her rocking chair, so close she could feel the heat he radiated. When they dated, they were Cara and Callum. C&C. Etched on paper, carved into trees, and chiseled into the railing of the bridge. He'd promised her forever, and she'd naively believed him. She had chased dreams of tomorrows: a couple of dogs, a home on the outskirts of town, and babies. He'd said two sounded perfect, but he'd negotiate for a third.

Cara had thought of them as one. Deciphering where she ended and he began had been difficult until they buried Ali. The collapse of their world left her with the hard truth—love's promises don't always endure. She was C minus C.

He slipped her mocha from her hand, setting it on the porch, and pulled her to stand. The quilt wrapped around her fell to her feet. He traced the tear's path down her cheek. He rubbed his hands down her arms and then pulled her to him and held her close. Leaning into his warmth, she closed her eyes and rested her cheek on his chest. She knew she shouldn't, but she didn't fight it, couldn't fight it. She let him be her strength. She basked in the comfort he radiated. His scent pulled her back to their country drives in his truck and movies on the couch.

"He was a faithful friend." Callum's low, reassuring voice and warm breath against her skin comforted her. He pulled back and tenderly brushed strands of her hair behind her ear. "Will you take me to where you buried him?" he asked.

Cara glanced down the lane. "Dad said he can still guard us from that shady spot."

They shared a comfortable silence on the short drive to Nestlé's grave.

"Hey, big boy," Callum started right in with his goodbye when he reached the large patch of unearthed soil. "Are you racing up and down the streets of gold now without hip pain? I sure hope God lets you flap your ears in the breeze on occasional drives in the bed of a Ford truck."

Cara nudged him with her arm and whispered, "Jeep."

"Sorry for that interruption, Lover Boy. You and I both know the truth—God loves Ford trucks best of all. I wish I could have given you an ear massage and said goodbye. God has one big-hearted companion now. We'll go fishing again someday in Heaven's best pond. Give Ali a sloppy kiss for me, will ya?"

"Memories can't replace being together," Cara said, staring at the newly dug mound of earth.

Callum turned to Cara, and she glimpsed his watery eyes. They both knew she was referring not just to Nestlé, but to Ali and to each other.

"I should go," he said. "Want a ride back up the lane?"

Cara shook her head no. For so many reasons, including the danger that she could easily get used to depending on him, being alone would serve her best right now.

Callum stepped toward Cara and cradled her hands. Cara's words caught in the tightness of her throat. Bending his head slowly toward her, his eyes softened. Opening his mouth, he hesitated to speak. Did he feel the comfort of the closeness between them, too? Her body drifted toward him. She closed her eyes as his soft lips rested heavily against her forehead. Care. Calm. Connection. All washed over her. Cara pulled him to her, tightening their hold on one another. The warmth of his tender touch and her desire for it consumed every thought. Callum's kiss couldn't possibly have said more. He'd kissed her soul.

"This probably isn't the best time to ask, but will you go on the second date with me? We could do something low key after church if you're not feeling up to anything more. Maybe go to the pond and tell Nestlé stories. Just an idea."

Looking away from his pleading eyes was impossible. Desire danced like flames between them.

"Yeah, that sounds good," Cara answered with too much anguish in her voice, a mix of Nestlé's absence and Callum's confusing presence.

"I miss you, Cara," he said and climbed into the cab of his truck. His eyes, overcome with sorrow, locked with hers. "I couldn't stay away from you today. I miss Nestlé, but I miss you more."

Cara uttered no response. Her need for life to rewind was too fierce to acknowledge out loud. The pain of wanting Nestlé back and wanting what she once had with Callum tore through her.

She forced the warm liquid in her eyes not to spill over her cheeks.

"Have a good night." He barely got out the words.

His truck revved down the road, and a choked sob escaped from her throat.

And I've missed you, Callum.

NINETEEN

"**I** keep expecting Nestlé to greet me every day I come home from work. The house feels so empty without him lumbering around. Nothing makes missing him better," Cara said, grabbing the grocery list from her sister, "but Friday night pizza might help a little." Cara glanced at the short list of ingredients on their way into the grocery store.

"Wait. We should add dessert to that list. Let's grab some Oreo ice cream!"

"You are so right! Being with you brightens my day, and not just because you're thinking of dessert." Cara gave her sister a side hug. Cara knew enough about grief to know it would slide from her heart in its own time, but she thanked God she had her sister now.

"We're making two pizzas, right?" Tori clarified.

"Yeah, one with only veggies for you and Mom, and one supreme with meat for the carnivores in our tribe."

"Don't forget the red onions. Maybe we could buy a pre-made cauliflower crust for the veggie one," Tori suggested.

"Cheater," Cara teased. "Mom loves our homemade thick crust we used to make for family night."

"She'll like the cauliflower crust. I promise. We'll tell her it's healthy for Dad," Tori said with a grin.

"As if he'd be caught eating a pizza without meat," Cara smirked, checking her watch again. "We better get moving. We have two hours until Mom's home."

At the grocery store, Tori surveyed the produce and plucked mushrooms, a bag of spinach, and a red onion from the display.

After a long search for the crust, Cara said, "I'll grab the sauce, and you grab the small can of black olives."

Cara surveyed shelves of sauces—so many choices. A whimper distracted her. She glanced to the very end of the aisle and saw a trembling ball of a boy crouched below the pasta selections. He hid his face between his knees and wrapped his arms around his head, shutting out the world.

Cara stooped low next to the shaggy, blond-haired boy and softly asked, "Hey, buddy, are you lost?" His whimpers quieted, but he gave no answer. Cara sensed her sister hovering over her shoulder and glanced at her, shrugging her shoulders. She wasn't sure how to reach the sad boy, but Cara tried again, even warmer. "Can we help you find your mommy?"

He released his arms from around his head, only to hug his knees. Dark brown, wary eyes slowly raised to Cara and Tori, darting between them, reading their faces. His unkempt clothes and bruised cheek hinted at a story, but Cara resisted rushing to judgment.

Cara touched his arm to help him stand, but he flinched and shied away from her. Cara and Tori exchanged worried glances. She'd remembered how important it was to tell little ones what she planned to do before touching them. This time, she softly asked, "Would you like to hold my hand? We'll take you to your mommy."

He gave a little nod and clutched her hand with his sticky fingers. She pulled him to his feet and smiled at the dinosaur on his shirt. He couldn't be more than five years old. Cara caught the distinct skunky smell of marijuana clinging to his clothes.

"I'll grab the pizza sauce and check out. I'll meet you at the front," Tori said low in her ear and hurried off with the grocery cart.

Cara bent down to the scared boy's eye-level. "That's a cool t-shirt. I bet you love dinosaurs."

A shy smile lit up his face. "It's a T-Rex. His name means tyrant lizard king." A little excitement tinged his sadness.

"Wow. He's fierce. My name is Cara. It means friend. What's your name?"

"Wally," his voice shivered.

"That's a fun name. What's your mom's name?" Cara gently asked, noting marks the shape of fingers on his arm.

"My mom's name is Annabeth. My dad is Walter, like me," he said with a pout.

Cara wasn't getting happy family vibes. She masked the alarm that was igniting her adrenaline rush with a cheerful, "Well, that's so cool to have the same name as your dad."

Unconvinced, Wally shrugged his shoulders but didn't meet her eyes.

"Let's go find them, okay?" she said, keeping a lookout for a panicked mom searching frantically for her little boy.

Wally didn't speak as they strolled hand in hand to the service center and waited in line for the store manager behind two other customers. His stiff stance and quiet fear ramped up Cara's unease.

Wally tugged on her shirt and pointed out the front window of the store. Cara followed his gaze out the window to a man leaning against a rusty truck, waving his hands wildly in the air. His face sneered at the woman he was obviously giving an unpleasant piece of his mind. Tori joined Cara in time to watch the scene play out before them.

"Are those your parents?" Cara asked, trying to disguise the dread gripping her stomach.

Wally nodded but didn't peel his wide eyes from the scene. Neither did Cara. Something told her he'd seen this behavior many times before, and she wanted to grab him and run far away from the store, to keep him from this kind of pain, but she couldn't abandon Wally's mom. She recognized Annabeth. They had gone to high school together. Cara wanted to help her, to kick her husband in the groin, but she knew Annabeth's kind of opponent wasn't easily beaten. Cara couldn't imagine fighting this foe.

Wally's clutch on her strengthened, and she glanced down at his quivering chin. She leaned down and wrapped her arm around him, snuggling him against her. "I got you. You're safe with me," she assured him.

Just as Cara looked out the window again, she caught his father backhand Annabeth across the face. His mom tripped backwards, knocked off balance, and spilled to the ground, catching herself on her hands and knees.

Wally whimpered. Cara shrieked, and both she and Tori instinctively grabbed for their phones.

"You dial, Tori," Cara whispered. She turned Wally into her, hiding his eyes from the painful scene, but Wally wouldn't be distracted. He pushed from her and bolted out the door to his mom.

"Wally, wait!" she called and raced after him, catching up as he knelt next to his mom on the asphalt.

"Get away from her, Wally. You'll turn into trash just like her," Wally's father seethed.

Wally cowered from his father's reach, staying as close as possible to his mom.

"I'm okay, baby," Annabeth slurred, lifting her head to Wally, attempting a small smile through her pain. She shifted her gaze higher to Cara and grimaced, her eyes shy with humiliation. "Go with the nice lady." Annabeth's weak voice begged Cara to take her son away from the scene.

"I promise I'll take care of Wally." If only Cara's words could comfort Annabeth like their high school pep talks did, but Annabeth faced the tragedy of a much harder life now. "Let me help you. Take my hand," Cara said, extending her hand to Annabeth.

Annabeth shook her head and started to get up. "Take him away, please," she begged.

Cara lifted Wally and the smell of alcohol overpowered her nostrils. "I got you, Wally," she said, wrapping him in her arms. She took fast steps toward the store, putting a cautious distance between Wally and his parents. Everything in her screamed she should not let Wally watch their exchange, but he wouldn't allow it, twisting and crying to keep his mom in his sights. Cara couldn't look away either. A dark red bruise swelled on Annabeth's cheek and a bitter sadness welled in her eyes.

"You're a sorry excuse for a mother, losing a five-year-old," Walter scoffed and scrutinized, performing for the onlookers. "What a sad sack of a wife. Did you even get my cigarettes and beer?"

"I got everything, just like you asked," she answered, rising to her feet.

Walter screamed more profanities at Annabeth. He had no idea or didn't care that a squad car, lights flashing, had blocked his truck in.

Callum stepped out and the tension in Cara's shoulders eased somewhat, but her concern for Annabeth quickly morphed into concern for Callum.

"Oh no!" Wally's innocent voice panicked at the sight of a police car. "Mom!" he pleaded, reaching for his mom.

Every eye turned their direction.

Annabeth started toward Wally, but his dad shoved her out of the way so forcefully she slammed to the ground again, hitting her head hard on the asphalt this time. Walter stumbled after her, spewing more expletives about her lousy parenting.

Cara cringed at the brutality and held her breath, fighting against racing to Annabeth's defense. Instinctively, she depended on Callum to protect Annabeth and settle their fears.

As Walter's fist reared back, Callum grabbed him from behind in a flash and forced him against his car, cuffing him behind the back. Walter continued his protest while Callum read him his rights and guided him toward the squad car. Walter wrangled against his arrest. He twisted to spit vehemence in Callum's face and spittle spewed from his lips.

As he guided Walter's head inside the car, Walter gave Callum a thousand-mile stare and spouted more threats. "Officer Hall, I'll be sure to remember you. Let me know if I can ever do your wife a favor."

Cara shivered at the pure evil in Walter's voice.

Callum's clenched jaw hinted at the only crack in his calm demeanor as he shut the patrol car door in Walter's face, muting his vicious tirade.

Wally's stare locked on his mom, and Cara tightened her grip on him. She was sure he'd curl up and shelter inside himself like he had in the grocery aisle, hiding from the pain that was sure to come.

Callum helped Annabeth stand and gain her balance. She swiped at the blood trickling down her cheek and hobbled to Wally. He ran to her, grabbing her around the legs as she spoke sweetly in his ear.

Memories of Annabeth replayed in her mind. Annabeth, the strong team leader who had offered Cara a hand up after a tumble on the field. Annabeth, a senior, always going out of her way to high five Cara, a freshman, in the hallways. It pained her to see Annabeth's spirit so drastically beaten down.

Callum smiled at Cara in relief, but she couldn't offer one back. Witnessing Walter like this scared her—such vehement ugliness toward someone you're supposed to love.

"Thanks for calling and helping this brave guy," Callum said to Cara and Tori, mussing Wally's hair. He bent down eye to eye with him. "I'm Officer Hall. I'm taking your dad with me for a while to help him cool off." Cara tenderly rubbed circles on Wally's back, soothing herself as much as him. "You and your mom will ride in an ambulance to the hospital. They want to check her head. I know you want to be with her." Callum did his best to reassure Wally.

Wally gave a small nod of his head and grabbed his mom's hand.

Cara wanted to promise Wally that Callum would make things better, but she knew her promises couldn't make Wally's life easier or make him believe her. He'd experienced this trauma before, she was sure.

An ambulance wailed in the distance and Wally tensed.

"It's going to be okay, sweetie," Cara said, but both Wally and his mom knew differently, and stared back at her in quiet disbelief.

Cara stepped out of Annabeth's earshot. Her words came fast, sharing with Callum the events in the store, the smell of alcohol and marijuana, and her concerns about abuse. A tremble that started in her hands had spread throughout her body knowing what Wally would go home to.

Callum leaned close. His lips fluttered next to her cheekbone. His breath brushed her skin, and she nearly rested her cheek against his, craving his gentleness. "I'll keep him safe, Cara," he said, attempting to dispel her fears.

"Don't make a promise out of your control, Callum." Her heart hurt at that truth, knowing how very little he could change for Wally and Annabeth.

"I tell you what. You pray." His words, voiced deep in his throat, oozed assurance and shivered up her spine. He caressed her arm, and her hopes of him embracing her were entirely inappropriate for this moment. "And I'll pray, too. I promise to do everything within my power."

The shield she held tightly around her heart slipped, and she nearly pleaded out loud, wanting to believe that Callum, the ultimate good guy, could keep them safe and make everything good again.

She felt her body respond to his confidence as her nerves settled. His mere presence had always done that for her.

Callum hustled over to the paramedics to get Wally and Annabeth settled. Wally waved goodbye to Cara just as the ambulance doors were closing. Cara prayed harder than she had in a very long time.

Please, Lord. You know the desire of our hearts. Keep them safe.

Callum returned and nudged her elbow, pulling her out of her heavy headspace. "Are we still good for Sunday?" His words invaded her prayer.

"Definitely," she answered unexpectedly eager, longing for the comfort the pond date promised.

Cara and Tori sat in silence inside the car for a few seconds after loading their groceries in the trunk, not sure how to navigate what they had witnessed. It was all too much, and she needed a good cry to release her pent-up emotions.

"That poor little boy," Tori sighed.

"He was so scared. He didn't know who to trust," Cara sniffled, her hands trembling. "Did you see how he reacted? You could tell he didn't trust his mom could protect him from his dad."

"I'm sure he's been caught in the middle of their battles before." Tori winced as if the pain of knowing this struck her physically.

"He wanted to take care of his mom. He's traumatized by his parents but still trying to take care of them. Did you know I played soccer with Annabeth in high school?" Cara quieted and stared at the rearview mirror like she was seeing the past. "She was happy then. Now look at her. I'm sad and mad for her. I feel at a loss to help her. And it's obvious she needs it. How do we leave them? Do we just tell them things will be okay, and then go back home, eat our pizza, and sleep with no worries? Did you see her eyes? They were so tired. Like she'd already lived an entire lifetime, and she's only three years older than me!"

"I'm angry for Wally. Five years old and scared and feeling responsible for your mom. Ugh," Tori groaned.

"Annabeth must feel so trapped. She was bubbly and the most encouraging captain we had on our team." Cara grabbed Tori's arm and asked, "Did you see the marks on his arm, right above his elbow? His little fingers clung so hard to my hand."

"It's a helpless feeling, knowing he will go right back to that horrible situation. Can you imagine what that man does and says to them behind closed doors if that's what he does in public? Annabeth loves Wally. I saw that," Tori said, convincing herself along with Cara.

Tears welled in Cara's eyes. "But is her love enough to keep him from harm?" Cara felt desperate to believe it would be. "You heard what Callum said. He'll call Children and Family Services. This cycle of trauma sucks. I hope they can help him, but chances are…" She couldn't voice the alternative.

"If he's taken from them, that will be another kind of pain—abandonment," Tori said.

They both stared blankly out the front window. They couldn't shake the jitters racking their insides.

"Whew," Cara blew out a long breath, trying to rid herself of feelings of powerlessness.

"Yeah," Tori agreed. Both were lost in a pit of what-ifs.

The last hour had felt like an eternity. Cara grasped the steering wheel and rested her head on her hands, hiding her now bloodshot eyes.

"One minute we're trying to drown our sorrows in pizza, and the next our hearts are breaking for this little boy. I can't shake the nervous feeling I have for him. God says He won't give us more than we can handle. This is a whole lot more than this little guy should have to handle." Cara reproached God and wiped away a tear with the back of her hand.

"It actually says we won't be tempted beyond what we're able," Tori gently corrected. "And right after, it says He'll provide a way out so you can bear it. To me, it sounds like He's guaranteeing our lives will have situations and suffering that we won't be able to handle on our own. But even if we have trials, He promises to be with us through them."

Cara contemplated the difference in interpretation.

"We'll have to trust His promise that He'll take care of Wally like we trust He takes care of us," Tori said.

"That's a lot easier to say than to believe," Cara fretted, her insides waffling.

"I agree," Tori said, pensive. "But just because bad things happen doesn't mean God isn't in control. Let's pray for Wally," Tori suggested.

And right then, Tori prayed out loud for God to be with Wally and protect him.

Cara bowed her head and fervently agreed with every word Tori prayed, even if doubt still racked her insides.

TWENTY

Cara and Tori made the most of their Friday night together. Chatting into the wee hours, they attempted to free themselves of their sadness over Nestlé and Wally. Cara dragged herself to bed as soft moonlight seeped through her curtains. She desperately needed Saturday to unwind. She begged for sleep to come when she rested her head on the pillow, and when it finally did, Callum invaded her dream, waking her. Unable to return to sleep at seven in the morning, she reached for her aunt's debut novel, *Girl Gone Gaga*, concentrating on Megan's latest escapade in Paris to push thoughts of Callum out of her head. After three paragraphs, she halted and flipped back to the beginning of chapter two to refresh herself on the plot details.

She cozied into her pillow, pulled her sheet up to her chin, and read the first couple of sentences aloud to focus herself. *"Alexander's absence clung to her like paint on a Monet canvas. She longed for the many hues her blushes took on as he touched her."* Oh goodness. This romance novel was not redirecting her focus from Callum. Cara wholeheartedly agreed with Megan, the main character, who went for a run along the Seine. Her body begged for movement, an energizing action, to drag her mind from the previous night's sludge. She hopped from her bed and fumbled through her clean clothes, still unfolded in the laundry basket, and pulled out running shorts and a wrinkled t-shirt.

When she sat on the rug to stretch, she spied her running shoes under the bed. Laced up, she bounded down the steps and yelled to her mom from the front screen door that she'd be back in an hour.

"Just a second, Cara," her mom called from the kitchen, urgent to catch her.

Stopping dead in her tracks, Cara stumbled over the threshold. She hung onto the screen door, did an about face, and sprang toward the kitchen, reminiscent of all the times her mom caught her sneaking out of chores as a kid. She nearly collided with her mom, drying her hands on a tea towel.

"What's up?" Cara asked, her voice cheery.

"You're in a good mood!" her mom stated optimistically, with a hint of meddling to follow.

"It's Saturday. I have an entire day to just hang out. I see you're enjoying it, too," she teased, pointing at the flour on her mom's shirt. "Look at you. You're baking?" she asked, snatching the tea towel and snapping her mom with it.

Her mom grabbed it back and popped Cara on the leg. "I'm making us a batch of oatmeal cookies."

"Mmm. My favorite."

"It never hurts to remind my girls of the joys of home. If you have time, Dad and I thought we'd plan a family night. Are you free to grab dinner and play a little Apples to Apples? Tori's free after work."

When she was a kid, Saturday nights were family game nights. Her parents called it bonding time. When she started dating Callum, her parents worked in random family nights again, mostly as a way to get to know him. Callum had looked forward to those evenings as much as she had. A true belly laugh from him made everyone break out into hearty laughter. Warmth suffused through her when he let loose and his playful goofiness took over. He was never so loveable as when he'd bellowed out loud over his own stupidity. Was she foolish to want those happy times again?

"That works for me. I'm going for a run, and then I'll check in with Hannah and Sarah. They're checking their work schedules. If they can't get off for the Music Festival next weekend, we're going to squeeze in coffee time together today. I'll still have plenty of time this evening."

"I'm glad you're getting time with your cousins this summer. I'll make dessert for tonight. You just name the restaurant."

"Filippo's Pizza—I could eat my favorite every night. My mouth is watering just thinking about their homemade meatballs. But I'm good with their pizza too. Whatever everyone wants."

Her mom's face lit up. "I'm looking forward to all of us being together. Even Gramps wants to play."

"Aww, I'm glad," Cara hugged her mom. "Hey, when I get back, I'm going to run into town to find a pair of jeans. Want to come?"

"Sure. I'd love to." Her mom checked her watch. "You better skedaddle if you're going to get all that done," she said, and whipped Cara on her bum with the tea towel.

Cara skipped down the porch steps, popped her earbuds in, and jogged the quarter mile down their lane.

She rounded the bend onto the country road, lined with the dappled shade of age-old oaks, and spotted Callum's truck headed her way. A cloud of dust met her as he skidded to a stop.

"Can you get in?" he asked. An odd combination of excitement and impatience sat on his tongue and punched through the social niceties of a polite invitation.

"Get in? Nice greeting." She shot him an exaggerated smirk. "Good morning to you, too, Cal," she mocked with polite cheer.

"Morning?" he choked on a chuckle. "I've been up for fourteen hours."

She bit her lower lip and didn't mention the fitful sleep she'd had, thanks to him. "What are you doing here?" she asked, more ruffled than inquisitive.

"Come and see," he pleaded and waved her into the truck, adding a mischievous flare to his grin she couldn't resist. "I promise it'll take thirty minutes, maybe less."

She glanced at her Fitbit for the time and considered his cryptic request. "Okay, I'll bite," she agreed and eyed him suspiciously.

The corner of his mouth turned up in a satisfied grin, and he bent across the seat to open the door.

"Not too hard, I hope," he joked as she hopped into the cab.

She made an impatient circular motion with her hand. "Get a move on."

Did he understand the trust it took for her to sit shotgun, to look into the rearview mirror at what they had once been? Every time he drew close was a terrifying tug on her heartstrings.

"Settling your doubts about me or roping the wind?" he mumbled through an exhausted sigh.

She glared at him, and he gripped the steering wheel with both hands, uncomfortable under her scrutiny. If God granted her a superpower, she'd choose to read minds. Her throat tightened as she choked down her skeptical thoughts.

Five minutes later, Callum cut the engine in front of a small white stucco home within eyeshot of the post office and three long blocks from the police station. Boxwood bushes spanning the length of the front, trimmed below the windowsill, were evidence of Callum's meticulous care.

Neither moved in their seat for five silent seconds, which might as well have been five minutes. He fiddled with his keys and his thoughts. "This is the house I rent. I have something I want to give you. If you don't like it, you don't have to keep it. Are you okay with coming in?"

She pursed her lips and pitched an assessing glance at him. Feeling gutsy, she consented, "Okay."

After she'd left town, everything changed. By all definitions, Callum had been a man then. Thanks to the college credit he earned in high school, he had earned his bachelor's degree a full year before Cara, and his hometown department hired him, courtesy of her dad, the Chief.

A more filled-out Callum walked in front of her now and not just physically. He'd created his own world, and she readied her mind to enter his first house.

She tried not to gawk as she surveyed his choice. Something like regret tightened her gut. She'd always thought they'd pick their first home together. This is nothing like what she'd choose. His immaculate care of the lawn and the trimmed bushes didn't surprise her, nor did the lack of flowers. She would have added those.

A short walkway, edged by freshly cut grass, led to a bright blue door. Callum opened the metal screen door and held it for her to take, inviting her closer into the small space on his concrete stoop.

"Teal blue, huh?" she said, observing the wooden door with a half-moon window.

A humorous challenge flashed across his face that she couldn't read. "Picked it out myself. Like it?"

"It pops, for sure! But I never took you as a beachy vibe guy."

Callum instantly laughed out loud. "You sure make a guy feel confident." He nudged her shoulder. "You know me well enough to know I didn't paint the door that color. It was like that when I moved in. I think the people I bought it from must have missed the ocean. If I had painted this door, it would be—"

"Black," they said at the same time, while she demonstrated the obvious with the wave of her palm to his truck.

"Or gray," she added.

"Another beautifully muted color. This one has the advantage of being easy to find when you give directions to your place, though."

He punched a code into the keyless entry lock, and Cara recognized the date of the twins' birthday. She hadn't thought to hide her eyes, but he hadn't hidden the code from her either. She felt like she'd invaded his personal space by not looking away.

"Do you direct many people to your front door?" Playful words spilled naturally from her lips in his presence. He instantly caught her meaning.

"Curious?" he asked as the door clicked unlocked. "Or jealous?" he added.

Her face flushed red and a snarky response caught in her throat. Why was she embarrassed?

"You're so easy to rattle," he laughed, and pulled her into his immaculate living room.

"Nikki," he called. His tone brightened. "I'm home."

Her head flipped fast to follow his expectant gaze. "You were serious?" She stepped back toward the door and grabbed the handle. "I thought you were kidding."

Callum grabbed her by the hand and pulled her through his house. "Come on. You'll want to meet her."

Every wall was white. All the curtains were black. The modern kitchen showcased stainless steel appliances, white cabinets, white walls, and a white porcelain backsplash.

"Nikki, come here, baby," he tenderly called.

A brown snoot and floppy ears peaked from behind a door. Callum squatted to puppy level and coaxed her from her hiding spot. She bounded to him, licked his neck and face, and jumped sloppily in circles until he cuddled her to his chest.

"This is my new girl, Nikki," he said, smiling coyly and placing the little cuddly bundle of thick black fur in Cara's arms.

"She's adorable." Nikki accepted Cara into the pack, licking every inch of her cheek. Relief washed over her at the realization that Nikki was an animal. Her misunderstanding irritated her.

"She's why I brought you here. She's your present."

"My present? Why?"

"She needs a home, and you need her. She can't replace Nestlé, but you'll love her well, and she'll be devoted to you."

I wanted you to be devoted to me.

She tucked Nikki close in her arms. "Callum, you can't give away your dog," she said as Nikki settled under her long caresses. "Besides, I'm leaving soon and my apartment doesn't allow dogs."

"She's not my dog. She needs a place with land to run and roam and someone to teach her good manners. Obviously…" he said, tapping Nikki's nose lightly to stop her from chewing the ends of Cara's hair. "This ten-pounder will outgrow my little place here in town in a few months." He leaned in close and tenderly lifted Nikki's muzzle and kissed her forehead. His warm breath fell against Cara's neck. He carefully swept Cara's hair behind her shoulder, out of Nikki's reach. His fingertips brushed the flesh on the nape of her neck and sent shivers down her spine as if he'd delicately kissed her.

Cara fought against the overwhelming sensation spiraling through her body. She squeezed her eyelids closed and sucked on her lips, lost in the memory of his touch. Counting to three, she inhaled deeply through her nose and slowly exhaled through slightly parted lips, regaining some composure and calming her heart rate.

His eyes studied her. Her body hadn't forgotten him. His stillness told her he'd not forgotten hers.

She pulled her focus from Callum to Nikki. "I think she needs some chew toys." She thought she might, too. Something else to sink her thoughts into. "What kind is she?"

"Well, she's a mutt, but she definitely has a lot of German shepherd in her. She was the most skittish of the five in the litter. Remember the house fire Dylan and I responded to yesterday? The family lost everything. Their animals were in their garage and were all going to the shelter. When they offered Dylan and me a pup, I thought of you—that you might like a new companion."

"A new companion, huh?" she asked, her eyebrows raised. She wondered if he understood how his words played in her head like rejection. Her body stiffened, and she felt betrayed like that day under the hickory tree at the cemetery when he let her go.

"Nestlé would be okay with it, don't you think? But if it feels too soon, I can take her to the shelter. I'm not home enough to care for her."

Cara couldn't commit to this cute pup, but she wanted to. Nikki was so small and alone and unsure. She would feel abandoned all over again if Cara put her down and walked away. Cara could relate all too well.

"Did you give her the name Nikki?"

"The mom said her two kids named this one Nik after Saint Nicholas, but when she told them the pup was a girl, they changed it to Nikki."

"Why Saint Nicholas?" she asked, confused by the Christmas reference for puppies born in June.

"I asked the same question," he shrugged. "The kids said they'd asked for pups for Christmas. They figured Santa was just late. I guess that's what you get when you leave the names up to three- and five-year-olds. All the others had the more classic saddle pattern of tan and black. She's the only one with an all-black body and tan spots at the eyebrows and socks for paws. The kids said Saint Nick got Nikki dirty sliding down the chimney."

"What did they name the other four?"

He laughed before he gave the answer. "Dasher, Dancer, Comet, Cupid."

"Kids crack me up," she said.

"Dylan said Dasher was the manliest name, so he took that one. He hopes to make a hunting dog of him. That remains to be seen." Callum smirked.

"How is the family?"

"They made it out safe, thank God. It was a terrible fire."

"What can we do for them?"

"Take good care of their pup."

Her fingers tugged at her lower lip, betraying her war between doubt and desire.

As if on cue, Nikki added her own form of persuasion, cozying into her neck and licking her face.

"Let's take her for a ride and see what my parents think. They'll have to raise her until I find a place that accepts big dogs. Gramps could use the company if they can stand the training."

"She gets excited when she first greets people," he said, and nodded to the piddle on the floor, "but she loves doing her duty outside. She'll be super easy to potty train. I bet your sister can accomplish that by the end of the summer. I promise to drop by when I can to take her for truck rides and run her at Lake of the Woods."

Cara moaned, not realizing her response was audible.

"What's wrong?" he asked and stopped mid-swipe while cleaning Nikki's mess.

She averted the truth—her intruding jealousy over Nikki getting to ride shotgun through the country with Callum—and said, "Well, let's see how this goes over with Dad. This could go badly for you, dropping a dog on your boss's doorstep."

"But he's a softy when it comes to canines, right?" he asked with a bit of a hopeful cringe.

Cara couldn't erase her biggest worry over adopting his pup. Nikki would be a constant reminder of Callum.

And darn if he didn't know it!

TWENTY-ONE

Cara sat on the porch step, cuddling a sleeping Nikki in her lap, and waited for Callum to arrive for their second date. When his truck rolled onto their lane at a leisurely Sunday afternoon pace, Nikki perked up, her chunky body wiggling with excitement. As Callum cut the engine and opened his truck door, she bolted toward him. Cara bounded down the steps to get the eager pup under control, but there was no need. Callum swept Nikki into his arms.

Nikki nuzzled into his neck for a calm few seconds and then started profusely licking Callum's face. Callum laughed and sweet-talked her. "Aww. I miss you too, girl! I hope you're behaving."

Cara cleared her throat and pulled her pup from his arms. "Little traitor. We don't have much time left together, and you're already replacing my affections." As if asking for forgiveness, Nikki snuggled into Cara's neck, but then chomped away at her fingers like they were a chew toy.

"She'd never replace you," he said, petting Nikki.

Cara halted Callum from following her up the steps. "Let me get this little escape artist settled inside with Mom."

Minutes later, when she hopped into the truck, he asked straightaway, "How does Italian sound? There's a new upscale Italian place—"

"We talked about keeping it low key and heading to the pond. That sounds plenty fine to me."

"Fine wasn't what I was going for. I was going for something more date worthy," Callum corrected.

"No need to impress me," Cara scowled.

Callum snickered. He always said her face couldn't lie.

"Do not impress. Got it. Whatever your heart desires."

The truth was Callum's suggestion of a pond date *had* impressed Cara. She needed a retreat from the heaviness of the last few days, and he knew it. Nothing was more "date worthy" than a night on the water under clear skies with him, even if she felt conflicted. It had been their place to relax, to hide away from others, to make out. Where they were "them" together.

"But first, let's at least stop for ice cream," Callum said.

"Ice cream is date worthy," Cara said, offering him a conciliatory smile.

There was a time when where they were headed was of little consequence compared to simply being together.

***

Cara could sense Callum watching her. When she turned to Callum and asked, "What'll you have?" he was leaning over her shoulder, eyeing the ice cream in the cases. His lips hovered inches from hers, close enough for him to kiss her. Heat flushed through her at the thought.

"I'm having trouble focusing on ice cream while I'm standing this close to you," he whispered into her ear.

This was madness, these dates. Get a grip. Who's getting revenge on who here?

"Concentrate on the menu board," she directed him without looking his way. She took two subtle steps away from Callum and said to the teen working behind the counter, "I'll take cosmic cookie in a waffle cone, please."

Callum turned a confused grimace on her.

"What?" Cara asked.

"Blue ice cream? How old are you?" Callum asked.

"It's healthy for you. It has spirulina in it."

He wrinkled his nose. "I don't know what that is, but it sounds like a virus I'd avoid."

"It's algae."

He doubled over and coughed. "Ew. Algae in your ice cream?" Turning his attention back to the server, he said, "I'll take a scoop of your Madagascar Vanilla."

"Vanilla?" she squealed in laughter.

"Mine's exotic. It's from Madagascar!" He grinned.

"At least you jazzed it up with a sugar cone."

"I know what I want," Callum said with a slow, deliberate voice, looking directly into Cara's eyes.

"Callum!" she cautioned. Cara's insides grew shaky at his implication, but she swallowed hard around the knot of nerves in her throat. If she responded with any hint of hope, he'd push harder.

He quit his pursuit as they walked down Main Street to his truck. The ice cream did the trick of sweetening her mood until Cara noticed a black Honda.

"Oh my," Cara stopped walking and covered her mouth, pinching her lips.

Callum saw Ali's car just as Cara gasped in surprise. Two teenage girls sang along to music blaring out the window. Ali's fish bumper sticker still covered the dent she'd made backing into a pole.

Neither spoke but watched the car turn the corner out of sight.

"Ali would love them enjoying her car," he said, flipping the sad narrative running through their heads.

Cara was envious of the girls. They reminded her of what she would never have with Ali again.

"You two certainly tested those speakers a time or two, much to my parents' dismay," he said, shaking his head.

"Hey, you were right there with us," she accused and caught his faraway gaze.

"I didn't dare get between you two and Taylor Swift. The entire town heard you three," he joked.

"Jamming on our ride to school woke us up," Cara defended. She could only listen to Taylor's new music now. The memories were too strong to sing alone to her and Ali's favorites. "We had good times in that car." They'd lived so carefree and confidently. Cara envied who she was back then.

"I loved being with you guys," he said, lingering over his words. "Being wherever you are is enough…"

Jolted by his admission, she turned to look at him. She couldn't deny the hope projected in his wistful eyes. It was for far more than a kiss in an ice cream shop.

Cara had no words for him, but she knew the feeling he tried to relay. Once upon a time, no matter where life took them, as long as she was with Callum, she'd go. That's how sure she'd once felt about them. Cara held back her tears. She wanted that unwavering security again.

I miss every easy moment I had with you.

Callum and Cara finished their cones in the truck on the short ride back to her house. They walked down the gravel lane to the pond, side by side, a safe two-foot distance apart. A palpable energy flowed between them and enveloped them like smoke from a bonfire.

His hand softly wrapped around hers, and she stared down at their clasped union with a kind of dull awareness. When her mind stopped spinning under his spell, she slipped her hand from his and plunged it in her pocket. Their familiar warmth and easy connection had been as natural a part of her world as the sun resting on the trees in the horizon. A strong wave of nostalgia had her wanting that connection too much. But darn, she didn't want to want it. Couldn't want to want it.

They walked without words and sat at the edge of the dock, as they had so many times before. God's light show was brighter than usual. Magenta and peach flames ribboned with lavender fell across the night sky into the royal blue heavens. A twilight watercolor palette painted across the tranquil pond. Its serenity was the antithesis of the energy rolling Cara's insides into a knot. Uncertainty and melancholy braided with a thread of wayward yearning.

"Are you ready for a little chariot ride in Apollo?" Callum asked, using the name he'd once given to the boat he claimed whisked them away from life's cares.

"Sounds nice," she said, thankful for a diversion.

Callum hopped from the dock to flip the jon boat. "Give me a hand," he called to her. His tanned muscles pulled at the sleeves of his white t-shirt. He glanced back at her out of habit, leery she'd push him in as she had in their past, in a moment of mischief.

Water had dripped off his dark, smooth chest. His playful smile had met hers when he whooshed from the water and flipped his long locks off his forehead.

Her skin tingled at the pleasant memory. She rubbed her arms and exhaled to rid herself of its effect.

"Certainly Helios," she teased, tagging him with that sun god nickname she'd given him one long-ago summer when he'd started taking his shirt off to tan.

Callum placed the paddles she handed him in the bow and reached for her. Feeling the strength of his grip, she looked up. Their eyes locked, and all the times he'd steadied her before flowed through her. She didn't want him to guide her with his same unwavering confidence. Not now. Callum steadying her would be the most unsteadying thing in her life.

Callum didn't immediately release her hand. With a sharp tug, she freed herself and found her balance. Grasping both gunnels, she positioned herself in the middle of the bench seat, forcing Callum to sit on another.

Callum easily climbed in, and they paddled through the still water, quietly in-sync, beginning and ending each stroke together. They paddled around the far bend and drifted lazily like an autumn leaf toward the bridge. Cara turned around to face him just as he scratched his bicep. She caught a quick glimpse of ink on his arm.

"What does that say?" she asked, nodding at his arm.

Callum looked at the side of the boat, confused.

"Your arm," she said.

"This is…" he flexed his bicep and hesitated. For a split-second, that movement made her insides flip, and she hated her unrestrained visceral reaction. As if unveiling a secret, he slowly pushed his t-shirt up over his shoulder and finished, "my way of always having Ali near me. I needed that. The pain from the needle was oddly healing."

In a bold move, definitely not guided by reason, she leaned toward him and traced each delicate angel wing surrounding Ali's name. He examined her slow movements, giving her time with her memories. Her finger shadowed the letters scripted in Ali's own handwriting, lightly flowing from the A to caress the L and then settle momentarily on the I.

Cara withdrew her hands to her lap. Callum's soft eyes understood her pain. Gathering her long sleek hair over her left shoulder, she shared her own personal memorial of her best friend, *Phil 4:8 Ali.*

"It's the most painful thing I've ever done," she admitted. "But nothing compared to losing her."

"I needed a permanent reminder of her," he said.

"I wanted the words she loved and lived by." Ali's favorite verse would forever be inked at the base of her neck.

"Very courageous. I saw your tattoo that day at the copier. I never thought you'd get one."

"Me, either, but life has forced me to look at things in new ways." Her response steered her back into the dangerous waters of contemplation.

"It's been full of changes, for sure," Callum said, looking expectantly at Cara.

Lord, don't I know that, she thought.

Callum paddled slowly for both of them as the afternoon sun began its wink goodnight over the western horizon. Ripples danced as they glided through the water, a perfect mirror of the skyscape. Geese squawked and scattered to the far edges at their intrusion. A frog croaked from the cattails, joining the symphony of the night—katydids' rasping staccato pulses, crickets' chirping, and cicadas' rattling tambourines.

"Let's stop here." Callum pulled his paddle into the boat, and they listened to the pond's serenade together. When he scratched his hand up the back of his neck and glanced at her with a grooved brow, she knew something weighed on him.

With trepidation, her eyes darted from him to the water. She waited with her hands heavy in her lap. Her chest rose and fell, and she counted her breaths until he spoke again.

And then the boat rocked, and he bridged the distance between them, moving hip to hip with her. Her stability wavered. A hundred different ideas of what Callum would say raced through her mind.

Guard your heart, Cara.

"Life with you back here feels good," Callum said.

A gentle wind nudged her to answer.

It's a deep dive off a cliff.

"It feels very shaky to me," she contradicted.

"Life is scary and messy," he agreed and linked his pinky to hers, "and good, all at the same time…"

Cara started counting her breaths again.

"Grief and grace are intertwined," he said, scooting sideways to look her in the face. "And I've realized I never want to survive those again without you by my side."

The truth that grace was needed for this messy and scary life tugged at her. The weight of his admission that he didn't want to do life without her sunk like an untethered anchor, pulling at her heart.

"I don't expect life to be neat and tidy," she admitted.

"But?" he prompted her to speak.

"But I want what I can depend on. When things weren't hard, we were good. But when Ali died, we crumbled."

"I was drowning. You couldn't have rescued me. No one could. And I knew you would try." His sharp answer sliced at her, and she braced against it. Cara could swear his dark eyes begged her to argue with him, but maybe she couldn't read him like she used to. Maybe he wanted something else that she couldn't define.

"I believed in us, but you shut me out," she gulped, unable to stop the petulant child in her, repeating the same argument. "More like pushed me and slammed the door."

"I got things wrong—saw things wrong. You had faith in me when I had faith in nothing," he said, scratchy regret in his voice. He hung his head and grabbed the back of his neck again. "But I have faith we can work our way back to one another."

Cara melted a little at his admission, but it felt necessary and urgent to share the depth of her fear. She wouldn't avoid it. "That faith faded for me," she confessed.

A sinking feeling engulfed Cara. With every utterance, she would dash Callum's hope just a bit more. Her intention wasn't to hurt him. The ugly truth she'd thrown at him—that she couldn't fully trust him—still didn't feel freeing when she said it this second time.

"I don't blame you for leaving," Callum admitted. "I don't want to be paralyzed by fear ever again, unable to love you the way you deserve. I always want to look into your eyes, no matter if it's disappointment or happiness looking back at me. I'll take anything I can get from you, so long as you're focused my way."

Cara understood that truth to her core now. Part of her wanted to let Callum in, but she couldn't.

"I see who I want to be. I want to be *yours*! Can we try? I'm not deserving. Heck, how you see me now, I don't fully know," he said.

"I've been angry at you. I blamed you for my heartache. I tried to shut you out. Anger is a steady place for me, but I want to let that go," Cara confessed.

"Can you take me back for who I am now—for what I'm telling you now?" he whispered. "For every day forward, I only want you. I'll fight your fear as long as it takes. Forgive me," he pressed.

His request was a step off a cliff.

"Callum, I'm trying to forgive," she rasped. A weight lifted after admitting that to him.

His voice broke. "I can live with that." Callum sat taller and his eyes shot to the heavens for a second. "It's maddening how long it's taken us to get here, to those words." He exhaled and Cara saw relief sink in. "I've missed being with you like this." He cupped her head and eased her against his chest, the soft weight of his touch comfortingly familiar.

"I'm sorry," she admitted. His closeness no longer magnified her pain.

"Shh," he comforted. "Don't say that. I'm the sorry one. You have nothing to be sorry for."

Twilight fell to sunset. Callum hopped back to his seat, and they rowed back to shore in silence.

They tied down the jon boat together like they had a hundred times before. Each doing their part. Cara listened to the familiar click of their shoes as they walked down the long wooden dock toward the gravel road.

When he threaded his fingers through hers, she didn't pull away, but the commotion in her chest skipped like stones across a pond. He stopped and turned, his ardent eyes boring into her. "Cara, I want only you sitting shotgun in my truck or paddling in my boat. I want to be your Friday night cuddle on the couch person. I want to spend every special occasion together."

She stopped, slipping her fingers from his, and turned to face him.

"Say there can be another us?" he implored.

She'd blame her dizziness on the tilting boat if she were still in it, but she stood on the solid wood planks at the start of the dock. Hope rose in her chest like a rising balloon, but fear quickly deflated it. She should be exhilarated, beyond happy, but she was terrified. Sweat beaded along her hairline. Her palms were clammy. Her ribcage tightened, and she felt like she was suffocating.

He rested his forehead against hers and softly whispered, "I never want to write 'I love you' to anyone else."

I can't imagine that I could either.

Cara stepped back and wrapped her arms around her waist. She needed room. Room to breathe. Room to think. Room to get away from the heat of his body and his breath on her neck.

"I want you. I want us," he said.

His steadfastness tempted her to give in to his longing. Her heart fluttered in her chest and her pulse thundered in her head.

"Are you okay?" he asked, but his voice came to her as if he stood at the far end of a tunnel.

"It's hard to hear the words I so badly wanted to hear you say two years ago—let alone trust them."

"I didn't let us go because I didn't love you."

"That's what it felt like," she coughed. She thought she just might suffocate.

"I have loved you every day, right up to this very moment. I never stopped."

Cara didn't understand how that could be. Her brain circled chaotically around Callum's words, like she couldn't quite find her orbit. Cara wished she could admit she wanted to give them a second chance, but she couldn't voice it. That had to mean something. What if Callum made the same mistakes? Was it foolish of her to trust he'd figured things out? She didn't verbally reciprocate his declaration of love.

Forgiveness felt like all she could trust him with, but he wanted so much more.

She turned to walk away, but he hooked a finger through her belt loop and gripped her waist with his palm, turning her into his arms. "Please, don't walk away."

"Why? You did!" Cara responded without expression. She didn't have to spew emotion at him. Her words alone hit the bullseye. She immediately hated herself for taking a cheap shot to drown out her hurt.

Callum flinched. "I did, but I'm taking every step I can back to you.

"When things get hard, I'll be standing here alone."

"No, I'll still be right beside you!" He grabbed her hands. "I won't let go again."

The war in her heart was obvious.

Callum vowed again more gently, "I promise. I know my words probably sound trite and sickening to you after I pushed you out of my life. But this is not the same promise that I made to you that night in my truck in college. In a way, this promise is so much more because of that one.

I broke that promise. I lost your trust. My words won't be good enough a second time around. This time, I've got to prove my promise to you. Let me do that."

The vice around her chest grew stronger, breathing grew harder, as if she was sucking in air through a straw. Her hands reached for him, crumpling his shirt, but quickly grabbed at the tightness in her own chest before she buckled to her knees.

Her neck strained with each breath. The warning signs suddenly registered. "Where's your inhaler?" Callum asked.

Through shallow breaths, she muttered, "Back pocket."

There was nothing sensual about Callum groping for the canister, difficult as it was with Cara bent over in tight jeans.

Kneeling beside her, he pulled her shoulders upright and said, "Expand your lungs. Now, inhale this." He searched her face for any sign of relief after the first puff of albuterol. He watched her shallow inhale and exhale.

"Again." His barely controlled insistence didn't help her racing heartbeat.

She held one finger in front of his face to stop him from directing her. Her heart rate slowed as she gained more air.

"Go again, now." He snatched her inhaler and held it inches from her mouth.

She snatched it right back from him.

"I'll manage," she puffed out between pursed lips.

"This is life or death, Cara. Go again." His breath caressed her cheek.

"Please," she insisted and settled one hand on his chest, keeping him at bay. She attempted to suck in air before speaking. "I got this."

He begged her, "No, please!" He pushed the inhaler in her hand up to her mouth.

Turning away, she assured him, "I'm fine. Give me a bit of time."

"Let's just be sure," he said, retreating a bit. "You're still working hard to breathe." His hands imitated taking a puff.

Resting her hands on her hips, she rolled her eyes, a clear warning to back off.

"I know my body."

"How often does this happen?" he gently asked.

"Not often," she said, "It's just a panic attack. They started after Ali died and…" She let her voice trail away. If Callum knew the true source of her panic, hoping again for the two of them, he'd work even harder to convince her.

"I want to be sure you're breathing okay," he said, searching her face.

But you keep taking my breath away.

"I promise to love you better this time," Callum pled, desperate to finish his thoughts. "Your absence forced me to face my fears. I want to continue to deal with my grief in a healthy way for me, for you, for us. I'm hoping where my words fall short, my actions and prayers don't. You have always been the stronger one of us—whether you believe it or not. You're more persistent than anyone I know. Lord knows, we wouldn't even be on this date if you didn't need to prove you could handle it."

He knows me.

"Give me a chance to erase…or…uh…replace the pain and doubt I've caused. I'll show up every day—every hard day!"

She raced back toward to the end of the dock like it would offer her an escape. Taking a puff on her inhaler, she stared at the moon shining on the water, waiting for full relief. Callum was right when he'd insisted she needed it. And that was irritating.

He walked up to her and stood between her and the water, anchoring her with his unfaltering gaze. With inches between them, for a split second, she thought to grab him and let the madness of her heart guide her. Let this be the end of their sad chapter. But she couldn't surrender to trembling hope.

Cara reflected on the life they'd once dreamed of when they sat on the bridge at this very lake. They'd build a home on her family's land, attend church on Sundays, canoe and fish, and raise their children. They'd grow old together, God willing, sharing happiness and heartache.

She had only wanted that life with the guy who'd captured her heart the moment he told her she was the best human he knew. He used to say God works good for those who love Him, and she was his good.

"Everyone talks about how hard it is to trust people after you've been hurt," Cara said, searching for her next words.

"Uh-huh." Callum sat back on his heels, absorbing each word she uttered.

Her lips stiffened. "But not very many people talk about how hard it is to trust yourself to make the right decisions after the ground has been cut out from under you. Do you know what thinking I was not enough for you felt like? One minute, I was determined and confident in the direction my life was headed. After you proved you could so easily push me away, I doubted everything, trusted nothing, even myself."

Without shifting her view from the lake, Cara slipped her hand in Callum's. "So trust is a real battle for me. The part of me that hopes we could have a future gets quickly ambushed by doubt." She wove her fingers between his and gently rested her head against his shoulder. Nestling against Callum, she nervously brushed her thumb back and forth against his, a kind of soothing lullaby played with their fingers. She pulled away from him a little and choked up at the gentleness in his eyes.

He slid his arm low around her waist and snuggled her close. Towering over her, his warm breath spilled over the crown of her head. She lay her head on his shoulder again, closed her eyes, and breathed in rhythm to the rise and fall of his chest. She felt him hoping for a hint of a promise.

Their breakup had taught Cara some important things about herself. She deserved loyalty. Above all, she should be loyal to herself, to her needs, to her plans, and to her emotional healing. And that conflicted with what he wanted from her, and even with what parts of her body were saying to her.

This is so unfair to him. To me. This has to be our last time.

As if in revolt, the need to connect with him rose like a flame. She overrode caution and did exactly what her heart desired, but her head cautioned her against.

Just once more.

She snaked her fingers through his hair, molded her palms around his head, and pulled him to her. Laying her cheek against his, she inhaled the scent of his skin and felt the hint of his smile. Then she lightly kissed the lobe of his ear. Goosebumps trailed along his neck. His nose caressed the side of hers, tickling her skin. His breath lingered on her cheek. Closing her eyes, she slowly slid her kiss across his stubble until she found the warmth of his lips.

She clung to him and kissed him her goodbye.

His urgent lips sunk into hers as if he'd read her longing. Her arms circled his waist, and she molded against him. His heat flooded through her, seeping into every part of her core. She splayed her fingers under the edge of his shirt, caressing the powerful cords in his lower back, and he moaned.

His grip loosened, and Cara's eyes fluttered open to his penetrating stare. For the longest time, neither had words to identify this moment.

His lips were still temptingly close to hers. "Don't overanalyze, Cara," Callum urged.

Cara surrendered and leaned into him. Their lips hastily found one another again. She matched his gentle intensity. Their kisses slowly subsided, but their power remained. Callum pressed a soft kiss on her forehead, lingering there while their breathing found a natural rhythm again. They nuzzled cheek to cheek at the water's edge as the night air grew thick with contemplation.

Silent minutes later, he breathed a plea to her. "Loving you every day will be my life's mission. I want to be better. I want to understand deeper. For the rest of my life, you're the person I want to be with. It's you, Cara."

Cara wanted to soothe his anguish, to smooth the confused furrow between his eyelids with a soft kiss, to trace her finger down his hairline, along his jaw, and up around the curve of his downturned mouth. She groaned at causing her own suffering.

His lips hovered against her cheekbone as he softly called to her, "Cara?"

She held still, very still, and savored the warmth of his chest and his nose cradled next to hers, releasing only a whimper when she pulled away from him.

He brushed a kiss on the tip of her nose, and still, she couldn't look him in the eyes.

Despite her shaky legs, she retreated from his embrace. When she opened her mouth, her vocal cords quivered with a croak. "I'll miss you," she said, and her heart tore an inch. A mist of tears blurred her eyes. Any further explanation was trapped in her throat.

He swallowed the plea to beg her for more. He waited, hopeful that she'd explain her retreat.

But darn if she just couldn't let go, lose control, and trust a second chance. Liquid stung her eyes, knowing she could not let her heart split wide open for him again.

From the heavy rise and fall of his chest, she could tell he held something back, something he desperately wanted to say.

He tugged her hand, asking her to look at him. His pull on her now was too strong. Desire had made her fragile. Avoidance was her only escape.

"This time, our goodbye is my fault." Cara pushed away from his chest.

Confused and off balance from her push, Callum stepped back to look into her face, wobbling on the edge of the dock. "Cara—" he started, but fell backwards with his arms flailing. He reached for her, but she couldn't grab hold fast enough to rescue him.

"Callum," Cara yelled in disbelief as he plunged into the water.

Callum's eyes crested the dark surface. A slow smile spread across his face. "Not again," he said.

Only then did Cara's laughter echo across the pond as she realized she'd succeeded a little too much in pushing him away.

TWENTY-TWO

Cara plopped on the edge of her bed, attempting to exhale the weight of the evening. Unlacing her black Converse, she half grinned at the memory of a fully clothed Callum falling backwards into the pond.

She'd profusely apologized to a dripping wet Callum, his clinging clothes outlining his muscles, as he squished down the lane.

A somber mood had settled between them. Years gone by, they would have giggled all the way back to the house. Tonight, their glances at one another had been pierced with sadness and heaviness—a heaviness that she'd chosen.

She nearly choked on that thought.

She'd shattered his hope for a future together.

Heck. She'd shattered her own. The gravity of her choice weighed on her heart. Did disappointment in her own decision even make sense? She'd spent weeks of mental and emotional gymnastics resisting Callum, struggling not to fall into comfortable behaviors with him.

Before climbing into his truck, he had captured her gaze seconds too long, reading the resignation in her face. He couldn't read the nausea growing in her gut. His bewildered expression had matched her own.

Cara had casually waved goodbye as if she'd done it every night and sighed in relief when she turned her back to him.

Callum is quicksand. The more I try not to think of him, the deeper I sink. This next week can't pass fast enough.

She could only blame herself for gutting her own heart. No tears fell this time. No all-night ruminating why he didn't love her anymore or why she couldn't be what he needed. Her decision might be a brave attempt to be true to herself, but maybe she was simply a coward, refusing to risk.

Cara pitched her shoe into her walk-in closet, hitting the doorjamb way harder than she expected.

"Oops. Missed. Dang it!"

Everything is so exhausting tonight!

She flung the second high top sneaker with more frustration, and it crashed against the wall on the other side of the door.

That figures, she exhaled—*this so resembles my night. I'm so off-kilter.*

Clearly, she was off balance if she couldn't even hit a three-foot opening from ten feet with a measly size-eight shoe, something she'd done with ease nearly every day since junior high.

Her competitive ire kicked in. She needed a win, even one small one like this, a little pseudo-confirmation that she'd made the right choice. Evaluating, she retrieved both shoes, recalibrated her hold, and bounced down onto the bed in the same spot and exact position.

I will pitch both shoes through that doorway. A win is proof that I did the right thing tonight.

No matter that there was absolutely no logic in this contest she had concocted with herself.

"One success to get on the other side of this challenge. That's all I need," she emceed her solo competition. She balanced the shoe in her palm, tossing it up and down, eyeing the target. Upon the release, the heel caught on her pinky. The shoe twirled in the air, hit the hardwood floor on its side, and bounced a foot from the entrance.

"Wait folks! All is not lost. One shoe in the goal is a win. Just one shoe. Proof positive. That's all I need," she pleaded, desperately adjusting her contest.

Her final chance. She lifted the last high-top in front of her face, juggling the shoe hand to hand, and blew hard on the rubber heel like a gambler's desperate attempt to influence lady luck.

Only she would know the success or defeat of this competition. Keeping her rump on the mattress, she leaned forward as far as she could. Swaying her arm forward and back, she cocked, loaded, and pitched the last black Converse between the doors. It flew hard and hit her hanging clothes, falling smack dab into the middle of the closet floor.

"Bingo! There it is!" she yelled, pumping her fists in the air. "A win! You did good tonight, girl," she roared, half-heartedly cheering herself on. Falling back onto her pillows, she swiped her hands as if ridding herself of the dust of the past, but she couldn't fool herself.

Okay, so it took me four tries.

It wasn't long before she chided herself, exposing her pseudo escape from the heaviness of the night for what it was. "Grow up, Cara. That's fairytale magic."

"Just so you know, I'm not the evil stepsister," Tori warned.

"Oh!" Cara jumped. "You scared me!" Cara sat up against her headboard, crossing her legs.

"You were so busy orchestrating your playoff round, you didn't see the spectators cheering you on! Now, that's focus!" Tori giggled, balancing her shoulder against the doorjamb. "You're so competitive, even with yourself."

Cara gritted her teeth and delivered a humorless smile.

"Whenever you're this focused, I know something's clearly got you wound up. Want to talk about it?" Tori grilled.

Tori plopped down on the edge of the bed, and Cara blurted out, "Callum asked me to give him a second chance." What he wanted went way beyond that. He'd asked her to choose him, together forever.

"And is that a...?" Tori asked, giving her sister a thumbs-up.

"No, not good at all," she squelched dismissively. "I'm leaving in a week. What's the point? I didn't accept."

Tori plied Cara with her frustrations. "I'm lost here. You admitted you two made some headway on your first date. Isn't this a major move in a good direction? Why didn't you accept?"

"I meant headway in reconciliation, understanding our breakup, being in one another's presence without wanting to yell at him. I wasn't looking to fall back into dating him."

"Okay," Tori barely got out before Cara continued.

"That's the fantasy I let myself entertain for a short second this evening. But we both know the tale—the agony returns when the clock strikes midnight."

"We're living in the real world here, sis," Tori encouraged.

"Exactly. The real world where my boyfriend broke up with me. Where he blamed me for my best friend's death.

Where he made promises and broke them, saying it was better for me," Cara explained.

Where my fear and pride don't let me trust. Where no matter how much I know that in my head, my heart is still scared.

"And what about second chances?" Tori said, raising her eyebrows in a challenge. "Maybe that's what you're being given here."

"That's all Hallmark and heartache," Cara assured.

"Maybe it's trusting and healing," Tori pushed back.

Since Tori threw it out there, Cara agreed. "Trust is my issue. What if I lose again?" Cara admitted and pulled both her legs to her chest, wrapped her arms around her shins, and rested her chin on her knees.

"I'm not surprised he wants more time with you," Tori said.

"Why not?"

"Because he still loves you? Why else?" Tori saddled up next to Cara and wrapped her arm around her. "What do you want?"

"What if he leaves me again?" Cara asked, still hesitant, still resisting. After a few seconds lost in her own thoughts, Cara sat up straighter against the headboard and resolved, "What Callum and I need is to move forward, not backward," she emphasized.

"As far as I can tell, you're moving backward, not forward," Tori refuted.

"How is not getting back with Callum moving backwards?" Cara cocked her eyebrow in disbelief and shot her sister a defensive glare.

"When you were dating, you swore to me—quite adamantly if you recall—that Callum was the person God had planned for you to share the rest of your life with. I was skeptical that you could be so sure back then. So now, I'm reminding you of your words. Either Callum is that man or he is not. Did you get that wrong back then or do you have it wrong now? Or are you saying that God got it wrong?"

"God changes our plans."

"Or maybe *you* got it wrong. *You* changed *your* plans. You're afraid of getting hurt again. Normally, you're such a fierce competitor and a relentless fighter. I get that your disappointment and hurt run deep. It's safer to blame him and fight against him than try again."

Cara's face blanched when Tori's shot hit its mark. Her lips opened and closed as she fumbled for a response. "I put too much trust in him and not enough in myself. I need to trust my gut."

"What does your gut tell you?" Tori asked, more counsel than question.

That I love him.

"I understand now how grief got in the way. But it's just a matter of time before we hit another complication, and then I'm the fool who trusted him again."

"That's what holds you back from giving Callum a second chance, fear of appearing like a fool? What seems foolish is not taking the hard shot when it presents itself." Tori paused and grasped her sister's hands. "In your heart of hearts, do you think the problem here could be you?"

Of course it is! Cara tried to pull away, but Tori wouldn't let her.

"I don't mean to sound harsh. Everything is really in your court. In any relationship, you have to choose the next step without seeing the end game. I guess you have to ask yourself if you believe you can create a better relationship with Callum? If so, there's hope." Tori started for the door but turned back. "And maybe a little hope will lead you to the trust you need."

"After he promised he'd love me forever and then he pushed me away, I don't know which words of his to trust."

"He can't earn your trust if you don't let him try."

TWENTY-THREE

With Callum on second shift, the end of Cara's last week at the police department had fewer of his disruptive, probing glances, but she still had to force thoughts of him from her mind. To complicate her life further, he left a short note on her desk every day. She caught herself hurrying to her desk, searching for her name in his handwriting. Each folded piece of stapled paper had one line, but she still pulled them from her pocket and read them throughout the day.

Monday: I hope no one gives you grief today.

Tuesday: I'm grateful for you, simply grateful.

Wednesday: Wacky Wednesday weans we waugh and waugh.

(She did laugh at his lame attempt at humor.)

Thursday: Cheers to you for remaking your life the way you want it to be.

Friday: I'll miss you.

Friday's goodbye scratched at her old wound of loss until later that day when Callum's truck barreled down their driveway. Her dad had shamelessly invited Callum to family game night. Cara suspected Callum was fully onboard with his tactics. Well, she planned on enjoying herself. She'd made it through her summer as planned, so no more fretting over Callum. She'd show them.

When Callum walked through the door, Cara volunteered to walk the leftover pizza to Gramps and let him know the games were starting.

I'm not trying to escape Callum, she counseled herself.

Callum elbowed her and asked, "Don't mind if I come along, do you?"

"Are you ready to lose?" she teased in defiance of her hammering heart. The way Callum could evoke so many warring emotions in her without trying was frightening. It made her elated that he knew her so well, but it also annoyed her for the same reason.

"I'm always up for good competition, but I'm hitching myself to you tonight. If we're on the same team, we can't lose."

He hooked his arm in hers as they made their way down the lane. "It's just a few days until you leave."

"I pull out Monday. Meetings start at the end of next week."

"Do you have any time for our last date?" Callum asked, bumping her shoulder again, nearly knocking the pizza box from her hand.

She rolled her eyes at him. "We could count tonight," she offered.

"Seems to me, your dad asked me to game night," he corrected.

"We could send in a picture of me beating you at Apples to Apples. Although, our best picture is of you totally soaked," she said and giggled.

"Well, tonight is kind of like a date since you've been checking me out. Maybe we should get a picture of us right now," he said, pulling out his phone.

She coughed a laugh. "What? I'm checking you out? You're just trying to get a picture of us together. I know what you're doing."

"Darn right I am. I need something to hope for. And I've noticed you looking. Don't say you weren't."

"That's respect. You look at the person speaking."

"You can't take your eyes off my sexy stubble," he added and winked, scratching his chin.

"Callum, everyone looks at you."

Callum tugged her arm, and she turned to face him. The fire in his eyes held her in place like an embrace. She was thankful for the pizza box taking up space between them.

"Cara, have you ever thought we were *meant* to be together?" The warmth in his voice drew her to him like a soft caress. His palm grazed her cheek, and Cara gripped the box harder, digging it into her stomach.

"Yes, I have, Callum. We settled this by the pond," she said with finality, more for herself than Callum.

"Hey there, young-uns," Gramps called out. Relieved, she headed his way.

"Your mom texted that my favorite pizza was on its way." He stepped onto the porch with the aid of his cane and took the box from her hand.

"Good to see you again, sir," Callum said and leaned in, cupping Gramps's hand with both of his. "I can set that inside for you if you'd like."

"I can manage. This here cane is mostly for looks, so I don't get yelled at. We'll get a chance to catch up during the games."

Callum smoothed the upturn at the edges of his grin, but Cara caught the twitch of his jaw, hinting of nerves.

Cara's lips danced around a smug smile.

"I'll come right up to the house for a rousing good time after I wolf this down!" Gramps lifted the box and shot Cara a cheeky grin.

"Let us know if you need any help," Callum offered.

"I don't need as much help as everyone likes to think I do, but I don't mind the pampering. As far as I can tell, you two are the ones that need the help," he said, pointing his cane between the two of them.

"Gramps!" Cara warned.

"Let me know if you need any advice," he said, pointing his cane at Callum. "I'm happy to share all my wisdom." Gramps chuckled or coughed. Cara wasn't sure which one.

"And I'd be happy to hear it," Callum enthusiastically offered. "Especially if it has anything to do with this one," he said, poking Cara in the side.

Cara inhaled a controlled, exasperated breath through her nose and barked, "Traitor."

"Just calling 'em like I see 'em, Cara Bear. Save me a seat on your right side, young man. Left side's my good ear," Gramps said.

Cara squeezed her eyes closed for a long blink and secured a little composure. "See ya shortly, Gramps," she said and clutched Callum's arm, pulling him back to the house.

"He's lively!" Callum said with a thread of laughter.

Pride surged in her chest. "He's definitely a straight shooter."

"You shut him down too quickly. I wanted to hear what advice he had for me," Callum said without a hint of joking. "I think I need it."

"Don't worry. I'm sure he won't be able to help sharing more at the table tonight. He's lost a bit of his filter as his hair has grayed," she said.

"I'm serious. What insight do you think your grandpa would have given me about you?"

Cara stopped short, set her hand below her chin, pretending to think hard for a second, and then lightly bopped Callum on his forehead with her palm. She clamped her hands to her hips. Her eyes sparked and shot a dart at him. "You know what? I'm calling your bluff. You don't want his thoughts. Let me tell you. If he gave his insight, you'd have been in the hot seat!" She grinned. "He's given it to me twice in the last month."

"I dare you. Call my bluff. Let's go back and ask him," he challenged, mimicking her tenacity.

She stared at his set jaw. Her gut-instinct was to say, "You're on," but instead Callum interrupted her, or more likely, rescued her.

"I'm just kidding. Let's go." Callum pulled her ahead to the house. Cara and Callum held the silence between them. She lost herself in the rhythm of their steps, the comfort of being at his side, and the ease of being with someone who doesn't have to fill every second with words.

Callum stopped and faced her, clearly going to say something, but Cara grazed his fingers to draw him along and sweetly warned, "Just keep walking, officer," not wanting this feeling to escape. The gravity of the dwindling number of days she had left in his orbit eclipsed her good sense.

"Foul play with your fingers," Callum teased, keeping humor foremost between them.

"Totally accidental. I assure you," she said.

"But it's all good," he said and gently brushed her jaw. "A touch for a touch." His flirty banter was quickly replaced with a look of determination.

Cara's heart raced, and not from fury or fright. Her hands became clammy and her thoughts jumbled. Their short walk exposed feelings she had hoped to rein in. She no longer trusted her herself and turned from the predicament she found herself in, heading for the safety of the house.

Cara started up the porch steps but stopped midway and turned around to Callum. "I want you to know that I'm glad we had this summer to clear the air between us. I was dreading being around you at the beginning, but I think it's been good. It feels good to let go of the anger and forgive you."

"Know that no matter where you go, Cara, I will miss you. I will want you."

Callum met her on the step. When he inched closer, she braced to hold her own space and not skip up the steps in cowardly haste.

Cara leaned into him, and a surprised smile brightened his face.

She took advantage of his silence and inserted, "At a loss for words?"

He pressed one finger to her lips. No words, just soft pressure. She yielded under the spell his dark eyes cast over her.

Wielding some magical power of persuasion, his arm wrapped around her side and his hand clutched hers, their fingers coiling into a familiar weave. She had no recollection of when she'd gripped the railing until the weight of him pressed against her. His chest crushed hers, spilling tingles throughout her body. His stubble grazed her cheek, and she settled against it.

He whispered low and reverently, "I'm not at a loss for words. Can I kiss you?" His syrupy breath coated her ear and undid her.

"Those are good words."

His fingers floated soft caresses down her hair and gently cupped her cheek. His thumb hitched under her chin and nudged her to look into his eyes. Every second he took to make his way to her lips felt like minutes. His lips met hers. When he softly sucked her lower lip between his, her insides trembled. She begged time to still as his mouth finally claimed hers.

Callum's kisses were never *a mere kiss*. His kisses were a fierce claiming, a joining, a belonging. With all that lay between them, she'd thought they wouldn't affect her the same way they once had, but each touch of his lips still spoke to her soul.

Soft flutter kisses climbed up her cheek until her eyes opened at the cool reality of his lips parting from her skin. She memorized his face. She'd remember this in her dreams.

"You're crying," he said in surprise as a tear dripped onto her cheek. With her face still nestled in his hands, he swiped the tear away with his thumb.

"So many goodbyes." Cara's voice cracked.

When she lowered her quivering chin, he lowered his head, trading questioning glances with her.

That same heart-wrenching loss of him—now twice. She'd sworn she'd never let herself lose Callum again.

"I don't want to let you go," he said. "I can't let you leave without a fight."

"Callum, I'm not going to fight with you."

"Not fight *with* you, Cara. Fight *for* you. For *us*. The thought of losing you again kills me. Living without oxygen would be easier than living without you." Callum scooted closer. A tiny but noticeable tic affected the lid under his right eye.

"Being strong, letting you go, feels like strangling myself with my own noose," Callum said, swallowing hard through a clenched jaw. "It's all so heavy. The loss of you. The years away from you. I see your fight for control, your fear of going down a path that might lead us back to where we once were. You won't take a chance for fear our relationship won't be the same—the way it once looked perfect in our mind's eye. So we look back and curse what we once had because it fuels our longing for what was and cannot be."

A growing loneliness gripped her with each word he spoke, an odd sensation as soft as his breath was on her face.

"We can't go back. It's gone, Cara. That's true."

Cara heard the desperation in his voice, a sad and seductive plea.

"Unless…" He lowered his voice and heightened his urgency.

"Unless?" she hesitated to ask.

"Unless, we choose to trust again, trust in a new beginning."

She heard the heartache and disappointment he tried to disguise. They had both grappled to tread water under the waves of grief. She'd had to get away to breathe, to not be pulled under in the riptide's wake…but surely…Oh Lord, she saw it now. She'd selfishly treated this man like he had superpowers, like he couldn't break. She'd pushed away from him as much as he'd pushed away from her when they were both just trying to hold their heads above water. Why had she not realized that?

"I'm leaving Monday," she said, almost stamping her foot in frustration at her inconvenient realization. Cara attempted to quell her feelings and let numbness protect her.

"Stay! I don't want to lose you again. I won't be perfect. I'm pretty sure I won't say or do everything right. But no man could ever try harder than I will."

"I have plans, a new job, a school that's depending on me."

"And you have me. So go."

His abrupt about-face startled her.

"Go to your new job. Help the kids. Discover all God has for you. But make a place for me."

He grabbed her hand, and the lines between his eyes sunk in seriousness. "I will want you every day. You and me—we're meant to be together. I can wait. I can trust God's plan, however He decides to play this out."

"You just cast this as God's doing. Pulling in the big guns now, are you? How are you so sure about our future? I want to be able to trust God with that same certainty about my life's plans. When you breathe this close to me…when you share your feelings, I fall back into letting you fill that void in my heart. You say the things I want to hear, but…"

"But?"

"I feel the chemistry between us. I do. We've had that from the very beginning. You overwhelm every part of me. You always have. Honestly, you were the happiest part of my life."

"Trust that. Don't be afraid. You make me braver, Cara. I want this. This is me fighting for us. I made a home in grief, but no more. You make me want to live better." He cradled her cheeks like he held their fragile worlds in his palms. "Will you take the risk?" he asked delicately. "Don't look in the rearview mirror."

Her lips parted to speak, but no sound spilled from them.

He waited expectantly, hoping for more.

In her heart, Cara knew there would be nothing good about this goodbye. Could she even live through it? Melodramatic as that thought sounded, her knees buckled even now. Her heart fluttered fast, arrested by his plea uttered a second time, making her unable to think in a logical sequence.

"I can't—I just can't—" she explained, nearly inaudible.

"You can't?" His shoulders slumped in defeat.

Did that gut-wrenching admission pour from her own mouth? Good God. Was trusting Callum some challenge to trust God? Her eyes darted from him to the heavens as if a clearer answer were written in the night sky. Panic rose in her chest. Could she dispel her regret, uncertainty, and doubt and believe that love always wins?

Everything about what he asked had her heart reeling. Plans were falling into place for her future. One she'd designed without Callum, and he was asking her to backpedal.

She wanted him—badly. There. She admitted it. To deny herself of him by her own volition was near impossible.

She'd begged God, promised she'd do whatever it took, if only He'd give her the love of her life back. But with each day of Callum ignoring her, she'd given up hope and turned her back on that prayer. Was this some twisted test of her pride and her patience?

Callum waited and watched and hung on tighter as the wheels of her mind and heart turned.

She gently grasped his hands and tried to explain her muddled mind. His touch utterly flummoxed her. She closed her eyes and started, "They say there's no love without risk, but—" With that one word, Callum heard her resistance. In the small space between them, she felt him hold his breath. She tightened her grip on his hands, mostly to persist in her resolve, and continued, "I can't risk–"

"You can't?" he echoed her.

"Stop interrupting! This is hard enough," she urged through an exasperated sigh.

She had prayed for God to take away her longing for Callum. Instead, He was giving her the desire of her heart. Confusion reigned. "I can't change—" she paused.

Callum drew closer, biting the corner of his lip, obviously working through something in his mind. He squeezed her hands tightly and blurted under his breath, "There's that word again. I love you, Cara. Deep inside, you know that. I have worked through things. I've changed." He ran a hand through his hair, his habit signaling frustration, and then clung again to her. "Can you trust me—have even a little faith?"

"I don't want to live through heartbreak again." She pulled her hands from his, assessing his anxious wince. "Ali's death and our breakup created a tornado, wrecking my life. I've fought to pick up the pieces, to feel safe." She paused at the confusion clouding his face.

"I need to trust myself right now."

Frown lines tightened on Callum's forehead.

She couldn't walk away from him without…without what, she didn't know. Before overthinking froze her in place, she wrapped her arms around his waist, cuddled his cheek, and locked this moment in her memory. "I love you. I probably always will."

"God, I love you," he whispered back. "I'm keeping the faith. We better get inside," he said, surrendering to her need.

TWENTY-FOUR

Sugar and salt accosted Cara's nostrils. She couldn't take the delicious wafts of sweetness much longer as she waited to eat lunch with Tori and her cousins. She should have told Bethany and Sarah to arrive thirty minutes earlier. They were never on time; each one blamed the other. She'd give them ten more minutes. If they didn't show, she'd find something to scarf down. They'd never be the wiser, but she'd be the better. With her bit of breakfast rumbling in her gut, she couldn't wait to get a gyro, too. She would grab a funnel cake during the concert. She looked forward to the sugary goodness of the Music Fest every year.

Tucked between the Community Center and the food court vendors, she propped herself against a telephone pole and watched all of Middletown saunter down Main Street, mingle with friends, select food, and set up lawn chairs in the field, anticipating the next band. She wrapped her arms across her middle, a poor attempt to assuage her hunger, and watched middle school boys whistle and point at unsuspecting girls. The high school football team strolled like a mob in their jerseys down the middle of the street. A star-struck kindergartener hugged his teacher. Local realtors and bankers handed out frisbees and magnets.

That's it. I'm not waiting.

Cara walked up to the nearest food vendor, selling pecan-caramel-covered apples, grabbed one from the table, and slapped a five-dollar bill into the hand of the teen cashier. Sinking her teeth into it, she tasted sweet relief.

Her mind wandered to an equally dangerous place, another kind of pang threatening to eat her insides. Somewhere, Callum patrolled this event.

Don't go there, she warned herself. *You leave in two days. Two days.*

The crowd in the street lightened for a brief second like clouds giving way to slivers of sunshine, and a fully uniformed Callum broke through, directly across from her on Main Street. He and Dylan stood at the edge of the Beer Garden like gatekeepers. Men and women passed by and shook his hand, probably thanking him for his bravery in protecting the town. Callum smiled at a long-haired blonde who stopped to chat. Pangs of jealousy heated Cara's insides.

All six-foot-two of him oozed virility—every stretched muscle, smoothly curved, ruggedly taut. Cara zoomed in on the sharp intake of his tanned cheeks, sloping to his stubbled, angular jawline. His eyes hidden behind aviator sunglasses, Callum was a trained surveyor with resolute focus, reserving his lopsided, boyish grin for only his most relaxed and private moments. He straightened, helped a woman with directions, pointing, and then rubbed his hands together like he was washing them. She'd bet money he had no idea he did that move at the end of all his explanations.

Women deliberately did double takes at Callum. She huffed at the appeal of the uniform. He satisfied that cliché, but she liked him better clad in boots, jeans, and a t-shirt—his comfort attire.

She couldn't take her eyes off him either. Maybe she was a little wrong to stare? Maybe a lot wrong, but it didn't hurt to enjoy a last look at him in uniform. She still appreciated that God had certainly outdone Himself when He created this man. Her safety lay in keeping her distance after her lapse last night, caving to his touch.

His gentle authority was so alluring. His full-on concentration and natural determination sent a thrill through her.

Lord have mercy.

That's how she had walked right into loving him years ago. He had caught her alone, sulking on the bleachers after a hard soccer game. He'd plopped down next to her, closer than he'd ever sat before, and searched her downcast eyes. "What's wrong?" he'd asked.

Cara, slumped with her head in her hands, swiped away welling tears blurring her vision. When the sting in her eyes softened, her flat voice cracked at the start. She looked into his kind eyes and her words gained speed, blabbing on about her missed penalty kick that sailed over the crossbar, failing to keep her team in postseason play.

He straddled the bleacher, focused solely on her, and listened without interrupting, as if there was nothing more important in the world to him than her team's loss and her fear of not getting a scholarship. Cara grew more candid with every "Uh-huh" he aired.

She finally took a deep breath and set her hand on his knee. "Thanks for listening. I'm much more relaxed. I think I got a little too worked up."

"Never!" he said, frowning at her apology. His simple declaration lifted her mood. He stood and pulled her up from the bleachers, sweeping one arm lightly around her waist.

Warmth radiated from her head to her toes. A shock wave of electricity bolted through her when he tugged her against his hip.

"But now for some fun." He flashed her a beaming smile. Cara's gaze slid to his lips. His devilish grin could have been a warning, but his mere presence and enthusiasm completely enraptured her. "Let's think of something good," he announced. He waited for her to make a suggestion, but Cara couldn't make herself think of anything but his full lips.

"Cara?" He snapped her out of her trance.

Embarrassed, she skittered backwards. Her legs hit the bleachers, and her arms flailed as she tried to grab onto Callum. "Ohhh," she yelped, fumbling to gain her balance.

Time stood still as Callum wrapped his arms around her and pulled her fully against him. Her heart jittered a dance instead of panic, and her brain stuttered to recover with an answer. Callum flickered a good-natured smile and declared, "That's easy, Cara Riley. Me and you. Together. That's what's good."

Every bit of time with Callum after that day on the bleachers had been oh so good—until it wasn't.

Guilt and regret rapped her gut. Last night on her back steps, Callum looked directly into her eyes, begged her to reach out to him once more, to see that he'd changed, to offer him hope. She couldn't give him what he wanted. Yet, today, partially hidden by festivalgoers, she secretly watched him go about his workday, his world, and dreamed, just for imagination's sake, of a life that might have been theirs.

She knew she should stay where she was, with her feet planted and her back flat against the pole, but her feet carried her toward the street. One step became two, two became four, and four became eight, like some magic drew her toward him. He must have felt her eyes on him. He turned and tipped his cap to her, like he knew she was coming.

"Hey, Cara," someone called from behind her, and Cara turned to her cousin and childhood partner-in-crime. "Where are you headed?" Bethany asked, interceding Cara's impulsive stupidity, but catching the red-hot line her stare seared through the crowd. "Oh my, yes!" Bethany concurred wickedly, following Cara's gaze. "Looking at him could keep a woman busy for a lifetime."

"Weren't we meeting in front of the fire department?" Sarah asked.

"Tori said she'd meet me here."

"But your eyes were fixed over there," Bethany taunted, pointing behind her.

Cara had been so absorbed in Callum that she'd lost track of watching for her cousins.

"Tori texted from work and said she found someone to take her place. She said we'd meet right here. I thought she'd beat you guys here," Cara explained.

"She said to meet you in the middle of the street?" Bethany called her bluff again.

"No, there by the kettle corn," Cara answered, pointing to the pole she'd been standing against before her harebrained idea to approach Callum uprooted her good sense.

"Are you two dating again?" Bethany asked, always a straight shooter. "I heard he hasn't dated anyone since you two broke up."

"Oh, wow," Sarah gasped. She slapped her hand over her heart, directing a look of amazement at Cara. "How sweet."

Bethany pointed at him. "Yep, he's got it bad for you, Cara."

All three cousins stared at Callum, and his head turned in their direction again, as if they had alerted him.

Cara slapped Bethany's hand down and frowned. "Don't point."

"Okay, Miss Manners," Bethany said.

"Who's the other officer with him?" Sarah asked, still staring.

"Dylan. He's his best friend," Cara answered.

"Oh, he's hot, too," Sarah said in her best suggestive manner.

Cara nudged Bethany with her elbow. "You didn't tell Sarah that Dylan asked you out?"

"Sarah, Dylan asked me to his family reunion tomorrow." Bethany's tone mocked Cara. "I took pity on him and agreed," Bethany joked with a wink.

"He is definitely not a pity date," Sarah said, still staring at Dylan. "But meeting the family on a first date? Yikes."

"Dylan got down on his knees and begged me to spare him the pain of his grandma and grandpa and aunts and uncles asking who he was dating." Bethany animated with praying hands.

"A penchant for drama, wouldn't you say?" Cara said, but she could totally imagine Dylan resorting to those silly tactics.

"It's better than guessing how a guy feels," Bethany answered.

"So much better. That's for sure," Cara said.

"Way easier to deal with," Sarah agreed with the obvious.

"Callum and I went out this summer," Cara blurted.

"O.M.G. What?" Bethany squealed, clasping hands over her mouth. "Go on!"

"My dad's on the board of the animal shelter. He hooked twenty dollars from me for two raffle tickets and laid them on dates with Callum. I won. I went. We went axe throwing, boating on the pond, and got ice cream. Two dates and they're over." Cara's matter-of-fact objectivity didn't fool anyone. She braced for their inquisition.

"If you say so," Bethany doubted, wide-eyed. "I wouldn't describe what I'd witnessed as *over*. The dates may be, but not the feelings you have for him. They're heading this way, and Callum's gawking at you, Cara."

Her heart thrummed roughly against her chest.

"If there's nothing between you two, then why are you panicking?" Sarah asked.

"I'm not panicking." Cara stared at the crushed popcorn at her feet, concentrating on slowing her heart rate before Callum reached them.

"You better find a place for those fidgety hands. They're almost here," Sarah whispered under her breath.

"Coming to listen to some Christian music, ladies?" Dylan asked, always friendly. "Ready for a good time?" he added, focusing solely on Bethany.

"Sure am. You going to join me?" Bethany suggested and nudged him with her elbow.

"The uniform relegates me to watching," he said and winked. Leaning toward Bethany so only she could hear, he added, "I'll keep an eye on you for sure."

"I know you'll be checking things out, too." Bethany prodded Callum. Her gaze darted from Callum to Cara.

Cara felt her cousins' eyes on her. Pressing her hands into her pockets, she avoided them by nonchalantly awaiting Callum's reply.

"I'm always watching," Callum said in his official demeanor. He feigned surveillance of the hungry masses milling about the food court.

Cara caught the trace of a smile in his voice and gathered his suggested meaning.

Her cousins grinned at her.

"Are you still introducing the band, Cochren and Company?" Callum asked.

"It's going to be short and sweet."

"You'll be great," Callum added.

Bethany and Dylan carried the rest of the conversation while Cara and Callum exchanged glances.

"I'm starving," Cara popped in, interrupting Bethany's flirting. "We have to decide which food truck will be dinner and get in line so we can grab a good spot on the lawn before the band hits the stage."

They said their goodbyes, and a wave of relief to be out from under Callum's watchful eyes washed over Cara. As they made their way to the gyro vendor, she pleaded with herself not to look back. Callum wanted her. She needed no affirmation of that. She had pushed him away, said her goodbye, just last night. The pressure in her chest wasn't nervousness over introducing a band. That would be numbingly simple compared to managing the pangs of regret twisting her insides. She told herself to stop obsessing about her decision. But she'd also always believed she should listen to her gut, and it was sending her mixed messages.

✶✶✶

Why her dad thought it would be great practice for her career to speak to hundreds of strangers from a stage, she didn't know. That's what she got for suggesting this band for Middletown's music festival. This would be her last official duty for him.

She'd played soccer in front of hundreds of shouting fans. Even though that was totally different, she could use the same tactics not to be unnerved by this crowd. She'd focus on the next play—in this case—her short, memorized lines.

An hour later, Cara tested the microphone as she called, "Hey, everybody." Cara fed off the jazzed energy of the crowd as she introduced herself. "Welcome to Middletown Music Festival. I'm Cara Riley. It's great to see so many people here today to support our Christian band." The concertgoers cheered and stragglers settled onto their blankets and lawn chairs. Cara went off-script. "I can't wait to hear them play one of my favorites, 'Running Home.' You won't be able to stay seated in your lawn chairs during that one. There's not one of us who hasn't felt broken at some point, struggling to pull life together but feeling like you're running in circles." A hush fell over the onlookers. "Maybe tonight you need assurance that God has a plan for your life." She turned to the band members who joined her on stage, and then got back on script. "Cochren and

Company's songs may have you believing in second chances. Put your hands together and give them a warm welcome."

Warm cheers and whistles rose through the trees as the keyboard hit its first notes to "Running Home."

Cara hopped down the bandstand's back steps and nearly ran straight into Callum at the bottom. He reached for her, wrapping his hand softly around her forearm, and slipped her away from the eyes of the audience, stopping behind the band's trailer. He moved fully into her space. Cara looked up at him, so close she could see tiny lines at the corners of his eyes, squinting in the sun.

"I want to say these last weeks with you are what I prayed for. I wanted a way for us to connect, to move beyond the biggest mistake of my life. Every time we're together, I can't stop wanting more." He thrust a hand through his hair, grabbing the back of his neck, careful with his next words.

"I'm thankful God's given you and me a second chance. It's been a different kind of second chance, for sure. It's been tough for you, but it's been good, too. You can see that, right?" His brow furrowed at his question.

Cara nodded in agreement. She could see that. The bridge they'd created. The progress they'd made in communicating. The forgiveness she'd offered him. The understanding they'd sought from one another.

"Before you leave for your new job, I was hoping to spend a little more time together. Tomorrow evening?" He leaned in close to her. His breath brushed her lips as he said, "But no matter how many times we're together, it'll never be enough for me."

How could she respond to that? His confession made her shake like she was alone on stage under a spotlight.

Loving this man used to be simple. She inched back from him, uncertain of what she'd say until she had spoken. His smoldering eyes reached for her. The weight of his urgency swirled around her.

She thought about what he'd said. *God's given us this summer. It's been good.* She agreed. It had been crazymaking at times, but she could look back and see the good, too. *It'll never be enough.* Traces of that sentiment disturbed her peace. *I could reach out to him once I'm settled. A long-distance relationship might be a start. It would be a tough hurdle.* Wrestling with that idea was too big to tackle at this moment. Right now, all he needed was a yes or no answer.

Callum tangled his fingers in hers. "Do you have time for an early dinner? We could grab Italian, your favorite. You'd call that a perfect farewell."

Her throat tightened, and she tried to temper the fight between her reluctance and her longing. She hated saying goodbye to him once again. With a voice far steadier than the heart beating fiercely in her chest, she answered, "I'll make time."

He kissed her lightly on her cheek and squeezed her hand three times, once for each word he didn't say aloud, but she understood just the same.

TWENTY-FIVE

Walking into church the next morning, Cara felt raw. An amplifying jitter coursed its way through her nerves. She hated this kind of drama—the never-ending goodbye to Callum. The relentless urgency to end the pain that made her feel she'd have to Houdini her way from chains or halt a careening semi-truck. Her chest pounded in a way that threatened to drive her to her praying knees.

Her eyes on alert for Callum, she stayed glued beside her shuffling Gramps as he greeted his way through the church foyer to her family's row of seats.

Several people wrapped her in hugs and politely inquired about her move. They had been the 'hospital' that mended her through those first months after Ali's death. They had prayed for peace—a peace that allowed her to continue with her schooling when she felt like quitting. She artfully kept the conversation on her new job and away from any closer personal inspection. That would lead down plenty of rabbit trails and colliding emotions over Callum. She wouldn't be able to hide her wobbling heart or searching eyes. Everyone would surmise she still loved Callum, and it would be true.

Cara had slipped a time or two into an unfamiliar church on campus, where no history connected her. No shared sorrow had slid behind the smiles of the greeters. No pastor challenged her to belong. No commitment had tied her to service. Her heart hadn't engaged with those families like it did with those greeting her now. She'd kept her sorrow carefully wrapped within her chest, a safe distance from people and a church.

But she had ranted plenty in the privacy of her apartment, rants she could only throw at God. She'd have entangled Ali or Callum in her crisis of faith, but her closest confidants, the only ones outside of her family she dared to show her weary, lacking soul, were gone from her life. That sanctuary of Ali and Callum no longer existed. Now it was just her and her broken heart before God.

Cara camped at the end of their row, watching her cousin's little boy in the next row vroom trucks up and down his mom's arm while Lexi cradled her newborn in a wrap, coal black hair and ruby cheeks peeking through. Cara admired Lexi's grit and determination and had always thought they were a lot alike. She'd been varsity captain of the volleyball team when Cara was a freshman. Everyone would agree that Lexi had led by example—a faith filled example that Cara remembered praying to be like. Now, she couldn't feel further from Lexi's kind of faith.

The pastor worked his way to the podium, and Cara glanced back at a click of the church sanctuary doors opening.

"Who are you looking for?" Tori asked, insinuation dripping from her voice.

"No one," she lied and turned her attention back to the platform.

Click.

Cara couldn't help but glance back at the latecomer.

"It's not like him to be late to anything," Tori puzzled low in Cara's ear.

"Who?" Cara asked. Tori was too astute to fall for Cara's innocent act.

"I'm not even going to dignify that question with an answer. If you pay attention to Pastor Caleb, you might get your mind off him—I mean the door," Tori giggled.

Cara completely missed the announcements. At some point, Pastor Caleb had transitioned to his introduction, typically a joke he'd craftily weave into the main points of his sermon. She missed the beginning of his sketch about a Pentecostal dog.

Click.

Cara squeezed her sister's knee briefly, and Tori, understanding her signal, peeked toward the sanctuary doors and shook her head no.

Calm your nerves, she told herself.

By the first point in the pastor's *Trusting God in Transition* message, Callum hadn't slunk into the back row. For a guy who prided himself on being punctual, Cara knew he wouldn't be joining his family this late into a Sunday service, so she stopped turning around at each click of the door and concentrated on the sermon.

Pastor Caleb led the congregation in reading from Joshua 1:1-9 on the large overhead screen. He asked them to repeat the phrase *strong and courageous* aloud three times, each time louder. She wasn't sure what that responsorial was supposed to do, but she repeated the words along with the rest of the congregation. She had always hated that kind of engagement, but this time she had to admit that hearing the collective voices declare those words in unison bolstered her somehow.

The questions from the pulpit captured her attention. "Are you moving into a new era? Facing changes and challenges?"

Yes and yes! She perked up and listened more closely.

"Then walk with God." Pastor Caleb answered his own question.

I haven't been good about that. If only it were that simple. Cara deflated a bit.

"Our life is always in continual flux even if we don't recognize it." Pastor Caleb pointed at the large screen behind him and encouraged the congregation to write down or take a picture of his next words. "The movement of God must never be measured by the slowness of a human life or by our inadequacies. God's plan isn't ours."

Continual flux is exhausting, unsettling, nerve-wracking. You can bet I'm like one of the grumbling Israelites in the wilderness. Thank goodness God doesn't wait on me to part the waters or understand what He's doing.

Cara missed a large chunk of what else the pastor said, but his use of the word *purpose* drew her attention.

"…The idea of finding our life's purpose gets thrown around a lot these days. While God certainly wants us to be inspired by the life He's created for us, above all, He wants us to be transformed. Continually." Pastor Caleb might as well have been speaking solely to her. "Some things we face in life seem like impossible struggles. It's natural to want to run from our difficulties, to reject pain and hardship. They certainly couldn't be God's blessing. Am I right?"

Most definitely.

"I caution you not to run away from your trials. Don't reject working through hard things. That may be where you find God's greatest blessing. That may be where He hones your resilience and strength. These moments are when He intends to transform you." The word rejection spun her thoughts back to Callum.

It was a huge leap from God to Callum, but she couldn't help where her thoughts wandered. *The domino effect on my life. Ali died. Callum's rejection. Not understanding God's plan. Refusing to trust Callum again.*

"Faith gets God's attention."

Doubt beamed like a neon sign in her skull.

Callum asked me to have a little faith.

"Faith is taking God at His Word in times of trouble, transition, changes, and challenges… In times of transition, when the waters' rush picks up or changes course, our faith will be greatly tested."

Cara read the Scripture that flashed on the screen: "And we know that for those who love God all things work together for good, for those who are called according to His purpose."

But reading Romans 8:2, and believing good comes out of suffering, is a mental marathon apart.

"We are not always grateful for change or for our unique challenges. We don't often choose to embrace them. We camouflage our discouragements, our despondency, our hard places."

Be grateful for death and rejection and loneliness? What purpose do those serve? Everything feels so upside-down, inside-out. Camouflage was the only way I got through. But Mom and Dad, Gramps, and Tori saw through my mask. And darn, even Callum saw my pain.

"But the Spirit sees and gives us the help we need."

When? How?

Pastor Caleb asked everyone to reflect and fill in the blank of the line on the big screen for themselves.

_____*has come to an end, but God's plan has not.*

"His promises haven't ended. They are still true. His promises don't end with you," he encouraged.

Cara inserted in the blank *Ali's life, my relationship with Callum, my life in Middletown. What is God promising me?*

As if he'd read her thoughts, Pastor Caleb answered, "God spoke something into your life. Now's the time to ask Him. To hear a response. God's a realist. He's not a Pollyanna. He knows your hurt, your uncertainty. He speaks so you understand, but doubt hinders us from seeing His work."

Cara felt recrimination. *But I have so much doubt!*

"Joshua 1:9 shows us that God will be wherever you go, but sometimes, He will make you fight for what you want."

Cara exhaled in exhaustion at that thought. Cara couldn't turn her brain off...the wanting Callum...the wanting to trust him.

"...But you must decide what you need to bring to the challenge," he said adamantly.

Instantly, Cara thought, *Trust. My trust is weak.*

"...Ask God what He is asking of you." The nudging from the pulpit continued.

A quick answer came to her. *Get your stubborn self out of His way.* This blatant truth hit her so clearly.

"...Our response must be to trust Him through the challenges."

And how do I do that, just step out of this shaking boat onto the ocean of oncoming waves?

God orchestrated this message for her. Remorse and regret wrestled in her heart. Cara bowed her head in case her watery eyes reflected a window into her soul.

God had interesting timing. He superseded her

overwhelm and humbled her defenses. When the congregation stood at the worship leader's direction, Cara followed seconds later, delayed by her shaking insides. Every part of her wanted to cry out *thank you* to God for His revelation. She closed her eyes and settled into the truth of the worship, communion with God.

As everyone started singing, "Rest on Us" hit her differently than it ever had. The words washed over her like a refreshing waterfall. The Spirit came down and whispered *surrender*. Something in her chest dislodged. Her heart pounded and then concession flooded through her.

With each song the congregation sang together, Cara felt the Spirit inch its way into her soul, urging her to be stronger, more courageous, more trusting.

Silently, she confessed to God her self-reliance and arrogance at expecting life to go smoothly. While relying on herself wasn't all bad, she knew she had to lean more on God. She confessed her need to trust Him more with her broken places, to believe He could bring good from her pain. She forgave Callum for his mistakes and asked God to help her trust him again.

She renewed a promise to Him she'd made at church camp at the age of twelve—to humble herself enough to trust and follow. For the last two years, she'd managed a tightly vaulted control over her heart. She vowed to surrender. To offer hope to others, she'd need to show more vulnerability with her own pain. Under her breath, she invited Him to mold her life from this moment on. This was a familiar giving again, a necessary bridge to a fresh start.

She prayed a promise to God that felt like a new

beginning.

I will trust that through my tears and anguish You will give me reasons to smile and laugh. I will trust You to teach me to praise You through the pain and doubts in my life.

Pastor Caleb ended the service with the benediction she'd heard every Sunday in this church. "The Lord bless you and keep you…"

Click.

Someone left before the benediction ended.

Cara hesitated in her chair after the benediction, her head down.

Tori wrapped her arm around her, pulling their heads to one another, and whispered, "I'm right here if you need me."

Cara smiled a thanks at her sister and hugged her right back. Self-conscious of her red-rimmed eyes, Cara fiddled with the bulletin and avoided onlookers by collecting her phone, purse, and keys.

When she looked up, Callum's parents were huddled together with her parents in the middle aisle. Cara's dad whispered into her mom's ear, concern contorting his face. Grasping his shoulder, her mom gasped and peered at Cara and then spun back to her dad, summoning an answer without words. Her dad caught her eyes, and she recognized his tender glance of heartache. He didn't speak to her. His jaw tightened, and he grabbed at his mom's elbow to loosen her grasp on him. Her parents locked eyes. An understanding passed between them, something she knew nothing about. He nodded his head, speaking without words as only a couple that had been married for thirty years could, and hurried through the minglers and out the door.

"What?" Cara asked as she and Tori made their way to their mom, who plastered on a masked smile for Cara.

"Honey, let's step outside," her mom breathed in a close whisper. "I need to tell you something out of earshot."

Her mom would not meet her eyes but grabbed her purse from the floor and headed down the middle aisle. A familiar dread overwhelmed Cara, and her heart pounded as she bee-lined to follow, impatient for news. Cara skirted around a group chatting about lunch plans, only to accidentally brush against a toddler darting across the aisle, knocking him on his bum. Cara pulled the stunned little blond boy upright and apologized. He saw it as nothing more than an inconsequential slowdown and carried on his running way. His cheerful mom popped from the row and apologized to Cara, creating another barrier between her and her flight to the door.

Cara's faint smile must have worked too well. She didn't want to be impolite, but she had little patience just now for social niceties. The young mom sped from one topic to another without Cara's input. This mom was one of those people Gramps would say could talk the legs off a centipede. Cara tapped her hand against her leg, ticking away the seconds. She shuffled from foot to foot, searching the sanctuary for her mom. Stretching to glance over her head, Cara interrupted her with a white lie, right there in church.

"It's been lovely meeting you, Karly, but I need to run. My Gramps needs my help getting to the car." Cara had no idea where Gramps had scooted off to.

She opened the door and peered outside, but her mom was nowhere to be found. She saw Gramps visiting with a friend on the parking lot. Peering once again into the sanctuary, she found her mom, purse clutched to her chest, chit-chatting with strained politeness on her face.

Cara saw Tori and pulled her outside. They waited against her Jeep.

"Mom needs to get out here and tell us what's going on," Cara said.

"There's Mom. She's coming," Tori said.

Her mom rushed to Cara, clutching her in her arms.

"Mom, you're scaring me. What happened?" Irritation tinged her voice.

"Cara, this is hard to say." She took a deep breath and continued. "Callum's been shot and—"

"No—" Cara bent to her knees, hiding between the cars. Nothing else her mom said made sense. She felt herself begin to implode.

Tori wrapped her arm around Cara. "Breathe, Cara," she said.

Her mom grasped Cara's arms and pulled her up. With a gentle fierceness, she said, "Listen to me. He's at the hospital. They're taking good care of him. We don't know anything more about the shooting." Cara lifted her head to her mom's determination. "Your dad is going to the hospital. He promised to call with information as soon as possible."

"I have to see Callum," Cara pleaded.

"I know, sis. Hang on. We've got you," Tori comforted, wrapping her arm around Cara.

"His parents headed to the hospital. Let's get Gramps. We'll go home, make lunch, and wait to hear from your dad," her mom said. "And we'll pray."

While they prepared lunch, her mom's nervous chatter

was a feeble distraction. "You know, we're a small town with a lot of rural area. We're easy access off the highway. Even though Chicago and St. Louis are just hours away, honestly, some of the worst crimes in this community have been committed by our very own citizens. We have our fair share of vandalism and burglary. I remember the days I left my keys in the ignition and thought nothing of it. I never locked the door to our house or garage. We can't do that anymore around here…"

Cara moved the food around on her plate and excused herself to her room when her mom ran out of steam. A cell phone rang, and Cara ran back down the stairs, miming for her mom to put it on speakerphone. She heard the nuance of controlled stress in her dad's voice.

"All I know is he's in surgery to remove the bullet in his arm. Neighbors on the porch across the street saw a man in a white SUV pull into the lot of the police department. He got out but remained leaning against his car until Callum exited the building. Neighbors heard two shots fired—"

"I'm coming now, Dad." Cara grabbed her keys and purse, and bolted out the door.

TWENTY-SIX

Cara's dad met her at the ER doors and pulled her into a long embrace. Relief and concern clouded his smile. "He's going to be fine after some therapy and time off. They'll keep him overnight to watch for infection. If all goes well, he'll go home tomorrow. He wasn't awake yet when I stepped in to visit. I'm heading out to give you and the family time with him," he said, doing his best to reassure her.

The elevator pinged and the doors opened slower than pond water flows. She dashed down the antiseptic corridor, black and white tile against white walls. Her clunky shoes echoed down the hall, mimicking the pandemonium wreaking havoc on her nerves and her stomach. She counted down the numbers to Callum's room and stopped to compose herself outside 1112.

Never once had she allowed herself to entertain the idea that Callum could be shot on her hometown streets. He'd accused her a time or two of Pollyanna thinking, but she preferred to define herself as a glass half-full kind of girl. Standing outside his door, she suspected she'd lived with her eyes wide shut. They were wide open now. Through the small glass window, she peeked into a heavy dose of reality—a bandaged Callum, eyes closed, lying statue still in a hospital bed.

Callum's mom perched on the edge of his bed; her hands clasped around his. Her head nodded while his dad's lips moved. Was his dad talking to him or praying over him? One of a million prayers in his lifetime, she was sure. Mr. Hall nestled close to Callum's bandaged head and carefully wrapped his arm around his shoulder. His entire left arm was wrapped in gauze.

Cara zeroed in on Callum's pale face and then searched for the rise and fall of his chest. She gasped at the wretched vise that constricted her chest, at the inconceivable thought that he could have died.

"Can I help you?" a quiet voice called from behind her.

She turned around to face a pencil-thin nurse in light blue scrubs.

"Is it okay to go in?"

The nurse flipped through papers on a clipboard. "What's your name?"

"Cara. I'm his friend." She flushed at the awkward label, such a distant term for what he meant to her. She recovered with a polite smile and a glance through the window. Unwilling to invade the intimacy of that moment, she leaned back against the wall.

They had huddled against these same cold hospital walls waiting on news of Ali. Hearts shattered, drowning in disbelief, they had limped through the awful reality they'd have to return home without their precious girl.

"You're on his approved visitors list. The restrictions are merely a safety precaution. You're welcome to go in."

Cara's lungs responded to her growing anxiety, constricting like she was siphoning air through a straw. She slumped over and grabbed her thighs, coughing to breathe.

"Are you okay?" the sweet voice asked and crouched to meet Cara's eyes, her sleek ponytail slapping over her shoulder.

Not in the least Cara wanted to shout, but she nodded yes and fished through the front pocket of her purse for her inhaler.

Cara took a minute to let the medicine take effect and said a quick prayer before entering. *Lord, help me now.* She lightly knocked and cracked the door open, stalling at the entrance. "I'm sorry to interrupt. Is it okay to come in?" she said in a near whisper.

"Come in. Come in," Callum's mom pleaded and hurried to wrap Cara into a cocoon of coifed hair, perfume, and tenderness.

Cara sniffled, suddenly weepy for so many reasons.

"I'm so glad you're here," she said, looking Cara in the face. Mrs. Hall's eyes were dark from where she'd swiped away running mascara. "He can use our healing prayers."

Shame mixed with regret. Before this shooting, the last time she'd actually prayed for Callum was before she'd made her decision to leave Middletown.

Mrs. Hall held Cara close as she escorted her to Callum's bedside, her manicured nails digging into Cara's waist, tethering them together.

Cara couldn't breathe when she saw the man she loved tied to monitors and machines, his arm and head wrapped in bandages. The proud and powerful man she revered lay vulnerable before her, a mere mortal. He'd lived in her head and heart as invincible. She clasped her hand across her heart, stunned at what could have been, but for a few inches.

It didn't matter that her dad had assured her Callum would be okay. She was not okay. Not in the least. Cara leaned her thighs against Callum's bed to keep her knees from buckling and patted down the panic in her chest.

Mrs. Hall hovered over Callum's face. She softly brushed his dark, thick eyebrows with her finger and then kissed him on his forehead above each eye. Cara wished Callum would open his eyes. She needed to look into them. To see his strength again.

His mom tugged him into a light embrace, resting her cheek gently against his, careful to avoid his arm. The corner of her mouth turned up in a slight smile as a tear spilled from the corner of her eye and trailed down her neck. Cara heard her whisper, "I'm so grateful."

Being near Callum and seeing his condition for herself sent overwhelming waves of relief through Cara. She fought to keep tears from streaming down her cheeks.

Experience told Cara that Mrs. Hall wouldn't tough love her agony away. She'd find an equilibrium between peace and pain. Like the tides, her grief had ebbed and flowed, waves placid one minute and crashing against her the next.

"I love you so much," Callum's mom said and pressed another lingering kiss against his forehead. Turning to Cara, she said, "We were just going to step out for a bit and give you a few minutes alone. They told us to expect the pain meds in his IV to make him groggy for a while." Mrs. Hall looked down at Callum, and a deep V formed between her brows. "He hasn't woken up yet, but he may go in and out of sleep."

Mrs. Hall whispered in Cara's ear before heading for the door, "The doctor said, except for the pain and mental trauma, he'll get physically better each day. God is so good. And you being here is an answer to prayer." She dared not ask whose prayer she was an answer to.

"I love you, son." A weary Mr. Hall studied his son as he squeezed his hand. His countenance hung like he carried the weight of the world. Of course, he did. He was the kind of dad whose kids were his world.

Cara hugged Mr. Hall as he rounded the end of the bed, saying a prayer for him to walk through the second hardest thing he'd faced in his sixty years. She prayed for the peace of Matthew 11 in her head. *Come to me, all you who are weary and burdened, and I will give you rest.*

She stood alone at Callum's bedside. Monitors beeped. Machines whirred. Lines spiked up and down electronic screens. She searched for the rise and fall of his chest. This rhythm was a welcome proof of life. She might be overreacting, but she didn't care.

Eventually, she pulled the leather chair Mr. Hall vacated closer to Callum's head and settled as close to him as possible, gently setting her hand on his chest. Just maybe he'd sense she was there. She couldn't look away from the blood-stained bandage wrapping Callum's forehead. His arm pinned to his side. The drip from the IV line stuck in his hand.

Déjà vu washed over Cara. She'd stood beside Callum's parents and witnessed Ali laid out, covered in a white hospital sheet like this, looking like she would awaken at Cara's whisper. But she hadn't. Sobbing, Cara had collapsed into her dad's arms.

She couldn't fathom the toll seeing Callum in a hospital bed was having on his parents. She knew the toll it was taking on her. She had to remind her own heart to beat. She wanted to wrap him in her arms and never let him go.

Less than twenty-four hours ago, before he lay injured in a hospital bed, she'd stubbornly said goodbye to protect her own heart. Now, she regretted turning away from him. The scab around the hole in her heart scratched open and her greatest fear poured out—a world without Callum.

Her eyes blurred and throat tightened. The words the pastor had spoken this morning came back to her clear as glass. "Faith gets God's attention." God had her attention. She was convinced this was the moment of faith He'd been preparing her to step into.

Cara pulled her phone from her pocket and read the words she'd taken a screenshot of. "Faith is taking God at His Word in times of trouble, transition, changes, and challenges." She had promised God a new beginning.

Nothing felt more like the new beginning she needed than this one with Callum.

She hated that she couldn't lay aside her foolish pride and stubborn fears until she was faced with losing Callum from her life forever. She'd taken it for granted that he'd always be around. Callum had asked her to have faith. Looking back, God had been softening her heart all summer toward Him and toward Callum despite her fears. Had He been slowly building her faith for this moment?

In response to Pastor Caleb's words, she'd promised God her trust. She would trust Him to help her smile through her tears. She promised to look for the good He created in her life. She knew that for the rest of her life, Callum would be her good.

"You and me. That's what's good," he'd once said.

The urgency to talk to Callum pulled her from her seat. She wanted to tell him about how God had been strengthening her, to explain her stubborn heart's change. Not being able to share the courage she'd found was akin to torture.

She sat on the bed, grabbed his hand, and spilled her heart aloud to him and to God. She prayed, not out of habit, but out of need.

"Thank you, Lord, for saving Callum," she started and so did her tears. "A world without him is unimaginable. I thought that even if we weren't together for the rest of our lives, I could go on, knowing he was alive and well. That was once enough. But I see now, nothing would be right if he were gone from my life. You've been guiding me to this point. To find the courage and faith to trust You and Callum. I see that a new beginning with him has been Your good for me all along. You've been waiting for me to step out and trust the gift You were giving me."

She paused and added a secondary plea. "Lord, Callum knows in his heart of hearts that this stubborn girl loves him. Help me continue to trust our relationship through You."

When she finished, her heart was slightly more stable.

She leaned closer to Callum. He'd always be part of her. She reached for him, masked in the shadows of the dim light and the sun spilling through the slats of closed shades, and grazed her knuckles over his stubble.

"I love you. Forever. Always have. Always will," she whispered.

"Same," his scratchy voice rasped. His eyes flickered open and clung to hers for a few seconds before falling back to sleep.

TWENTY-SEVEN

Before God and a sleeping Callum, Cara admitted she wanted him—a longing she'd squelched before today. Sharing her hidden desire out loud had fueled the smoldering ember of hope in the pit of her stomach that told her things might not be over—not really, not if she didn't want them to be.

Now that she'd given oxygen to her desire, she could barely contain the urgency to talk to him, to figure out how this would work. She glanced at her watch for the tenth time in five minutes, watching Callum for any waking expression. She paced the room as time ticked away. She wanted to talk with him before his parents returned.

One question cycled more than others through her mind. *Am I changing my whole life for a man?* And only one answer streamed through her brain like a neon billboard. *Yes, because that man is Callum!*

Alone with her own thoughts, the error of her ways haunted her—her rush to judge him, her lack of forgiveness. Coming back to Middletown, she thought they'd feel like strangers, distant and unsure of each other. At the beginning of the summer, they were. Angry, she'd fumbled through even talking to him, but as weeks passed and they spent more time together, she glimpsed the closeness they once shared. The intimate moments flashed through her mind—Callum brushing her hair back to see her tattoo, his entwining his fingers with hers, his touch anywhere on her body tugging on her heart. Each moment had left her craving another. She hadn't prepared for his resolute pursuit. She'd kept him at a distance, danced around their deep connection. When her heart had whispered it couldn't hurt to give Callum another try, her head had screamed it most certainly could hurt. She never thought being pulled in two directions would end like this.

"Cara?" he called, and her heart leaped.

They locked eyes, and every nerve of her attention fixed on him. She couldn't look away. Callum blinked heavily like he might close his eyes in sleep again and panic rose in her throat.

"You're here?" he asked and tilted his head, working through something in his mind.

"There's nowhere else I could be," she confessed, relieved to hear his voice.

Callum patted the bed for her to sit closer to him. "Come here."

As much as she wanted to race ahead with her thoughts and feelings and share her heart's revelations, she treaded lightly. "I didn't know you were working today?"

"I covered Dylan's shift." He attempted a half smile and struggled to pick up the weight of his arm to rest his hand on hers. He slowly jiggled his fingers poking from the wrap covering his entire arm and half of his hand. He winced and exhaled a heavy breath. "An angel was watching over me," he said, his voice shaky.

Cara captured the inside of her cheek between her teeth and steadied her shaky voice. She couldn't speak the words aloud, but her eyes held her meaning. "I'm so thankful nothing worse happened," she added.

"I hope my guns don't cave in when I wear a tight t-shirt," he said and shot her a wide-eyed goofy grin. The pain meds caused him to speak with a bit of a drawl. Callum never acknowledged the danger in his work or talked about the fear of it. Despite the life-threatening morning, he was attempting to appear upbeat.

His good-natured humor eased her anxiety. "Oh, brother. Do guys ever get over their guns? Your guardian angel was working overtime today."

"I'm thinking my guardian angel might be a little off kilter. Might need more training. Maybe he needs glasses."

"Your parents stepped out for a quick bite. My dad was here earlier, but I had to see that you were okay. You really scared me." She stared at him in concern.

"And what's that look for?" he asked.

"I'm worried about you. How are you doing? Really."

"It happened so fast. It took me by surprise." Callum cautiously shifted to sit up higher in the bed.

Cara adjusted his pillows and gently kissed his cheek.

"You can't take anything for granted these days, I guess," he said, contemplating his own words.

"No, we can't," she agreed wholeheartedly. Cara was ready to share her change of heart, but Callum continued.

"Middletown has always been a small town with low crime, but a couple of things that happened here would curl your eyelashes. A guy killed his mom and hid her in a barn. A little girl was murdered, and police were able to solve that case using DNA."

"My dad told me about that. Good police work."

"The day seemed so normal, then I took two steps outside the department and heard a pop. This shooting blindsided me. That guy I arrested for beating up his wife at the grocery store tried to kill me. I knew he was bad news, but I didn't think he'd come looking to settle a score."

Callum stopped his story when the nurse entered. She greeted him, checked the machines, and offered him some water. She smiled at Cara and scooted out.

"I dove behind my squad car for cover. When I stood and returned fire, he had his gun fixed on me. I got a shot off before I dropped, or he may have gotten me again." Callum rubbed his bandaged forehead.

Cara felt sick to her stomach.

"Next thing I remember, Lieutenant Harris was holding my head and telling me to stay down and that an ambulance was on the way. He told me I got the guy."

"Did it hurt?"

"At first, it didn't hurt that much. I guess my mind was so focused. When I saw how much blood there was, I wasn't convinced I'd only been shot once. I looked at my arm and that's when the red-hot pain hit. That's all I remember. I guess I passed out."

"He ambushed you, Callum! He was a monster! You could have been killed!" Her high pitch sounded more unhinged and argumentative than the desperately grateful she hoped to convey.

"But I wasn't." His eyes chased hers until she looked into his. "I'm still here with you." She read the hope he'd wanted his words to mark.

"And I'm glad." Every fiber in her meant it.

"I know you are," he asserted. Their eye contact held a weight and a promise she'd not felt between them for a long time. Then Callum broke into a slow, satisfied grin as he said, "If I recall, you plan to trust me with a fresh start."

He'd heard every word of her prayer. She wasn't sure exactly what he recalled, but now was the right time to make sure he understood.

"Callum, I can't make a guarantee that things will work out between us. I guess no one can really do that at the start. I want a new start with you. I know you want that, too—"

"Yes. Yes, I do."

"I lied to myself. I told myself I couldn't trust I'd be safe with you. Honestly, I don't want to hurt that badly ever again, so much so that I thought keeping you out of my life was the surest way to avoid that kind of suffering."

"I'll never hurt you again."

"But it would hurt more not having you in my life. The truth is that I couldn't dare to be near you because I love you. Always have."

"Always will," he said finishing their line, and she could see a smile blooming on his face.

"You deserve a love that will risk her heart."

"Cara, you are that woman," he refuted.

She pushed ahead despite his protests. "Someone who doesn't want guarantees but guarantees she's all in."

"I want you—" he started, mustering strength to convince her, but she didn't need it.

Cara plowed ahead. Her mind was made up. "And I am that girl for you! You're my first love, my only love."

Cara kissed him long and tenderly. When she pulled away, he pulled her right back to him with his good arm for another binding kiss.

"I'm never, ever letting you go," he sighed contentedly.

"You'll have to. I hear your parents in the hallway." Cara stepped to the foot of the bed.

The door opened and his parents' voices floated into the room. They stalled in the doorway, greeting the doctor.

When they finally turned to enter, his mom cheered, "I'm so glad you're awake," and nearly ran to his bedside.

"So am I," he said, his eyes glued on Cara.

A young doctor extended his arm and shook Callum's hand. "Hi, I'm Doctor Max. I'll give you all an update and let you get back to visiting. The bullet grazed your humerus causing a comminuted shaft fracture right here in the midportion of your bone." He pointed to a spot in the middle of Callum's upper arm. "That means the impact from the bullet broke your bone into multiple pieces. You have some pins and screws in there to stabilize the bone. We cleaned up the damage to the surrounding soft tissue. Everything looks clean. We'll go over everything again before you leave. Do you have any questions so far?"

When Callum didn't respond, his mom looked suspiciously between Cara and Callum who gazed at one another as if no one else were in the room. "Callum, did you hear what the doctor said?" she asked.

Callum didn't look away. "Sure did."

The doctor continued, "We'll keep your arm in that splint while the swelling goes down. You'll go home with a sling for comfort and arm support. I'll see you in my office in a week to see how you're progressing."

"I couldn't be better." Callum beamed at Cara.

When all eyes turned to Cara, she ducked her chin at the embarrassing blush heating her face.

The doctor raised his eyebrows and chuckled, "That's the attitude we like to hear." Doctor Max lowered his eyes and studied his chart for a few seconds. The energy in the room Cara and Callum created was distractingly palpable.

He cleared his throat and continued, "We'll switch you to some bracing, depending on how things are progressing. Someone from PT will drop by your room in a little bit to give mobility instructions. We want to restore muscle strength, mobility, and flexibility. Fortunately, there was no nerve damage. I suspect you're used to working out, but you must go slowly for a while."

Cara pursed her lips in a pouty frown and shook her head.

Doctor Max caught her warning out of the corner of his eye and cautioned, "I don't normally have to say this, but so long as you don't overdo it with the exercises, you'll see great progress in the days ahead. The nurses will review things in further depth. But the best news is—"

"Oh, I already got that, Doc," Callum said, doubling his smile.

Only Cara understood his reference.

"Well, I'll give you some more. I don't expect there to be complications. We'll keep you on pain meds, but for now, rest is the best medicine," he said, looking pointedly at the three visitors in the room. "If you continue to do well throughout the night, we'll discharge you tomorrow." He shook Callum's hand again and headed out of the room.

"That is the best news," his mom agreed.

"Sure is." Cara took her first deep breath since she'd entered the hospital. She crept up to his bed.

His mom followed Cara's movements, a sparkle of mischief in her eyes. She tweaked the doctor's instructions. "You'll get to go home," she paused for emphasis and grinned, fluttering her eyelashes at Cara, "as long as you have someone stay with you."

Cara smiled conspiratorially at his mom and said, "I got the doctor's hint that you need to get some rest. I'm going to leave and let you rest up for your big homecoming tomorrow."

Callum frowned at her announcement.

Cara planted a slow, soft kiss on Callum's cheek, lingering close, cherishing their connection. The love she'd held for this man wanted to explode from her.

"We'll figure it out," he whispered.

"Yes, we will, you and me together."

TWENTY-EIGHT

Waiting to visit Callum again was a long twenty-four hours. She'd spent her morning making plenty of arrangements, running errands, and finally at four o'clock, she loaded a box in her Jeep and set off to greet the rest of her life.

Before she got out of the car, Cara bowed her head in a quick prayer, barely able to ignore the pup's sharp yips and wagging tail pounding against her back seat. She clasped the steering wheel and spilled a ramble of a prayer to God—as if He didn't already know.

Lord, help me with this new beginning.

Although it wasn't an audible correction, the loud voice in her head might as well have been. "Trust Me," flickered through her brain.

Yes, Lord. See, already I need clear directives. I'll trust You—with my future—with Callum—with all of it.

For certainty's sake, and knowing how deep her independent streak ran, she begged the Lord to take away anything not orchestrated by Him.

A college friend once asked Cara if she really believed prayer changed things. Cara didn't understand all the workings of God, but she was convinced of one thing.

Prayer may not change the circumstances, but it could certainly change her. She'd witnessed that transforming power.

I changed my mind because He changed my heart.

The battle Cara had waged inside her heart hadn't really been with Callum but with herself and God. She'd trust this second chance with Callum to God, not solely to her own control. She knew there were risks, but she was ready to work her way through the hard things.

Nikki pulled hard on her leash, gasping for air, to get to Callum's front door. When they made it to the stoop, she ran circles around Cara. "Sit, girl," Cara commanded. "I know you're excited. So am I." After a couple of sad puppy dog glances between her and the front door, Nikki flopped on her haunches. Cara untangled her feet from Nikki's leash. She knocked on Callum's door and waited, sitting on the bottom step of his porch with Nikki in her arms.

Callum was shocked to see Cara when he finally opened the door. "I thought you were my dad. My mom told me the big boss was coming."

Cara rose with a sparkle of excitement in her eyes, intoxicated at the mere sight of him. "She has you on a short leash, huh? So I'm the boss now? I like that," she giggled.

"Very short leash. I don't mind letting my mom do her thing, but I told her no spending the night," he said, raising his eyebrows in a dramatic flair. He stopped toe to toe, towering over her, and then bent even closer, nose to nose. They stood as one, reading each other's smiles. Callum waited for the slightest hint of a reach for him. When she tilted her chin up, he planted a light, undemanding kiss on her lips.

"But I don't mind being hitched to you. I'll let you boss me around all you want."

Then Nikki yipped and jumped up on him.

"You jealous girl," Callum said. Cara picked Nikki up, and Callum wooed her with his sultry soft voice and kisses to her noggin.

"Come in. We don't need to stand out in this scorcher for the entire shift my mom gave you," he said, holding the door with a coy smile of invitation.

Nikki couldn't contain herself being back in Callum's house. They sat together on the couch and laughed at her as she zoomed around the entire house until she tuckered out on the rug under the coffee table.

Cara asked, "Do you need anything?"

"How are your nursing skills? I could use a chest massage." He gave her a mischievous grin and rubbed his chest.

She smirked. "Are you still on pain meds? Maybe you need to cut back a bit."

"Remember your bedside manner."

"I'd make a terrible nurse. You, sir, should remember *your* manners," she teased, poking him in the chest.

"Just in case you believe otherwise, I have my full faculties, but having you this close and not being able to wrap both my arms around you makes the ache in my chest a hundred times worse."

"Down boy," she sassed.

Callum scratched the stubble along his jawline. "The boss would tell me I need to shave. But I'm not sure I trust you with a razor. Maybe I'll take full advantage of my time off work and grow a beard. How long do you think it took Gandalf to grow his beard?"

"Ew. No. Don't do it."

"But the strokability factor! It'll be like a puppy dog tail. Hagrid and Dumbledore dignified the long style."

"As long as you don't let creatures sleep in it, I guess," she said, curling her lip.

"It could double as a pillow when I go camping." Callum settled into a much more serious tone. "But I'm not going to complain about my recovery time. I had a long chat with God last night. We wrestled about why He would allow this to happen."

Cara loved when he shared his faith. "Was your talk comforting?"

"Somewhat. I don't always understand His ways. But I do know, peace doesn't come right away."

Cara and Callum used to have long talks about God. He'd challenge her to grow deeper in her faith. When she listened to his wisdom, she handled difficulties better. After a long sit at the pond or a long trek on the trail letting Callum be privy to her inner frustrations, their conversation soothed her turmoil. She laughed at herself, realizing she was jealous of God's close relationship with Callum, of Callum spilling his thoughts to Him.

"I'm sure your dad is going to make me go to counseling again. I'm not gonna lie. I'm shakier now that it's over and I'm home than when it was happening or even at the hospital." Callum grimaced at his confession.

"More quiet time to think? I can't even imagine dealing with getting shot and having to shoot someone."

"The extent of it all hasn't quite sunk in. It's a void my brain can't or won't let me address. Not yet anyway. No officer wants to be in this position. We train for it. We know the risk of our job, and we know the sacrifice. Neither makes it easier when it happens."

"Is it bad to say that I'm glad that man's not around to ever hurt you again?" she confessed.

"Absolutely not," he smiled at her. "I like when we're on the same side."

The tension in her jaw loosened, and Cara moved closer on the couch, settling her hand in his, wanting to be his comfort.

Callum's grasp tightened, and he stared at a sleeping Nikki. "It's hard knowing I killed a man." His shoulders slumped. "It makes me sad to think about Wally and all he's been through."

"I'm really sad and angry for Wally and for you," she said, unsuccessfully concealing her edginess. "But, most of all, I'm grateful you'll be okay. The good guy won."

"You know, when people find out I'm an officer, they ask, 'Have you ever shot someone?' They want to hear some riveting story. But that's the question no cop wants to be asked, let alone have to answer 'yes' to."

"Do you feel guilt over killing Wally's dad?" Cara asked.

"Absolutely not. I know that's not a popular answer. Guilt is for when we think we've done something wrong. He gave me no choice. He intended to kill me. It was my life or his. I get riled when people assume police officers don't mind shooting people. They have that all wrong. We do mind! We mind a lot! I take my training and mission to serve and protect the community very seriously."

"Are you sad?" Cara asked a little more delicately.

Callum jumped on that question. "Definitely! I'm sad he thought that was the way to handle his anger. I'm sad about the way he treated Annabeth and Wally, and that his parents probably treated him that way when he was young." Callum hung his head as he continued, "Mostly, I'm sad for his family. Wally and Annabeth do not deserve the pain he caused. It's like a scab that never scars over. Things scrape it and break the pain of it open again. I hate that Wally will live his whole life with this kind of pain, living without a dad at his little league games, on parent days at school, when it's time to teach him to drive."

"Something makes me think he wouldn't have been good at those things," Cara said, a poor attempt to help Callum feel better.

"Doesn't matter. It's sad that he will never have the chance to make better choices, to give his son the better life he deserves."

Callum continued without Cara's prompting. "But mostly, I feel disconnected," Callum reflected. "In the movies, police go right back to chasing bad guys and living their lives after shooting people. And that's what I have to do. Put it behind me. But it's not as easy as those shows make it out to be. I'm a cop, but the last thing I want to do is use deadly force. I'm proud of my ability to diffuse tough situations, but that man didn't even give me the chance." His face grew pained at recalling the horrific moment.

"Well, you just may have saved Annabeth and Wally's lives," Cara consoled.

"And that makes what I had to do worth it," he conceded. "Do you mind if we talk about something else?"

Cara suddenly hopped up and ran to the front door. Nikki followed fast on her heels. "No, you stay here. I'll be right back in a second," she said, pushing the pup away from the door.

"You better be. Do I get a second kiss hello when you come back?" Callum kidded.

"We'll see," she winked.

"I'll even wag for you if I have to. Hey, wait," he called, and she paused with her hand on the doorknob, "What time do you leave today? We need to figure out this long-distance relationship."

"We will. Promise. Hang tight! I'll only be a sec." Cara dashed out the front door and grabbed a box from the back of her Jeep.

Callum stood in the doorway, waiting for her. "What do you have there?"

"No peeking," she said, setting the box on the coffee table.

"Now you owe me a door tax," he commanded with false bravado.

"Door tax? You know tax collectors aren't liked, right?"

"A kiss. I promise you'll like this tax collector."

Cara stood at his good side and wrapped her arms around his waist, pulling his hip bone into her stomach. She melted into him, sharing a long and deep kiss.

A satisfied smile crossed his face. "Paid in full," he said.

"Do you trust me?" she asked, a bit of a quiver in her voice.

"Always have," he said, handing her confidence back.

"Do you believe God can change our hearts and minds?" she asked.

"Always will," he uttered with conviction. His chest constricted, afraid to hope for her next words.

Her palms caressed his cheeks, and she searched his face for an answer to a question she had not asked. Her thumbs brushed away the tension at the corner of his eyes, and he held his breath for every word she had yet to speak. She wrapped her hands around the back of his head and softly rested her forehead against his.

"Then trust me on this," she said.

"I do," he promised and waited for the rest.

Cara broke away from him, and he groaned at her retreat. Grabbing a paint can and brush from the box, she held it up to him. "I can't date a guy with a teal blue front door," she stated. The corner of her mouth turned up in a wry smile. "So I'm hoping you like this black. It's called Forever Charcoal."

Confused, Callum glanced at the can. "You're going to paint my door? Don't you have to leave for your new job?"

"I hope to start in a couple of weeks. I have plenty of time to paint this door while I adult-sit," she said, setting the can back in the box.

"I thought you said the new hire meetings started the end of this week?"

"Plans have changed," Cara said. A wide smile beamed across her face. "I have an interview with Children and Family Services, here in town, tomorrow."

Cara's enthusiasm flowed freely as she watched the corners of Callum's mouth turn up in realization and spread into tiny crinkles at the corners of his eyes. He grabbed her with his good arm. "Think of this as me lifting you off the ground and swinging you in circles."

Cara was equally as giddy with delight. Her insides fluttered as if he had actually spun her around.

"Callum, I want this. I want us. I trusted in my own plans long enough. I see now that mindset kept me from trusting God. I took so long to make the leap to get out of my own way. Under all my trying to push you away, my heart still hoped for us," she said, nearly breathless with excitement. "For a split-second, I thought of a long-distance relationship, but then I asked myself, 'Why?' I refuse to take one more second for granted between us."

Callum nodded his head and leaned it against hers with a joyous moan of agreement.

"Being with the only man I'll ever love for the rest of my life, in the town I've loved my whole life, feels perfect. I can't leave you. You and me, here together, is God's doing. Whatever the future brings, I'm fighting like crazy to trust Him. And you," she smiled. Cara looked squarely into Callum's eyes. "I love you. Always have, always will."

"I love you doesn't even express all that I'm feeling," he breathed against her lips.

Nikki yipped in agreement and jumped at their legs, begging to join their celebration.

"I'm never letting you slip away from me again," she vowed with a contented sigh. "I promise to run to you every day."

"And I promise to hold on this time." With his words, Callum embraced her, body and soul, and became her sanctuary once more. He planted a kiss on her lips and whispered, "Let's start forever right now."

And once again, Cara believed in the transforming power of a moment.

EPILOGUE

One year later, September.

Cara stood in Gramps's house, staring into the mirror. Updo hair, pearl earrings, and a white lace, open-back wedding gown. It was simply elegant, just what she'd wanted for their special day.

The bang of the screen door startled her. "Gramps? I thought you rode on the golf cart to the dock with Mom."

"I told them to come back for me. I want a couple of minutes with you alone," Gramps said. He walked to her and took her hand. Gramps wasn't worried about the wedding day schedule. He always said he refused to live in the shadow of time.

"Here is your something old. Grandma wanted you to have this." He pulled a wooden box from his pocket. A slight tremor shook his age-spotted hand. If this sweet and steady man could be shaken, talking about losing the love of his life would do it.

"I wish Grandma could be here today." She squeezed Gramps's hand like a hug and took the box. "It's beautiful," she whispered, tracing the gold leaf of the rose petals carved into the wood.

"You'll need this." He handed her a small gold vintage key.

Cara inserted the key into the gold lock. When it opened, she didn't recognize the tune that began playing. Plush, dark blue fabric cradled Grandma's wedding rings. Her eyes misted over, recalling how they'd graced Gram's long fingers.

"I bought her the biggest diamond I could afford," he said. "Years later, I offered to switch it out for something bigger, but she always refused. She said nothing bigger would prove my love better."

"They're beautiful. I used to watch the sun sparkle off the diamond and rub my finger across it when she held my hand. She let me try it on once. That's when I found out it reflects a rainbow on surfaces. When I was little, Grandma told me it was a princess diamond. I thought it had been made for a princess."

"Well, she was a princess…my princess. Now it's yours, sweet pea." He patted her hand.

"I'll treasure it," she said. Cara slid it perfectly on her finger and smiled at him. "What's the song?"

"'I'll Be Loving You Always.' That was our first dance in the church reception hall."

"And I'll be loving you always, too," she said and squeezed his hand.

A honk from the golf cart pushed them along.

"That's my ride. I'm so proud of you, Cara." Gramps squished her into a hard hug.

"For finding my way back to Callum?" Gramps had thought Cara should be with Callum from the start.

"For being strong. You've—"

"I wasn't as strong as Gram," Cara apologized, twisting the ring she'd placed on her right hand.

"Oh, rattlesnakes, young lady!" he corrected her.

Cara giggled at Gramps.

"You work dang hard to get what you want. You found your way. If that meant changing your mind—then so be it. Your head finally tuned in to your pounding heart. Don't be negative about yourself. You're a strong woman. When you couldn't change the past, you found a way to change your future. You're my little dynamite, just like your grandma. It takes a mountain of trust in God to live in the messy unknown. Today, you'll walk down that aisle to conquer whatever comes your way in life with Callum. Strong is knowing God's strength overcomes our greatest weaknesses."

He was right. Trusting love, both God's and Callum's, made her feel strong.

Minutes later, Cara exited the golf cart and stood at the end of a long, lace runner. She looked out to the pond and the bridge where Callum and she spent so many hours together. With Tori as her maid of honor, Dylan as the best man, and surrounded by close family and friends, it was a simple wedding—just what she wanted.

She made her way to the edge of the dock on the steady arm of her dad and under Callum's loving gaze. As she passed the two empty seats in the front row that she and Callum had decorated for Ali and Gram, a pang of sadness hit her.

Cara's dad kissed her on the cheek and then whispered in her ear, "You chose a good one, Cara Bear."

"I sure did. The best." She bear-hugged her dad and reached for Callum's outstretched hand.

When the time came, Callum gave his vows without a hint of nerves. He unfolded the sheet of paper he pulled from his suit pocket and cleared his throat. Then he grabbed the handkerchief from his coat pocket, balling it in his fist. Grinning at Cara, he said, "This may take me a while."

He held her hand as he said, "I first loved you that day I found you on the bleachers. You swiped away a tear you were too embarrassed for me to see. From that moment on, I never wanted you to hide from me again. I wanted to know all your secrets and emotions. I wanted to take away all your sadness, but I've learned that's not possible. I almost lost you until I learned sharing our sadness lessens its sting. I promise to forever be seeing you, finding you, and sharing with you, Cara."

His honest words empowered Cara. She stood taller beside him and tugged his hand three times.

He acknowledged her signal with a smile and continued, "Because you are by my side, I will never again struggle to look ahead in life. You make me braver."

Cara couldn't imagine anyone braver. He'd worked through losing his sister and getting shot and still had such a faith-filled outlook on life.

"I'm a knight in dented armor," he said, clearing his throat, "but I'll stand by your side and fight for us every single day for the rest of our days together. I want to work through every hard thing in life with you. I'm not perfect, but I'm close." He winked, and everyone laughed. He'd clearly memorized most of what he was saying, rarely glancing at his paper.

"So, when I make mistakes, I will I ask forgiveness from you, always. I promise never to let you win on purpose, unless it's my heart. I know what it means to you to earn your wins. But know this—you will never have to earn my love. I give my love freely. It was your fierce heart that brought you back to me. You refused to believe you couldn't do the difficult thing. I'll always cherish that."

He leaned close and whispered, "Hold on, don't let those happy tears fall just yet." She laughed at his antics and the tears fell anyway. Callum carefully wiped the tears from her eyes and then continued.

"I will be by your side to honor you, support you, and grow with you. I'll respect your dreams, your deepest desires, your strengths, and your weaknesses. I give you all my drive, resilience, and willingness to smile and cry through our journey. I give you myself, humble, raw, and open, to experience all the blessings of this life with you. I love you."

He leaned in to kiss her and Pastor Caleb teased, "Oh no, you don't, not yet!"

Cara handed Tori her sunflower bouquet in exchange for the vows she'd written to Callum.

Cara exhaled a deep breath to calm her nerves. "How do I express in just a few words how much you mean to me? I can only hope that you and everyone here can feel the overwhelming love I have for you, even if my words fall short. We were the three amigos—me, you, and Ali. And hanging together was the best part of life until the day you asked me to go for ice cream, just the two of us.

"That day, you saw through my sadness. You encouraged me when defeat overwhelmed me. You have a way of looking deep inside to the mess I hide, even from myself.

"I lost my way with Christ and you for a while. I had a distorted understanding of love. But you were patient and persisted until I realized the truth of forgiveness and trust.

I should have known we'd end up here the moment you pulled me over at the pig sign last summer. You took off your sunglasses, stared into my soul, and welcomed me back home. I should have known at that moment I'd come home for good because years before you'd arrested me, heart and soul."

She turned her paper over and took a moment to wipe away a tear. "When you decide you want something, you go after it. I'm thankful for your tenacity and fighting spirit. You prayed for me and fought for us when I refused to battle. You fought for me to find my faith and my way, even at the risk of losing me. Everyone here knows the storms we've battled. Looking back, it's those tough times that will remind us how cherished we are to one another. Because of them, we've learned to love each other better. We've relied on our friends and family for wisdom and guidance through those rough seasons, and we will absolutely continue to seek their support from this day forward."

Cara heard the clink of tags on Nikki's collar and turned to see her bounding down the dock. Both Cara and Callum bent over to stop her from jumping up on them. With one command from Callum, she laid at his side as if she'd always meant to be his best man. Callum nodded at Cara to continue.

"I promise to love you even when it gets hard. I promise to communicate my thoughts and feelings and needs with you, even if I need some alone time first. I promise to keep the fridge stocked with sweet tea and sweet corn. I promise to dance with you in the kitchen until we're old and gray. I promise you the last scoop of ice cream." Cara let her sheet fall to the floor and clasped both of Callum's hands.

"The first time you whispered 'I love you' to me was a sacred moment. And so was every time after. I promise to return that sacred vow to you now and every day. You are my good. I love you, Callum. Always have. Always will."

With her last words, Cara wanted to fall into Callum's arms, rest her cheek against his chest, and let the world fade away.

Callum opened his arms and said, "Come here." Hearing those words, Nikki sat up and leaned against Callum's leg.

Cara's chest swelled at the way he knew her thoughts, but as she took a step toward his waiting arms, she hesitated, looking at Pastor Caleb first.

Pastor Caleb relented with a heavy sigh, knowing the rings had not even been exchanged. He chuckled, "Oh, go ahead. Nothing says we can't do this part twice. I'll even make it official. You may kiss your bride."

Cara leapt into Callum's embrace, and they found trusting love made for the sweetest kiss.

"You're safe in my arms. You always will be," Callum whispered.

Cara pulled back to peer into Callum's eyes. "I know," she said, "I think I've always known."

BOOK CLUB
DISCUSSION GUIDE

1. Cara and Ali's favorite Scripture was Phil. 4:8. *"Finally, brothers and sisters, whatever is true, whatever is noble, whatever is right, whatever is pure, whatever is lovely, whatever is admirable–if anything is excellent or praiseworthy–think about such things."* What Scriptures do you cling to? Why?

2. Losing her best friend altered Cara's world. How has the death of a loved one affected you?

3. Would you get a tattoo? What would it be? Why?

4. What role do dreams play in your life? Should we place significance on dreams? Share the effect a dream had on you.

5. Siblings shape who we are and how we see the world. Share how your siblings impacted your life.

6. Cara has a special relationship with Gramps. What special relationship with an older person or mentor has helped you?

7. Why does Cara think she can handle working with Callum? Was this a misconception on her part?

8. What do you want to accomplish before you die? What would you want included in your Celebration of Life? What is the measure of a life well lived?

9. Callum explains why he broke up with Cara. Are his grief and reasoning believable to you?

10. Cara thinks they could have gone through the grief together. What do you think?

11. Cara loves music of all kinds. What songs inspire you? Why?

12. What is the significance of the pond? Do you have such a place?

13. If you were Cara, what would you have done differently with Callum?

14. What role does the setting of the story play in the novel?

15. Tori challenges Cara. Who challenges you in a good way? Can you give an example of a time someone pushed you to do something you didn't want to do, but it ended up for the best?

16. Do you believe first love can survive a lifetime? Why or why not?

17. Is love a worthy risk? Explain.

18. How does trusting God help us trust others?

19. Why is forgiveness necessary in relationships?

20. Which of the main characters' responses were you most sympathetic with and why?

21. Romans 8:28 says, *"And we know that for those who love God all things work together for good, for those who are called according to his purpose."* Do you believe God can transform bad things into good, or use suffering to bring people to a place of wholeness? Give an example of how God has done this in your life.

WITH GRATITUDE

Each novel I've written has been a long winding road of a journey, born from a passing thought that maybe a story could grow from a seed of an idea. While writing is a very solitary evolution, to get this novel in readers' hands involved a slew of people who helped in so many ways.

I cultivated the plot for *Trusting Love* from a book title my husband had in a dream. Even though the finished novel has little resemblance to the story we brainstormed from his dream, conjuring ideas together was fun. Thanks, Rick, for sharing your dream title and for being my dream come true.

My adult children, their spouses, and my grandkids fill my life with love, joy, inspiration, and encouragement. Ricky and Lena Roberson, Ariel and Dustin Kinkelaar, Daniel and Kayla Roberson, Niah and Jace Kinkelaar—you are the backdrop to my beautiful life!

I can't give a big enough bear hug to those who have dedicated endless hours scouring my manuscript to hone this novel. Thank you to Chrissy McClarren, Kim Baer, and Megan Montgomery for your editorial passion, pragmatism, guidance, and wisdom (and for scraping me off the editing floor and reminding me to wear my big girl pants).

Shh! Somewhere it's said you shouldn't pick a book by its cover, but I do! I love the cozy warmth of the cover for *Trusting Love*. I'd pick this book a thousand times. Thank you, Lena Roberson, for embracing my vision and making it come to life. Thank you for formatting my second novel and for your hard work creating and managing my beautiful website.

I am blessed with family who brag about me and my writing. Thank you to my biggest fans: my parents, Tom and Rose McClarren; my sister Chrissy McClarren and her husband Andy Reago; my brother Kevin McClarren and his wife Karen McClarren. Thank you to my in-laws for their encouragement: Brent and Theresa Roberson; Cindy and Larry Ingrum; Cammy and John Sherrill; Kari and Dirk Veldman; and all my nieces and nephews.

Writers need an audience of readers, and I am blessed to have such a supportive group of family, friends, and fans who read, attend local events, write reviews, and spread the word.

Through my years of teaching, I've been inspired by my students. Cara's character was born from a mix of three of my prior students. They are bold young women with big hearts and a love for life and people. (Thank you Cara, Kaitlyn, and Karly.) Thanks Kaitlyn Duchien and Carlos Guarin Castañeda for the inspiration of your vows.

Thank you to God and my church family, who tend to my heart and the Relationship that matters the most.

ABOUT THE AUTHOR

Cherie Roberson lives with her husband in the growing small town of Mahomet, Illinois.

After retiring from teaching, Cherie loaded up on chai tea and fulfilled her dream of writing a novel. Her debut romance novel, *Man in the Mist*, set in Scotland, is an ode to her heritage and finding joy after loss.

Cherie's second novel, *Trusting Love*, celebrates small-town living and first love while exploring themes of grief, forgiveness, and trust in God's providence.

When not venturing to faraway places, a mountain, or a beach, you'll find Cherie playing games with her grandchildren, taming her extensive garden, walking with headphones blasting music that's too loud, or reading for inspiration.

To order her debut novel, *Man in the Mist*, follow her blog, or subscribe to her newsletter, visit her website at www.cherieroberson.com.

Every review has a tremendous impact. Share a few lines about your favorite parts of *Trusting Love* on Amazon.

Find Cherie on social media:

Facebook   cherierobersonwrites

Instagram   cherierobersonwrites